# HUMANITY RISING

## THE SKYWARD SAGA
### BOOK 5

## A.R. KNIGHT

# 1 / HOLD THE LINE

I catch the black-glass spear, duck under the flailing claws of the furry creature and jab. The Flaum's armor, meant to guard against the fiery death of miners, does little to keep the spear's point from striking home. My enemy's skittering hits a halt as I withdraw the weapon, and before it reconsiders whether to live or die, I hit it with a kick and knock the Flaum off the mountain cliff.

"Nice catch!" Viera calls from my right as she whips out one of her silver pistols and fires.

The bullet cracks over my left shoulder, and I whirl to see another Flaum, just landing on its magnetic boots and about to deliver a shot to my back, stumble away as red blooms across its chest.

"That's your fault!" I shout, this time keeping my eyes on the landing craft above, but the attack's reaching its end, and this shuttle, along with the other three scattered along the wide cliff, are turning and heading back to orbit.

They'll return in a few hours with a fresh supply, while we count our wounded and wonder how much longer we can last.

"If you stop breaking your spears, I won't have to congratulate you for catching them," Viera, in her deep blue-dyed leather armor, short-gray hair snapping in the breeze, says to me as I climb back to her level.

"Tell that to the blacksmiths," I reply, glancing up to make sure the Sevora continue their retreat. "The armor we're cutting through doesn't break as easy as our leather."

I take a quick count of our losses, and while we have a hundred warriors out on the ridge, more than a dozen are being helped away, with another four or five unmoving on the cold gray rock, between drifts of snow. They won't be sent down the rope hammocks to Marilo—their bodies will be pitched off, same as the Sevora. You can't bury someone in rock, and it's too much risk to burn them.

"It's always too many and too few at the same time," I say, then shiver despite my own attempts not to. Ignos is heading towards darkness, and the mountaintops are always cold. "Does Avril have any idea why they're not attacking at full strength?"

"I haven't asked her, Empress," Viera replies. "Maybe they're scared?"

"They could raze us from orbit." I start the walk to the ladders down.

It's the duty of the Empress, or so I tell myself, to be the last one off the battlefield, but even as I leave the next shift of soldiers climbs their way over the lip. These warriors are tightly wrapped in animal skins, and bear packs of firewood on their backs. Ready to wait out the night.

"I'm grateful they don't," Viera says. "While this isn't the best life, it sure beats death."

"So far as you know."

"Exactly."

At the edge, with fighters streaming in and out beside me, I look into the burning forges, the bustling fortress of Marilo, capital of the Lunare and, at the moment, all of humanity. Heat rises up through the massive hole punched in the mountainside by the same aliens we're now facing on a daily basis; the Sevora, creatures that take the minds and bodies of other species and bend them into slaves.

I had one in my mind once and thought it was a god. It couldn't control me, and never figured out why. Now its friends are here to find out.

Or kill us all.

The rope ladders hang for a dozen meters, hooked in with long grapples bored into the stone. We lost a few brave fighters on the first expedition to set them up, but we couldn't give the Sevora the option to camp out above the city, even with all the captured miners we have being used to defend that hole.

At first the climb was daunting—stepping up over and over again as sure death from the fall lies below, but it's hard to be afraid of dying when it's so often around you. We've all become numb by now.

At least the blisters on my hands have calloused over.

Viera insists on following me and not the other way around, so I make the descent, staving off the bone-weariness that comes after every shift. A responsibility I don't have to take but do because when the survival of your race is at stake, rank isn't something to abuse.

Marilo's adapted to the life of wartime the way a warrior culture does; by tightening diets, getting the old, the young, and the unhealthy out of the city to one of the distant towns networked by caves to the Lunare capitol, and by coming to grips with the grim reality that they're fighting to delay the inevitable.

"Another caravan left today," Avril tells me when I meet the Lunare leader in Marilo's capitol building, a spiraling feature with many levels overlooking a wide central space where, in more normal times, people like Avril would be proclaiming this or that to a listening throng of governors and officials.

Now it's all but empty, save for our Shadows—guards appointed to follow us while remaining as inconspicuous as possible—and a few officials drafting orders or delivering reports. Avril's sitting at the central table, looking just as tired as I feel, though her battles have been with logistics rather than invading aliens.

"Have we heard from the others?" I reply.

Avril shrugs. "Yes, and no. They're making progress, but none will get to the boundaries for days yet."

By then, who knows if we'll even be around to receive those messages. We've been pulling together caravans of artisans, farmers, and what people we can spare and sending them to explore. To go to the edges of the map and draw it further, hunting for new places for humanity to take root if our current hold is pulled up.

Neither Avril nor I would see our species destroyed.

"Otherwise?"

"The city continues," Avril says, and I think her hair's even whiter than before, as if the stress is turning the Lunare leader slowly to snow, and when she suddenly smiles, the pale pink of her lips seems at terrible odds with the fire-lit dim of Marilo. "There's even some hope. Several more merchants came in today, traveling back and selling wines. I bought a bottle. The dream is to open it when the fighting ends."

"Or when the Sevora finally choose to break through."

"Still no sign, then?"

The daily ask, and my daily reply comes with a shaking head. "The Vincere haven't shown yet."

If humanity is going to survive, we're going to need outside help. A week ago, I'd sent the signal. T'Oli, a Ooblot who'd traveled across the stars to bring me back home, said the Vincere would hear the message and respond, but even it has no idea how long that might take. We might be flattened, or we might be saved.

"Then why are the Sevora playing with us?" Avril says. "They attacked with so much ferocity before, but now it seems like they're just testing our lines, making sure we don't forget about them."

"I've asked the same question," Viera cuts in—she never leaves my side anymore, and I don't mind. "Their corpses, though, don't talk."

"Does that have anything to share?" Avril points at the thing on my wrist, a dark emerald bracelet.

The Cache holds more information than I'd ever be able to peruse, and using it draws me into a kind of trance, as the knowledge I'm searching for floats like projections around me. It's incredible, and dangerous, and I only use it when I'm alone or under tight protection. The Cache is also the reason my eyelids droop and my muscles sag—too many recent nights spent swimming through its endless oceans.

"It has no clear answer for why the Sevora are behaving like this," I say. "But I'm still looking."

The rest of my night passes in much the same way; passing discussions with other officials, an unsteady wander through the city to the haphazard room that's been designated as my quarters, with my Shadows and Viera watching me the entire way. Eventually I collapse on the mat of clotted straw that serves as my bed.

It's a far cry from the grand treatment I received when I was an Empress in more than name, and falls well short of the comforts I had in the various space ships and alien cities I've seen during my bumpy journey across the galaxy. The mat is, though, human. Made by human hands, with no hidden purpose other than relaxation, other than giving me the opportunity to lie down and, for just a moment, shut my eyes.

"Empress," Viera's voice, coupled with the grimy smell of scrappy coffee, brings me blinking awake.

Viera doesn't need to add anything more than that. Routine kicks in and I'm up, reaching for and pulling on my own light suit of armor, pulling the leather over the Cache, which never leaves my wrist. I don't wear a cape, but one of the priests from my old city, Damantum, took my emerald necklace with them when they evacuated. Last time, I left the jewels in the city because I was afraid of losing them.

Now I fasten them around my neck, the glittering ensemble the one concession I make to my rank, the one luxury I give myself.

T'Oli, a surprise guest, is waiting outside the apartment this morning. The creamy Ooblot looks mostly like a puddle with a pair of rounded sticks jutting out of it, though these sticks have eyes and the puddle follows me as we walk towards the rope ladders.

Marilo in the morning is the same as Marilo in the evening—a bevy of cookfires, moving bodies, and the occasional hawking of wares, though the trade now is less in gold and more in necessities. Up ahead, I can already see the shift changing underway as warriors climb and descend.

No hammocks this time, I note; either there's no wounded, or there wasn't an attack last night.

"They're pulling back," T'Oli says as we walk.

"The Sevora?" I allow myself the slight flutter of hope. "Why?"

"Panic," T'Oli replies. "Something's going wrong on their home-world. They're being careless with their communications, leaving them open and I've been able to listen on the shuttle. I'd say there's no clear leader left up there."

"I didn't think the Sevora were supposed to panic," Viera says. "Isn't that their whole deal? Order and control above everything? Boring as dirt?"

"They like to act that way, but the Sevora are as full of passion as we are," T'Oli replies, its Ooblot skin forming the sounds by smacking against itself, as the creature has no mouth. "On Vimelia, Clarity's Dawn saw more success playing the slugs against one another than pushing forward by ourselves. A rival is a rival, no matter the species."

"If they're losing control," I speak slow, thinking through the possibilities. "What happens if they give up on us?"

"Oh, they'll probably burn this entire planet," T'Oli says. "It'd be trivial, and safer."

"Then we need to evacuate," I start to speed up my walk. "Get everyone deeper into the caves."

T'Oli laughs, a strange, barking slap. "I wouldn't worry about it—they'll superheat the atmosphere. We'll all die, no matter where we go."

## 2 / A MEETING OF CLAWS

They were made. Grown, one by one in hanging hatcheries, to the designs of beings who sought to, who did, use them. Claws, talons, tails and razor teeth, all chosen for their murderous efficiency. A plan that has worked well, has instilled the creators with all the power they could want.

Yet the Amigga want more, and the Oratus, their creations, would give that to them.

Except for Sax. Except for Bas and the growing numbers realizing that a galaxy under the control of a species with no respect for natural life makes for a dangerous, deadly place to live.

Sax stands, with his midclaws resting on a long, round silver table in the middle of the frigate's sole meeting room. The table itself is polished clear, and it's hard enough that even the unnatural metal of Sax's claws doesn't scratch it. The sound of those claws, though, makes Sax wince. Reminds him of who, of what he is not anymore.

Around the table, white circles align every one-and-a-half meters, waiting for their occupants to give them life. Sax's own rises all three meters with him, supporting his legs and meeting his back while leaving a gap for Sax's tail. It's a gesture that shouldn't be necessary, but given that Sax's gray scales are routinely interrupted by patches of interwoven titanium, there's plenty of reason for the Oratus to be tired.

Across Sax's chest, six vents separate wide and gulp in recycled air, touched with a bit of flowered scent from the surface of Solis, the planet not far beyond this ship's hull. As he finishes his deep breath, a circular door on the left shunts open, revealing a sole guard and her miner. The Flaum, small, furry and with her two claws wrapped around the handle of the weapon she holds, leads in a trio of other Oratus.

The first, golden-scaled and confident, gives Sax a nod as she enters. Rav's the lead officer on this frigate, a three-letter Oratus like Sax who chose command over getting her claws dirty. She's the only reason Sax is still alive, and Rav is probably hoping Sax can convince the two Oratus following her not to destroy this ship and everyone on it.

The second Oratus bears deep blue scales, except for a series of scars cutting across his chest that have since healed into ridged black lines. His beet red eyes catch Sax's, and while they widen in recognition at the face that's been blown across the galaxy's wanted screens, the Oratus doesn't pause or demand Sax's immediate arrest.

The third, and oldest, bearing weathered brown scales, does stop when she sees Sax. Her look, though, and the slight baring of her razor teeth, is long and thoughtful. She keeps her claws at her sides, her tail placid on the floor behind her. Sax is looking for signs, but sees none.

"So you weren't lying," the brown one says to Rav, still standing in the doorway.

"Please, Cacia, sit," Rav says.

Sax freezes. A five-letter Oratus? He's never met one before, and knows there has to be less than a dozen in the entire galaxy. What Cacia would have done to earn those letters, he can't . . .

"Stop," Cacia says to Sax, and the Oratus catches himself, lowers his tail back to the ground. "I'm not worth getting all worried about.

Just like you, I earned my letters doing my duty. Unlike you, I plan to keep them by doing the same."

"I told you that's what she'd say," the deep blue one, who's made his way to the white platform across from Sax and sat down as it conformed to his body, says. "Cacia's never going to turn on the Amigga."

Rav, seated on Sax's right, giving the nearest seat to Cacia, shakes her head. "I think, Hul, she's going to surprise you."

"Nothing surprises me anymore," Hul hisses. "I'm too bored sitting out here by Solis to get surprised."

Cacia ignores what they're saying and heads to her own platform. Unlike the other two, which sit like Sax, Cacia's platform billows out around her, letting the Oratus recline such that she's almost lying on her back. It's an incredibly vulnerable position, but once she's in it, Cacia's expression relaxes, her claws lie flat, and her eyes close.

"Sax," Rav says after a moment. "Go on. Tell them what you told me."

Sax isn't much for speeches, unless it's a battle-cry or an order to eviscerate his enemies. Here, though, he's fighting for something more than himself, which lets Sax reach deeper into an oratory he didn't know he had.

"We're winning the war against the Sevora," Sax begins. "Which is only the start. The Amigga brought us, the Oratus and the Vincere, into existence to fight the battles they never wanted to. We have done that. We have kept the galaxy safe from anything the Chorus has deemed a threat for a long, long time."

Sax watches his audience as he talks; Hul is interested, Rav looks a little bored, and Cacia still has her eyes closed, as if she's sleeping.

"What happens, though, when the threat is the Chorus itself?" Sax continues. "What happens when they decide we've served our purpose, when they decide we're more trouble to keep around than we're worth? Do we let them end us?"

"How?" Hul interrupts. "They're a bunch of Amigga. Only the

best of them can even wield a weapon, and they don't do that very well."

"I barely survived a mirrored Oratus that came for me on this ship," Sax counters. The encounter with the light-bending Oratus, a version of Sax's species bred to handle the sort of dark-edged, shadow missions regular Oratus had little taste or knack for, left Sax ruined and needing metal plates grafted across rent gaps in his scales. "It claimed the Chorus had branded me a traitor and that my only possible end was death."

"As a traitor deserves," Cacia hisses from her seat.

Sax takes another long, slow breath. He wants to take his claws and shake them all. He wants to tell them that, right now, his pair is on her way to sabotaging their entire race because the galaxy's other species think the Oratus can't be trusted. Anger, though, won't work with these three—if Sax gets too dangerous, they'll just kill him and move on.

So he tells a different story instead.

"As part of a mission, I delivered a Sevora specimen to an Amigga station, called *Cobalt*. On this station, the Amigga was growing a new species. Ones they could control on their own. That had no free will."

Hul laughs, a hissing snort. "Yes, yes, we've heard the rumors. We're all going to be replaced by slime creatures from a tube?"

That's unexpected, but just because the target's discovered his gambit doesn't mean it won't work.

"They were more than slime creatures," Sax hisses. "The familiars, as the Amigga called them, were deadly, and they were getting better. It was working on disguises, so that you'd never know if the Flaum beside you was real or an Amigga slave. How long do you think the Chorus will keep us around when it can crew its frigates with endless hordes of blind followers?"

"And how, Sax, can we stop them?" Rav says. "Even if we believed you—and I'm not sure we do—would you have us take our small fleet, leap to the Chorus and fight them? Die for nothing?"

Sax blinks. He'd been focusing so hard on persuading them to see the truth that Sax hasn't spent any time on what to do when the other Oratus actually saw it.

"Help us," Sax says finally. "There's groups spread across the galaxy, working in small ways to grow our numbers, to find ways to take down the Chorus. Cacia, with your ship, you could help break the Chorus' hold on the current batch of new Oratus. Hul and Rav, you could keep Cacia safe, keep Solis safe until the Vincere as a whole can be turned."

Sax never planned on giving a speech in his life, but having his first and only, thus far, attempt at it greeted with a dull silence isn't what he expects. Rav responds to the quiet with a slow look at the other two Oratus, judging their reactions. Which aren't much: Hul takes a long breath through his vents, and Cacia keeps up her lounging. Not a word comes from either.

Silence heats quick to anger. Sax's blood pulses. Why aren't they talking? After all Sax fought for to get here, to earn a spot at this table, their reaction is to do nothing?

After another second passes, Sax slaps the metal table with his midclaws. The metal from his claws makes a ringing noise that echoes around the room, and it's weird enough to draw the eyes of Rav and Hul. Even Cacia cracks a single iris.

"I'm not giving you a choice," Sax hisses. "You either agree, now, to save our own species and the galaxy in which we live, or Rav and I will end you and find someone more willing."

Threatening a five-letter Oratus. An instant death, at least by Vincere protocols. Sax, though, isn't in the Vincere anymore. This meeting, in fact, is about as far from the Vincere as he can get. The question, now, is whether anyone else in the room feels the same way.

"Sax, I didn't—" Rav starts before Sax issues a loud growl to cut her off.

"I'm asking them," Sax hisses. "Accept, or die here."

Perhaps Rav realizes she's gone too far to take any other course but Sax's, as she stays quiet. Her claws are tight, as are Hul's, though the latter's keeping his gaze on Cacia. Whatever course the five-letter takes, he'll follow.

As for Cacia, she finally decides to make a move. At a twitch from her tail, the platform beneath her folds back into the ground like melting snow, leaving Cacia standing tall on her talons. She swings her head towards Sax and bares her teeth.

"I will not be led by a three-letter. Your argument has merit. Your plans have none."

Sax has been in enough fights to know when he's in one, even though this is being fought with words instead of claws.

"It is what I have," Sax says. "We're reacting, now. Trying to stay alive until we can strike at the Chorus."

"That might have worked when you were in hiding. When your only members were of lower species." Cacia gestures a foreclaw towards the Flaum guards at the back of the room. "Now the Chorus knows you exist, and as soon as they finish with the remnants of the Sevora, you will become the Vincere's sole target."

"I already know the situation," Sax says. "Either help us find a solution, or don't."

"If the Chorus is removed, there will be a vacuum. New leaders will be necessary. New commanders." Cacia's tail begins to swish back and forth, making a scraping noise as it glides along the metal floor. "I'm tired of sitting around this planet, Sax. I long for bigger, brighter things. I can begin to pull the levers that will bring the Vincere itself into our grasp, and in exchange, I would lead it."

Sax has no right to make the promise, no power to give it. Cacia's words, though, hint that they think Sax must be a high-ranking member of this resistance, that he must have some sway. So Sax says the words and gives Cacia what she wants.

Bas always says he needs to become a better liar.

I climb the rope ladders for my shift, making it to the top and into Ignos' light on another clear, windy day. Snow drifts, growing thicker as the seasons trend towards winter, gather in the gray rock crevices, burying sprigs of grass. In the distance, beyond the smaller foothills arrayed in front of me, I can make out the slightest shade of green on the horizon.

My true home. Somewhere in that deep jungle, my parents might still be alive. My tribe, my people might still struggle. The Sevora took that area first, with the refugees fleeing to the Lunare and their mountain shelters to survive. Many of my own former subjects made the long trek too, crossing plains and desert before the woods.

Many more did not.

So now I stand with unfamiliar allies, wielding bows, spears, curved kukri knives and flintlock rifles. Nothing compared to the arms I've seen, the weapons I'd made in Damantum, lost in the rapid escape. Yet for all their primitiveness, these tools have served us so far.

"That's not usual," Viera points up and I see what she's looking at.

The Sevora normally send a few shuttles through the

atmosphere, buzzing down and hitting our cliffside position with plenty of laser fire. We duck and cover, using the rocks for protection, then burst out and engage in a sloppy melee that lasts until the Sevora decide they've had enough and retreat.

This time, though, instead of four shuttles, there are dozens. Behind them, too, greater shapes are descending through the clouds; larger spike-like things, coming towards us with their round bottoms shimmering as reflected light bounces away.

"Looks like they're done playing with us," I say, then turn towards one of the warriors. "Send the signal—we need everyone ready to hold here, and the city needs to empty."

Avril's going to wake up to a thrill, but better that than not waking up at all.

"Cover positions!" Viera shouts as the first shuttles scream closer.

Everyone, myself and Viera included, dive into carved out niches in the rock. Some hang over the hole's edge back towards Marilo, resting their feet on notches made for the purpose. A hundred fighters disappear in a moment, and good thing too, because the Sevora start shooting in the next.

Lasers don't make noise when they scream down. There's no crackling, no whistling from an arrow's feather. There's only a flash and a spray as rock fractures and bursts. The hiss as snow vaporizes. Explosions, like when the Lunare use their cannons, don't erupt— rather, small fires start as the ground literally melts.

I see several fighters on the unlucky end of a near strike—the laser superheats the air around where they are enough that their fur-lined armor bursts into flame, prompting a frantic roll-around. My own shelter, beneath a thick slate slab, keeps Viera and I safe, and I try to ignore the screams of others less lucky than us.

"Think this is the end?" Viera asks as the flashes continue.

"I don't think we've come all this way to die here," I reply.

"Hope you're right." Viera glances at her pistols. "There are so many cool weapons out there I haven't used."

I can't stop the laugh.

The fire dies away as the shuttles get close. Once the flashes stop, it's a sign to burst out of our hideaways, and I go, black-glass spear in my right hand and a kukri looped at my waist. Viera has her pistols ready, a more conventional Lunare sword hung over her back.

"For Malo?" Viera says as we leave cover.

"Always!" I call back.

The spirit of my friend, who fell getting us off of the Sevora's home planet what feels like years ago, guides my spear as I rush towards the first quartet of Flaum dropping from the shuttles overhead. Their boots flare and catch each of the furry creatures, about my height, though of slighter build, as they land.

My first target sports clotted amber fur, which blows across its face as it's exposed to the mountain wind. Those distracting strands offer me the opening I need to slip the point past its guard, which amounts to a thrown up arm with a small hand wrapped around a miner's trigger. The stab connects and I start to pull back for a second jab when the Flaum pinches the spear into its side, pressing the point in further.

It's a move that has to be incredibly painful, but when you're being controlled by something else, something that can ignore your suffering for its own ends, such maneuvers become viable. I'm not expecting it, so when the Flaum twists away from me, the spear's torn from my grasp.

I draw the kukri, a knife that bends along the blade, ending with a heavier, flat point ideal for the more mundane tasks of life like chopping fruit or clearing leaves. I use it to perform a slashing cut, one that doesn't so much hurt the Flaum as force it back, giving me a meter's space to adjust.

On either side of me other warriors engage with the rest of the Flaum, using our numbers to drive them back towards the cliff's edge. Viera works her pistols, along with other Lunare marksmen, to keep other Sevora shooters from picking us off from the shuttle doors. This is the instant stalemate I've come to expect, and one that gets thrown awry as more Sevora shuttles blow in above and behind us.

The amber-furred Flaum makes its move, ignoring its wound and the spear sticking out of it to aim the miner towards me. In that instant, though, I jump forward, kukri swiping at the Flaum's weapon-wielding arm while the rest of me barrels into the light-weight creature.

I'm not a large person either—most of the warriors on this cliff face have me beat handily in height and weight—but Flaum are more fur than anything. The kukri's swing gets the Flaum backpedaling, and my left-shoulder charge hits its chest, knocking the Flaum into a falling stumble. With my left hand, I grab the handle of my spear as the Flaum chitters out a panicked screech, and draw back my weapon.

The Flaum, and the Sevora inside it, tumble over the cliff. There's a chance those boots it has can find enough metal in the mountainside to stabilize its fall, but I'm willing to live with that risk; there's more pressing targets.

"This isn't working, Kaishi!" Viera's yell cuts above the madness, and I see her wielding her sword in her left hand, a pistol in her right.

Viera ducks under a Flaum firing as it descends to land near her, then sweeps with her blade, taking the creature's legs out from under it. A quick finishing shot at the tripped Flaum buys my friend a breath, which she uses to tell me to run.

"There's too many!" Viera calls.

I rush back to the line, which now is more of a circle around the long hole back to Marilo, getting pressed in on all sides by the Sevora forces. Miners flash their bolts and our warriors fall, the Sevora forming a defensive line and allowing the ranks behind to lay down covering fire.

I'm passed back, Viera pulling me along. I try to turn, to stand with my own forces, but my friend won't let me, until I shake her off, twist away and look in the faces of the creatures gunning us down.

"Kaishi," Viera protests over the screams, the shouts and rings of metal-on-metal. "We run now, or we die!"

I've run before. Left my people to fend for themselves against a hostile galaxy, and I'm not doing it again.

"Then I die with them." I push back, get to the front when the warrior in front of me, a bulky man in a white-furred Fassoth cloak, bursts into flame and collapses.

The fighter's death reveals a grim line of Flaum with their buzzing blades drawn, the edges glowing with the same laser-light shooting from their miners, and behind them, aiming weapons, are the true killers—the Sevora gunning us down.

There's not enough of us to win, but there are enough of us to buy Marilo a little more time.

"Together!" I shout, thrusting the black-glass spear high, where it catches the light of Ignos.

And the shuttle above our heads explodes in a shattering boom, the shockwave sending all of us, human and Flaum alike, to our knees. Shrapnel rains, scattering burning knives into the crowd. That first boom is quickly followed by two more; another shuttle pair immolated out of the air.

Before I fully process what's going on, the Flaum in front of me are erased as rock explodes and a great ship—larger than the Sevora shuttles, with a pointed, glimmering front—drives into the side of the mountain. The sides of the vessel slide up and open, and creatures I never expected to see again leap out.

Oratus.

Four of them, followed by more furry Flaum and slug-like Whelk, though the latter species are accessories to the brutal show the Oratus put on. The three-meter tall lizard-like monsters, with their four clawed arms, two jagged talons and long, whipping tails deliver mortal punishment to the Sevora force at a speed I can barely comprehend.

The Sevora shuttles continue to detonate from a series of fast-moving slivers shrieking by and delivering concentrated fire. The aerial squad travels in a line, each in sequence firing at the same spot on their way by, eventually boring a burning hole in the Sevora ship until it explodes.

The response to the events comes in flavors—there's my numb, stunned analysis of what's going on, there's my soldiers, who alternate between cheering and retreat, and the Sevora, who abandon what composure they had and resort to panicked flight. They leap from the cliff, diving off the mountainside and running away.

They don't get far—the Flaum and Whelk that came down with the Oratus set up their longer miners and clean up the cowards, leaving us, after frantic seconds, in a blood-soaked, burning battlefield bereft of enemies.

"I don't believe it," Viera says, and I'm thankful she's found her way back to my side. "They actually came."

All I can do is nod and turn my eyes upward, at the light show continuing in Earth's upper atmosphere as the Sevora force that's haunted our every waking moment since I came home burns in systematic, fatal fashion. Like watching flowers burst into bloom on a spring day, the gray-black ships pop into oranges and whites against the blue sky.

I wonder if Ignos, the Sevora that once lived inside my head is up there.

I'm surprised to find I hope it's not.


The clean-up goes by quickly, with me spending most of it watching as the Oratus go about their bloody business. Our warriors quickly find their own efforts outmatched and settle back, watching their enemies both nearby and up above obliterated by these new players.

"Stay back!" I shout eventually. "Don't engage. These are . . . " 'Friends' seems the wrong word, but I need to say something, so I go with, "Allies!".

One of the Oratus, with glinting green scales and looking cleaner than the others after the carnage, finds its way to me once the Sevora threat is eliminated. I've forgotten how tall the creatures are—this one is nearly twice my height, and it stares down at me with its teeth visible, those vents lining its chest opening and closing to suck in the air.

My Shadows—the three left, anyway—step up around me, and Viera, behind me, has her hands on her pistols. I hold up a hand, telling them not to start something stupid.

"You are the leader?" the Oratus asks, its light hiss mingling with the whistle of mountain wind.

"I am," I reply. "Thank you for coming."

The Oratus cocks its head to the side. "We should thank you. This was the last Sevora fleet. With its destruction, their ability to expand is ruined."

I'm not sure how I feel about that, so I settle for a stare. The conversation, though, has passed beyond the easy introduction, and treads into awkward territory. The Vincere came, destroyed our enemies, and the only thing I want from them now is to leave and let us recover.

Diplomacy, however, requires compromise. Requires being polite.

Then the Oratus speaks and turns my plans to ash.

"You do not seem surprised to see us," the Oratus says. "Unlike the others of your kind, you do not shrink away. Tremble in fear." The emerald creature glances at Viera. "Neither does she."

A second Oratus, a darker blue in color, steps up behind the first. "They ought to be scared."

"Gar," the first Oratus says. "Stop. You've had your fill."

"Always ready for seconds," the blue one, Gar, replies. "These don't look so furry either, with more meat on their bones."

Even as my warriors shift around me, I know a joke when I hear it and crack a smile. "I've seen Oratus. Once before, some of you stole me from here."

I'm expecting a question, but what I get instead is a sudden tightening from both Oratus. Their tails touch, and then the green one crouches low until its eyes meet mine.

"Who stole you?"

"There were two," I say, feeling like this is a bad idea, but that lying would be even worse. "One with gray scales, called Sax, the other a pink-gold one named Bas. They took me and a couple of my friends to a station called *Cobalt*."

The emerald Oratus straightens, looks at Gar, who offers a slight baring of teeth. That seems to send a message, one that causes the emerald Oratus to expel a lot of air from its vents in a heavy sigh.

"We did not expect to find our ambassador so quickly," the Oratus says. "You will be returning with us, human. Gather your things, and pack carefully, for I don't know how long you will be gone."

# 4 / SAVING A SPECIES

The surface of Solis comes through as the shuttle breaks the heavy clouds. It's a sight Sax hasn't seen in a very, very long time. A long stripe of verdant green, a gash on an otherwise dry and rocky brown landscape. On one end of the scar, a giant mountain rises, and on the other, a low-lying lake marks the destination of the wide streams and rivers running through that strip of jungle. A kilometers-wide valley carved between two rising cliffs.

What catches the eye most, though, are the series of arches spanning that valley, rising up over the jungle from cliff to cliff and covered with stone-like armor. They look natural, brown and weathered by the often and turbulent storms that break and flush from one end of the valley to the other. Adorning each of these arches, and hanging like ripe blackberries, are the bulbous chambers that brought Sax to life.

"You have a particular target in mind?" the Flaum pilot, an ashen-furred one with scarred ears, asks.

Sax leans over her, staring out the shuttle's windshield. Crash netting hangs behind him, forgotten in the moment. Like how Sax is going to find his pair. Her mission was to exterminate the source of the Oratus, to prevent the Chorus from making newer, more loyal versions that wouldn't hesitate to cut Sax down. A task like that doesn't lend itself to being conspicuous.

"I . . . don't know," Sax hisses.

"You're going to have to make a choice soon," the Flaum replies. "I can't just dawdle up here. Cacia's entry code's only going to work for so long."

"They wouldn't shoot us down."

"Solis doesn't play around, Oratus," the Flaum says and Sax gives a low warning hiss, but the furball doesn't flinch. "Can't scare me—if they think we're not normal, they'll blow us apart and figure it out later. Which makes your threats all kinds of worthless."

The Flaum has a point, and so Sax chooses the farthest arch, the one closest to the lake. It would make sense for Bas to start from there, work her way up, rather than go to the Mountain and deal with all the Oratus-in-training coming her way.

Sax expects the shuttle to land at one of the hatcheries, but instead the Flaum targets the near side of the third arch, settling in for a landing at the very edge of the rocky mass. As they draw in closer, the ground beyond the arch, devoid of plants and anything other than gray dirt, shifts aside to reveal a small docking bay. One that, going by the speed of the door and the lack of lights inside, hasn't seen visitors in a very long while.

Yet, when the boarding ramp lowers and Sax sets foot on his homeworld for the first time since his birth, he's not alone. Another Oratus, the deep green bracelet of a Cache wrapped around his teal-colored left foreclaw, waits for him. What little lights there are frame the only exit, a single large door clearly meant for hauling small amounts of cargo. The Oratus stands in front of it and watches as Sax descends.

"Your wounds mark your status, Oratus," the greeter says. "What business do you have on Solis?"

"I'm looking for someone," Sax replies, talons settling into the packed-dirt floor of the bay. "Though if you'd seen her, you would be dead."

If this surprises the Oratus, there's no sign.

"You doubt our own skill? Solis has remained unconquered for its duration," the Oratus says. "We've trained thousands and thousands here. Any one seeking to attack this place would find themselves both over-matched and out-skilled."

"She doesn't want to fight you," Sax says. "She wants to kill you. I need to tell her not to."

That gets the Oratus to cock his head. To puzzle for a moment. Then, slowly, he speaks, "If what you say is true, then you should come inside. Leave your pilot out here. No other species is allowed on Solis, save with our consent."

Sax has no problem with that. Flaum are always more trouble than they're worth.

Sax follows the Oratus down the dim, rock-ridged corridor. The air's cool and still, and it's nice to walk, for once, without the clack of talons on metal floor. Hard-packed dirt might be primitive, but it feels soft on Sax's feet—the sand brings back brief memories of his start.

His birth, if Sax wants to call it that.

The next room, the main one for this hatchery, is huge. Like the top half of an onion, the room's sloped walls rise to a point far above them, the section anchored into the arch itself. Spaced throughout the chamber, both on the floor next to them and sitting in honey-combed creches along the room's sides, are large purple-red sacs. Each one has a small machine—no larger than Sax's midclaws—attached to it, showing a gradually-greening ring.

"This is your first time back, isn't it?" his guide says. "Most never return to Solis."

"I'm not here for the memories," Sax replies. "Have you seen her? Bas?"

"You're in such a hurry," the Oratus says, pausing near a bulging sack, its ring almost fully green. "Part of the problem of our species, I think, is that we're always running to the next conflict."

"What else is there?"

The Oratus laughs at this, but Sax picks up plenty of disappointment in the low hissing. "Do you know how they choose us? The ones who watch the hatcheries, who guide the new-formed Oratus?"

Of all the topics Sax has never once considered in his life, this has to be close to the bottom. What use would such a thought be? Knowing how these hatcheries are maintained won't help him beat the Sevora, won't help him destabilize the Chorus.

Sax is about to tell the guide to take him to Bas and be quiet while doing it, but there's something in the Oratus' expression, a light in its eyes and an eager twitch to the creature's tail that tells Sax this one's gone a long time without real conversation.

"I have no idea," Sax finally says.

"We're the failures," the guide hisses. "The ones that survive, but crash out of training. We don't make it through the wheels, don't find pairs or lose them. This is an exile, when it should be an honor."

Sax takes a step back, more at the tone than anything else. There's genuine anger coming out of this teal Oratus' mouth. The same sort of frustration Sax might express if he were left to rot on a background planet doing nothing but watching Oratus grow day after day.

"Don't you wonder how we stay sane? What they do to keep us happy?" the Oratus continues.

Sax, though, realizes now how quiet it is in here. Aside from the shifting of the occasional sack, there's no noise. No other Flaum, and Sax recalls plenty of those when he first emerged.

"I don't have time," Sax manages a reply as the strangeness twists in his gut.

Sax adjusts his stance, widens his legs and loosens his claws. He brings his tail down to the ground, subtly pressing it into the earth so that, if necessary, Sax can use it to push off.

"Nobody ever does, for us," the Oratus says. "So when she came, when she explained to me how forgotten I am, how unappreciated we are, I heard the truth."

"What truth?"

"That we need to spare them all," the Oratus gestures around the hatchery. "All the Amigga give us are lives of violence and death. Why should we allow that to happen?"

"Where are the Flaum, Oratus?"

"Gone, Sax." The sac next to the Oratus shifts along the floor, and the Oratus gives it a dire look. Raises a talon, as if to destroy it. "They aren't necessary anymore. I don't need their help for this."

Sax springs forward, tackles the Oratus and drives the guide into the ground. Pins the guide's claws back against the dirt, making sure to keep his own head high enough, away from the guide's sharp teeth.

"Their lives are not your decision," Sax hisses.

Sax expects resistance, struggle, but the guide only looks confused.

"When Rav sent the message you were coming, Bas said you would support us?" the guide says. "You want to end our pain as much as she does?"

"Change of plans," Sax says. "The Oratus need to survive, so we can make sure the Chorus does not."

The guide twists his head on the ground to look at the sac, almost ready to hatch. "So you would give us a new purpose?"

"We're trying to give you freedom to choose."

"Then Bas? Why would she?"

"Because at the time we thought you better dead than fighting against us," Sax says. "Turns out you can change an Oratus mind."

Sax makes a quick calculation that the guide isn't ready to fight anymore and slowly stands up, lets the guide get his claws back. The guide, for his part, takes his time climbing to his talons, shocked in more ways than one.

"Bas doesn't know," Sax continues. "I need to find her."

The guide shakes his head. "She's not here. By now she's probably on the farthest arch." The Oratus stares at Sax, raising his foreclaws up as if only now realizing what he's done. "Bas was . . . very convincing. She made sure we took care of our own assistants. You have to stop her."

"Call the other arches. Tell them what I've told you," Sax hisses, though he's already turning to run back to his ship.

The Flaum pilot hasn't raised the boarding ramp, and she's napping at the controls when Sax's heavy bounds startle her up from her sleep. In moments Sax has the story told and they're lifting off, out through the doors and up into Solis' sky.

To the first arch.

They're barely aloft before the shuttle's communications array crackles through the speakers embedded in the front line of terminals.

"Coming from the ground," the Flaum pilot says. "They're hailing."

"Answer it." Sax checks the screen—the identifier's blocked, which, in a way, identifies who it is.

The Flaum taps the flashing orange screen, which shifts to a lighter green to show the connection's been made.

"Sax, you came for me," Bas's hiss comes through the terminal. "You weren't supposed to do that."

"I made a different deal," Sax hisses. "We're keeping the Oratus alive."

Bas hesitates. "Nobody told me."

"I'm telling you," Sax says. "Where are you?"

"The first arch."

"Wait for me? And don't kill anyone?"

"You're the one who can't control himself, Sax." There's a bit of laughter in Bas' voice, but a tinge of uncertainty too.

She's looking for something.

"I'm not a hostage," Sax says. "I'd die first."

That gets a happy sigh through the call. "Glad you don't have to," Bas says.

They meet not long after, on the ground outside the first arch. Sax descends the ramp to find his pink-gold pair standing in the small bay waiting for him, Bas' own shuttle making the space crowded. It's the longest Sax has gone without seeing his pair since they've met. Days passed, either on Rathfall, trying to find his way back into civilization, or on Rav's frigate, nearly dying and then being pieced back together. That's the first thing Bas notices, her yellow eyes going wide as her midclaws touch the missing sections in Sax's glinting gray scales. She runs those eyes up and down her pair, and Sax stays quiet for a moment as he does the same. Their foreclaws clasp and the tips of their tails wrap around each other on the floor.

"I hoped, but didn't think we'd ever see each other again," Bas says first. "They said you would go to Evva and try to bring down the Chorus. From here, I'm supposed to go up and try, somehow, to destroy the Oratus training ship."

"You don't have to do that anymore," Sax says. "They tried to get me to do what you said, I refused. Violently."

"You didn't kill them all."

Sax cracks his razer mouth open in a smile. "They're still alive."

"Then what now? Evva?"

Sax nods. "That was the deal. I'd come here and stop your part of the mission, then we'd both head to the Chorus and tear them apart."

"You almost took too long," Bas flicks a glance behind her. "I never realized how close all of these caretaker Oratus are to losing their minds. All I had to do was explain how we were being used, and they were ready to cast it all away."

"They'll have a better purpose once the Amigga are gone."

Bas laughs. "It's that easy? Once they're gone?"

"Bas, I managed to get the Vincere leaders orbiting this planet to join us. If I can persuade people without using my claws, then we're destined to win."

Bas asks more questions and Sax answers, then they swap roles and talk more. Eventually the Flaum pilot comes down and asks whether they'll be staying long, as she's getting hungry and they didn't pack much food in their craft. That serves as enough of a cue to grab a snack, climb back in their shuttle, and pack off to orbit.

On the way up, Bas dishes one more long communication to the caretakers she'd just turned against their own race. It's a short one, an ask to stay their claws, to keep the new Oratus growing, a promise that they'll be hatching into a better future.

A promise Sax knows they'll keep.

R ight, except I'm not going anywhere." I don't flinch away
from the Oratus, despite the fact that its claws could eviscerate me before any of my Shadows could intervene. "I
just made it back here, and my people have been under attack."

The Oratus stares at me. Regards me as I would a particularly
interesting plant.

"Human, you are a new species," the Oratus hisses. "You are,
right now, apart from the rest of the galaxy. Do you know of the
Chorus?"

I've heard the term, mostly back on Vimelia, the Scvora homeworld where the Chorus was mainly mentioned with disdain.
Supposedly a group of Amigga—those round, strange creatures—
make up the Chorus, and use these Oratus to force the galaxy to do
what they want.

There's also the fact that one of those Amigga, one named Ignos,
may have created humans.

"I've heard of it," I finally say.

"They will need someone to speak for your species. If that will
not be you, then who?" the Oratus says.

"I'll do it," Viera announces from behind me. "She doesn't have to go."

"Viera?" I look back at her, confused. "What?"

"Told you, Empress. I'm a traveler—that's why I left the mountains for the jungle so long ago. If we're not going to get attacked, then it seems like all we'll be doing is putting humanity back together," Viera shrugs. "That's not what I'm interested in."

Could I let Viera go as the ambassador for humanity? Alone?

"Come back," I tell the Oratus. "Tomorrow. When the light rises again, we'll be back here, ready to go."

The Oratus delivers a low hiss, "Acceptable."

Once the declaration is made, the Oratus wastes no time; it roars a command, and its troops pile back into the craft. Its doors slide shut as we back away, and I'm wondering how the shuttle is going to break free of the rock it drove into during its landing, when a loud grinding noise begins. The ground beneath our feet shakes, loose rocks rattle and snow slips from its perches as the ship drills itself free.

I expect the shuttle, as its front loosens away from the rock, to fall over and slide down the hillside, but an array of small orange circles across its bottom hull spark to life and let the shuttle straighten out while hovering in the air. It rotates, floats a small distance away, and with a smoking burst of crackling sound, the craft roars up into a sky still spotted with the fading remains of the Sevora fleet.


"You don't want me to go?" Viera says later, as we're back down in Marilo sharing large glasses of wine.

The city's turned itself out in celebration. Nobody cares to consider that the Vincere could turn and attack us just like the Sevora did. Instead, the streets are full of people in drunken revelry. Runners riding the great white Fassoths have been dispatched to every corner of the mountains, and those Solare and Charre tribesmen who wish it are making ready, between dances and songs, to return to their homelands.

I'm watching a band of them right now from our balcony in Marilo's capitol building, a band of several dozen; Warriors, children, priests and more. Solare preparing to see if anything's left of their home. They're taking weapons too—nobody's assuming the last Sevora on the planet died on that mountainside today.

"I can't let you go," I say, taking another sip. The wine's acidic, harsh and stressed, but still welcome. "Not alone."

"So you don't trust me."

We're sitting in soft woven chairs, and mine crinkles as I lean back in it and toss Viera a smile. "I don't trust you to keep your hands off your pistols."

"Did that fine when I was staying with your tribe."

That takes me back, briefly. Avril's already sent scouts to see if my parents, if my home village still stands, but I'm not clinging to it. They never appeared in the mountains, and the Sevora struck first at the jungles and plains.

"We didn't threaten you," I say. "These things, you saw what happened on *Cobalt*. They'll try to bend you, break you. They'll want humans to accept them as masters."

"So?" Viera nods at the bouncing happiness over the edge. "If that's what we get, does it matter?"

"Dalachite, the Amigga on *Cobalt*? It was making copies of us. And you know what's on the other side of these mountains—evidence that the Amigga made us, and tried to destroy us. What's to say they won't again when it's convenient?"

"Do you think we could stop them if we wanted to?"

There's the truth I've kept from telling myself. No. No we could not win a war against those Oratus or their army they call the Vincere.

"That's why I have to go," I say, and now that the words are out, it's obvious. "You and I are the only ones that know the truth. We have to present ourselves as equals, we have to guarantee our future."

"You're going to fight for your people by leaving them again?"

Viera laughs, but it's a sad sound. "You're the only Empress I've known who spends all her time avoiding her domain."

Not because I want to.

Avril doesn't object to the plan, and I wonder if it's because, again, I'm handing her all the power she wants. The Lunare, now, have every advantage over the other tribes and while Avril says she's not going to embark on an immediate chain of conquests, I'm not sure I believe her.

I came back to my people and found them ruined once, and the next time I might find them gone entirely.

There's one more person I need to talk to before the morning: Vee, an Oratus that we found when we returned to Earth, trapped in the desolate remnants of the Amigga base that led, I think, to the human species.

Vee's been taking turns during the night, preferring the cold dark to the bright day, and his presence up there, I've heard, has saved countless lives. Even so, I'm nervous opening the door to the squat building whose highest floor, at one point a series of apartments, has been given over to him.

Vee's already awake by the time we arrive, standing ready.

"T'Oli, you want to explain?" I offer to the Ooblot, who joined Viera and I after our glass of wine.

"Oh no, I think you'll do a far better job," T'Oli says. "I have no gravity for these sorts of things."

I sigh, but T'Oli's right.

"What things?" Vee hisses.

"The Vincere are here," I say.

"So that's why it's so loud today." Vee nods towards the small windows.

They have no glass, so the sounds of happy drums and celebration bleed through. Probably quite the change from the dead quiet, doomed atmosphere that's hovered over the city before now.

"They want Viera and I to leave with them," I say, after

describing the Sevora's destruction. "I thought you might want to come too?"

Vee takes a long moment. Closes his eyes.

"I lost my pair in the attack on the base," Vee says finally. "The Vincere left me down there. I assume they believe I'm dead. I had nothing to live for until you found me and gave me a purpose."

The Oratus takes a long stride towards me and sets its right fore-claw on my shoulder. It should be comforting—I know Vee's not threatening me—but the sheer strength even in that one limb forces me to suppress a twitch.

"I have friends here now, the ones I've been fighting with," Vee says. "And as you say, there may yet be Sevora on this world, in the jungle."

"You want to stay here?" Viera blurts. "Really?"

Vee laughs, a rumbling, hissing thing. "Is that so surprising?"

"Frankly, yeah."

"I understand," I say, shaking my head at Viera. "Tomorrow, I won't tell them. They'll never know you survived."

Vee gives me a nod of thanks, then looks over at the Ooblot. "What of you, T'Oli? Are you staying, or going with the human?"

"Oh, I'd prefer to leave," T'Oli says. "Humans are awfully fragile, and after I've gone through this much trouble keeping Kaishi alive, I want her to stay that way."

"It's not easy," Viera mutters.

"Hey," I say. "I could order you both to stay here, you know."

"We wouldn't listen," Viera replies.

I know they wouldn't, and I'm glad.


The next morning comes faster than I'd like, especially with the results of several more wine glasses dancing in my skull. Viera's in even worse shape, and she spends most of the walk to the rope ladders with her eyes shut, hands pressed to her head.

"Why do you humans consume things so obviously harmful to yourselves?" T'Oli says, oozing along with us.

"Because we have to listen to you," Viera says.

I don't bother to say anything, because, really, I don't want any more noise. Not even my own voice. Every sound brings with it another knock of my headache.

Climbing the rope ladder, though, does some magic to make me feel better. Maybe it's the exertion, or the requirement to focus my unwilling body on a life-or-death task. Hitting the mountainside, with its blistering chill air, banishes the remnants of the hangover, and I face the brightening sky with a steady face.

The dozen warriors we stationed up here—because Avril refused to trust all the threats were gone, and I agreed—wave at us, but don't approach. I return the gesture, and I'm not offended they're not coming over—there's a shuttle swooping down towards our section of the cliff, and the open doors show the emerald Oratus is waiting. Nobody would want to get any closer to that if they don't have to.

The emerald Oratus jumps out of the shuttle, which stays hovering about a meter off the rock. With its claws, the Oratus helps us board, lifting first me, with T'Oli riding on my back, and then Viera into the craft.

The inside, like the first Vincere shuttle I rode in, gives its own definition to the word 'sparse'. There's simply nothing in the back save netting, though I notice the shuttle seems far taller on the inside, with a series of bars stretched across the top. The cockpit on this one is situated to our right, at the rear, where a pair of Flaum sit in tight quarters above the engines. To the left, the translucent view shows the shrinking mountain as the shuttle begins to withdraw.

"This is all you need?" the Oratus asks, staring at our small packs.

"We haven't been in one place long enough to gather possessions," I say, though I bring my hands to the emerald necklace. This time, I want to keep it, and I figure a little sign of royalty won't be a bad thing when I show up in front of the Chorus.

The Oratus nods. "We keep nothing for ourselves, either, except those weapons we deem most fit for our abilities." There's a pause as the Oratus sucks in some air, and Viera settles into a section of the hanging netting. "My name is Lan, and I welcome you, ambassador of humanity, to the Vincere."

I gather there's supposed to be something ceremonial in the sentiment, but right now I'm leaning against some draping black net as I leave my home far too soon, and I can't quite get there. So I ask a question instead.

"You know Sax?"

By the way Lan twitches, I know I've surprised the Oratus.

"We served together," Lan says, slow. "For a time, until he became a traitor to the Vincere and to his race."

"That doesn't sound like Sax." What I remember of the Oratus is his dedication to the mission, to the destruction of any threat. "He did everything he could to keep us alive."

Those words prompt more questions, and the rest of the shuttle ride is spent swapping stories of the Oratus, first of Sax, then Bas, and finally of the four of them, the last being Gar, who's waiting for us on the lead cruiser in the Vincere fleet above Earth.

If there's one thing I get from the conversation, it's that Lan isn't quite the soulless machine she makes the Oratus out to be. Regret and confusion permeate her memories as she tells them, and I sympathize; every night I turn over the time with Ignos—the Sevora—in my mind, wondering whether anything it did was out of concern for me or humanity, or whether it was all in self-interest. Whether the Sevora could care about me or my people.

*Nunilite* is the cruiser's name, supposedly, so Lan tells it, because that's also the name of the Amigga who discovered and designed leaping technology. As for why this specific ship gets the noble name, that's because of the giant bulb built on the front end of the cruiser. It's visible from the shuttle as we approach, largely because its copper shading sticks out from the bright-white of the rest of the hull.

"Leaping sends a ship through folds in space-time," Lan says, and the excited hiss in her voice tells me she prefers this to the sad discussion of her former partners. "This technology inverts the science." At my vacant look—Viera's asleep and who knows what T'Oli's thinking—Lan pauses for a moment, then tries again. "Rather than pushing a ship through a wrinkle in the universe to move from one place to another, the *Nunilite* can create a new fold between two points. It can bring them together."

"Why?"

Lan stares at me. I must have said something dumb. The Oratus opens her mouth to explain, then shuts it.

"Perhaps it's better if you don't know," Lan says. "You're not yet on our side, after all."

If Lan's expecting me to push the issue, to pester her about what sort of cosmic miracle the *Nunilite* can unleash on the universe, she's disappointed. Right now, I'm looking at Viera and feeling awfully jealous about her trip to the world of dreams, and with a simple statement I tell Lan I'm going to the same place.

The Oratus says she'll wake us when we arrive, but I'm already asleep before she finishes the sentence.

I've now landed on three places apart from Earth—*Cobalt*, a nightmarish space station where an Amigga tried to turn my species into carbon clones for its own ends, Vimelia, the Sevora homeworld where two factions tried to use my friends and I to inflame a war or end it, and now the *Nunilite*, which becomes my first glimpse of the Vincere in their element.

The shuttle doors open and Lan is the first one out, her emerald frame serving as a guide in the harsh docking bay lights. Unlike some of the others I've seen, though, this bay is empty of other ships. It's not large, either, with deep black floors, steel-slat walls, and a cross-section of Flaum and Whelk soldiers waiting for us to exit.

What's more surprising is the amount of artillery present for our arrival. Miners aim in our general direction, and at least two of the

Flaum are encased in larger . . . suits that give them longer limbs and larger cannons through metal extensions.

"Is this a threat?" I ask Viera as we slowly exit the shuttle.

"Maybe they think we're the danger."

"You're an unknown," Lan hisses as she steps back from us to remove any chance she gets hit by a stray shot. "The Vincere do not like to take unnecessary risks."

"That's right, we might just go crazy and blow up your ship right here," Viera says, shaking her head as she does it, a motion that stops as soon as all those miners snap to attention and the low whine of charging weapons fills the bay.

"I would not make jokes." Lan nods towards the docking bay's only exit, a thick clay-red door that appears very much shut.

"Touchy," Viera whispers to me as we follow Lan towards the door.

"The Vincere have never been known for their cheer," T'Oli states from my back, where the Ooblot's adopted its customary perch. "Some say you have to murder your sense of humor to join."

"We save our laughter for the battlefield," Lan says without turning back. "Where we mock our enemies as they fall."

"Remind me not to invite them to our next party," I say to Viera.

Beyond the red door, which opens only after we've been scanned and Viera's had her pistols and sword confiscated, there's one of what I gather to be many, many hallways. It's a wide one, and full of shuffling troops, floating platforms covered in crates, and the occasional buzzing drone shooting by above our heads.

Messages ordering individuals, squads, and other nouns I don't know echo overhead. Nobody bothers paying us any attention. At first, given our reception, I'd have thought we'd be the stars of the ship, but Lan informs us that as we've been cleared, we're no longer worthy of note.

"Where are we going?" I ask Lan as we keep walking and I lose myself in the maze.

"We're taking the long way to the bridge," Lan replies.

"Why the long way?" Viera asks.

"So you understand the scope of the ship, and your place within it."

I could choose to take the words as a threat, but our slow pace and the endless activity around us give me a chance to mull them over. We're on a military vessel, part of the so-called 'Vincere', and Lan's told us the point of coming with them will be to present humanity to the Chorus as a species worth having in the galaxy. Around us, Flaum and Whelk, along with scattered few other species whose names I don't know—stick-like ones with tiny limbs, and large, lumbering things that look like living rock—yet all of them defer to Lan's presence. They move out of her way, don't meet her eyes, and generally act like my own guards do around me.

Where would humans fall in that hierarchy? Lan's words seem to say we'd be right in that same mix, clustered among the species meant to serve and support the Oratus and their force. Assist the Amigga in any way they desired.

"Just what place is that?" Viera asks the question as I reach the conclusion.

Lan hisses a laugh. "Whatever place is chosen for you. The Chorus sets the galaxy's purpose, and the bounds of the lives within it."

The cruiser's bridge is unlike anything I've seen before—the triple-wide doors open onto a raised platform that splits a broad, silver-blue pit in which dozens of Flaum and other species work at various stations. Overseeing all of them, at the end of the platform, is a rust-colored Oratus whose scales are so scarred as to make me wince at all the pain it has to have felt.

Beyond the leader, as the rust-colored Oratus, by its straight-edged stance and slow panning gaze, makes clear that it is, sits a vast transparent shield showing, in its lower right corner, Earth's soft blue edge. Coming into view dead ahead is Nomis's bulk, her gray surface looking pocked and dark from this distance.

Lan leads the three of us out onto the platform, then bids us to stop about halfway to the end while she continues on.

"Maybe our species isn't good enough to go all the way," Viera says.

"We've been discounted before," I reply. "We proved them wrong."

"Undoubtedly, your past results will be indicative of future success!" T'Oli says, though only through the quietest of tapping talk.

"Are you being sarcastic?" Viera says the words to the Ooblot on my back.

"Yes." T'Oli shifts up onto my shoulders, so its less like a pack now and more like a cloak. "The odds of a species with your level of technology making an appreciable mark on the galaxy are slim."

"Yeah, well, you're a living puddle. So there."

I can't quite suppress a laugh, which causes a smile to spread across my face when Lan and the rust Oratus stomp up and stand over me.

"Lan tells me your name is Kaishi," the rust Oratus says. "I am Kolas. Welcome to my ship, my fleet, and our galaxy."

I don't know what the protocol is here—if this were, say, a leader of a Solare tribe back home I would bow. However, I'm also an Empress. I'm here representing all of humanity. And our species should bow to none.

So I give Kolas a nod instead, and hope that's sufficient. When I look back up at the Oratus, I notice Kolas has steel-colored eyes, an unnatural blue-gray shade that seems as hard as the metal. Its mouth is full of sharp teeth, though many of these are jagged or broken.

"You're an ugly one," Viera says from behind me. "Lan here's saying that we're low down on the species pecking order. Thing is, I don't know how we can be beneath something like you, seeing as you're all beat up and broken."

I close my eyes tight. Sigh. Hope that Viera's words don't get us eviscerated right there, right then.

Instead of death whistling towards me, though, what I get is a loud hissing laugh. Kolas, when I open my eyes, is nodding, still laughing, towards Viera.

"What is your name, little human?" Kolas says. "Your bravery does your species credit."

"Viera," my friend and current exasperation, says. "Figure we ought to start negotiations off strong."

"If only it were I that you needed to persuade," Kolas says. "I am the Chorus' vessel to lead the Vincere, but I am not the Chorus itself. Keep your courage for them, and they will treat you well."

"Will they?" I ask. "Because I don't think they wanted us to exist."

That prompts the first surprise I've seen on an Oratus face. Lan's mouth pops open slightly, her vents sucking in a bunch of air. Kolas, though, only gives me a dead stare, what remains of its humor dying away quick.

"You were a failure," Kolas says. "A species far more independent than the need called for. Look what we already have—Flaum, Whelk, Vyphen. All of these are as capable as yours, and more pliable still. That is why you have a tough trial ahead. You must prove the galaxy needs you."

Kolas' answer doesn't tell me why the Chorus made humans at all, what that need was, but before I can ask the question, the Oratus turns and barks an order down to the pit of Flaum. A call to prepare the cruiser and the fleet for a leap. Kolas glances back at us.

"Lan will take you to your cabin for the leap," Kolas says. "When it's done, you can return here to witness the end of the longest war in galactic history."

## 6 / THE GALAXY'S CENTER

A familiar ship floats beyond the pair of frigates. The *Mobius*, coasting in space like the head of a trident, waits for Sax and Bas well out of range of any surprise Vincere attack. Before they dock, Sax manages to send one last message of thanks to Rav, though when the commander asks where they're going next, Sax keeps quiet.

"The next mission," Sax hisses through space to Rav.

"There's always another one," Rav replies. "Good luck, Sax. I hope I don't have to rescue you again."

"You won't." Sax doesn't add that if they need rescuing where they're going, it'll be too late.

The Flaum pilot doesn't bother asking either, and the creature seems relieved when the airlocks open and the two Oratus make their way out of her ship. Knowing the bloody chaos that tends to follow him around, Sax doesn't blame her.

Standing on the other side of the airlock is a familiar site: Plake, her rainbow feathers furled around her arms stands center, with Agra-Red, a crimson, jelly-like Whelk whose body holds a gigantic miner embedded into its side, armed and ready beside her.

"Engee and Nobaa are busy back near the engines," Plake says when Sax looks around, curious. "I left Silver and Black on Rathfall." Plake winces for a second. "Really, they left me. Apparently your bug-hunting strategy is earning them more than running cargo ever would."

"Coorvin?" Sax asks.

The older Flaum is the only one of that species Sax likes. Coorvin's long tenure under the vice-grip of a psychotic Amigga has made him an infinitely preferable companion to the chattering madness of his brethren. That, and Coorvin's uncanny ability to slip around unnoticed through the side ways of spaces would make him a valuable asset for their mission.

"He's gone ahead," Agra-Red speaks for its captain. "The little guy is quiet, but I think he's burning for a bit of revenge. Wouldn't like to be an Amigga caught alone with him."

"He's a Flaum," Bas says. "What could he do?"

"Species have been killing each other long before your claws ever showed up, Oratus," Agra-Red replies. "Coorvin's clever enough to find a way."

Rav donated Sax and Bas a couple of miners and masks, but that's all the gear the two Oratus bring onto the *Mobius*, so after a minute's worth of prep, the airlock breaks from the Vincere shuttle and Sax's former pilot takes no spare time in jetting back towards the frigates.

The rest of them form up in the cockpit as Plake powers up the engines for a leap. The captain makes a quick call to Engee and confirms they're good to go. Crash netting falls down around them and Sax straps himself in.

"Anyone ever been to Aspicis?" Plake asks as she hovers a hand over the terminal.

"Never," Sax says and Bas echoes his sentiment. "Nobody would dare attack the Chorus, so we were never called there."

The Amigga's home and, by default, the galaxy's capitol world; Aspicis is almost a place of myth. Sax figures the limited information is by design—to even get onto the planet takes a whole set of clearances. Even Caches, those stores of knowledge kept on ships and, occasionally, individuals were generally wiped clear except to list what had to be done to gain entrance to the planet.

"One time," Agra-Red says, and Sax jerks his heard to the Whelk, surprised. "Before I knew you, Plake."

The captain removes her feathered hand from the launch button. "Anything we should know?"

"We wanted revenge," Agra-Red said. "The Sevora ruined our planet. So we went to Aspicis to plead for a place in the Vincere, a chance to get our own vengeance. It worked, more or less. That's why you've got Whelk in the Vincere now. I was packed into a freighter, and what I know is that we never made it to the surface. The Vincere stopped us well outside of orbit and we did everything over long range communications."

The Whelk's burbling story matches what little Sax knows. Aspicis isn't so much a place to visit as a fortress that only opens for a few.

"So we can't expect to be let in." Plake closes her eyes for a second, then presses the intercom button. "Engee, Nobaa, change the leap target. I want to get as close as possible to the planet itself."

"What?" Engee's voice comes back high and bright. "You know that's dangerous, right?"

"This whole thing's suicide," Plake says. "If we're going to run a blockade, we might as well start as far through it as we can. You like puzzles, Engee. Solve this one."

The Teven says they're getting to work on it, and Plake turns back to the stars. "Funny thing, I never thought I'd do anything worth anything after they took us out of the Vincere. Guess I was wrong."

Sax threads his tail through the netting, wraps it around Bas. "We will never part again."

She hisses a laugh. "Sax, don't make promises you can't keep."

"I'll keep this one." By the slight shake of her head, Sax knows Bas doesn't believe him, but that doesn't matter, because it's his promise to keep.

Engee beeps back, says the calculations are done. Plake's good to launch.

"If this goes wrong," Plake says. "We won't get a chance to say goodbye, so make your peace now."

The countdown starts at ten, but drops to zero faster than Sax thinks possible. Mere heartbeats and then the universe twists and warps around them, the leap folding the *Mobius* through space to the exact point Engee has them set to go. A point that could be occupied by an asteroid, by a passing ship or any number of things. Normally, worlds kept leap corridors clear of incoming vessels and debris, but here they're dodging the designated route. Here, they're going right into the teeth.

When everything snaps back into focus, the only thing Sax can see out the front of the *Mobius* is a huge, glittering hull. A battle cruiser, more than double the size of a frigate—the analysis runs through Sax like instinct—and more than capable of blowing them to bits in moments. Plake, though, gets this too and sends the *Mobius* into a spiraling dive, pulling the deep green world of Aspicis into view.

"Stations!" Plake shouts as the crash netting sucks back up into the ceiling.

There's no gravity on the ship, so Sax and the others depend on hand-and-foot holds to get around. The *Mobius* has a few weapons scattered about its hull, and the two Oratus and Agra-Red head to the respective spots. Sax launches himself towards the rear, where a claw press against a single large terminal at the back of the cargo bay sets up some stabilizing crash netting and sets Sax into place. The terminal shifts to a clear view out the *Mobius'* aft, where scrambling Vincere fighters show as blips between the five-cruiser phalanx extending back into the distance.

At least their leap gives them a bit of surprise. The Vincere fighters are slow turning around towards them, and Sax has plenty of time to settle on the closest trio. And pauses. These aren't the normal Flaum claw fighters, essentially three-pronged hooks, that Sax is used to. These, rather, look like needles. Their profile is long, thin and tiny. They also don't seem to have any weapons.

"Are you seeing these?" Sax hisses through the intercom in the terminal.

"I don't recognize them," Bas says, she's on his right, on the edge of the hull. "They must be new."

"Don't care if they're new or old," Plake says. "Get rid of them!"

The first bright flashes of hot energy lance out towards the *Mobius* from the nearby cruiser, though the shots are wide and travel above and below their ship. Sax isn't surprised—the cruiser would have a hard time hitting the tiny target, but if it could keep the *Mobius* trapped into a narrow lane, the Vincere fighters would have an easy job taking it down.

So Sax focuses, aims and starts a stitching hot fire through space back towards those needles. Behind the first trio, there are another dozen and they're closing fast. Too fast. Sax can barely see them, and the terminal's having a hard time picking up those small profiles on its scanners, so the Oratus is essentially shooting into the dark and hoping.

On either side, Agra-Red and Bas open up too, their streams having a harder time getting close to the needles, which are doing their best to stay right behind the *Mobius*. Sax can't tell if he's getting hits until one shot gets lucky, nails one of the needles in its cockpit and sends the fighter into a sparking, swirling dive away from them. Only the strike comes at point blank range, with the needles so, so close.

The needles haven't fired a shot, and they're still coming closer.

"They're going to ram us!" Sax hisses as he realizes just why these fighters have those long, pointed shapes.

"What?" Agra-Red manages to say before the first needle fighter punches into the back of the freighter.

There's a wrenching, popping sound as the housing around one of the *Mobius'* engines tears away and the pointed end of the needle rips through. A hot second later, as high-pitched Teven shouts come through the intercom, a steady whine fills the freighter and Sax's terminal sparks and dies. It's not hard to tell what's happened, and the sucking sound of vacuum makes it clear the *Mobius*, with a single strike, is done.

"Get to the evac mods!" Plake's yelling as she comes running out of the cockpit.

Her voice barely carries over the noise of the *Mobius* pulling itself apart. There's two of the escape craft, both latched onto the cargo bay like leeches. Sax talon-and-claws his way to the first one, slaps at the panel to open it. Hard-wired to the evac mod's own batteries for issues just like this, the panel still works enough to open the escape mod's door. Bas crashes against Sax, and together the two Oratus tumble in.

Agra-Red joins them a second later, and the Whelk slaps shut the door and sets the evac mod to ready for launch.

"They're all in the other one," the Whelk says as Bas and Sax hiss questions at him. "We're going."

An evac mod is weaponless, essentially a floating tank with a rocket on one end. If they spit out into space filled with lasers and fighters, they'll be easy targets.

"Don't launch yet," Plake's voice comes over the intercom—short-range communications between the two craft. "Wait till the last minute. I put us into an unstable dive towards the surface."

As if playing to her words, the evac mod begins to shake as Aspicis tugs against its fall. As they descend, the rumble increases until the evac mod jolts hard, too hard for atmosphere. Agra-Red does something then that Sax doesn't think is possible—the Whelk gets even redder, as if the blood in its gel body literally boils.

"That was the *Mobius*," the Whelk oozes. "Plake and I spent a long time earning that ship, running cargo for other idiots and saving our scratch till we could get her."

Sax, whose been a part of many Vincere ships lost to the explosions of war with the Sevora, can't empathize. He's never put much value in any craft—there's an inevitability that they're going to go up in a burning fireball someday.

"You'll find another," Sax hisses.

"You've never had to earn anything in your life," Agra-Red replies. "What would you know?"

"I earned my name," Sax says.

The pair glower at each other while Bas watches out the front viewport as Aspicis fills every available view. Sax follows his pair's eyes—no sense waging a war of wills with the Whelk, as Sax could shred the creature here in a second, and the ability to end, permanently, an adversary is the most important calculation in any argument.

What Sax does notice, though, as he looks out into space is that there aren't any other shots streaking past them. The Vincere fighters aren't, apparently, following them towards the ground and the cruisers aren't attempting to immolate them either.

"Why?" Sax says to Bas. "They should be able to destroy us before we hit the ground."

"Two evac mods," Bas says. "That's it. This can't be an invasion, and no doubt they're tracking our landing zone. They'll be waiting for us."

"They'll be getting more than they expect," Agra-Red burbles, its floppy arms wrapped around its miner.

"Interrogation?" Sax asks the only reason that comes to mind.

Why let an opposing force make landfall on your own turf unless you'd benefit?

"Either they don't know who we are, and they want to understand what would make someone try to leap that close to Aspicis," Bas says. "Or they do, and want to make an example of us."

Ah. The last makes sense. Sax has been party to plenty of those. Little pockets of resistance; planets or species that decide they'd like to make their own decisions rather than abide by the Chorus' demands. Those bursts of independence live until a few sets of Oratus show up and the sky bleeds as Vincere cruisers obliterate cities from orbit. Then, with video broadcasting everywhere, Sax holds up the leader of the cause with a claw to whatever part is going to make the most compelling demonstration and either extracts a loyalty pledge, or exacts the costs of refusing one.

"They won't have that chance," Sax says. "If the situation is impossible, then we must prevent them from taking us alive."

"I'll do the honors," Agra-Red says. "Wouldn't mind getting to blast a couple of Oratus before I go."

If there was any way Sax could make the Whelk's demise in this evac mod plausible, he'd act on it, but since there isn't, he settles for a glare at the crimson blob.

The evac mod postpones their fight, though, by entering the heavy part of Aspicis' atmosphere. Outside, blue-orange fire rings the viewport while, inside, the three occupants jostle on their benches. Sax uses his claws to grab holds, except his left midclaw, which is reserved for Bas. Agra-Red simply bobs with the motion, its wide, sticky base serving to keep the Whelk set on the bench.

They're silent for a while, listening to the roar and pop of the world coming into place around them. There's something about being so close to instant death that stays Sax from any cutting commentary, any tactical considerations for when they land. It's one of those things that happens on every atmospheric insertion, and on most ship-to-ship assaults; the point where, if a species has a god, they ought to be reaching out to them.

The Oratus have no deities, worship at no altar save the bloody one of survival. Sax doesn't mind this, even here. With Bas beside him, and a purpose waiting on the planet's surface, Sax has all he needs. Though that doesn't keep his vents from issuing a small sigh when the rumbles quiet and the stress of diving through an atmosphere fades away into a bright, clear descent towards the tangle of giant vines that shroud Aspicis' surface.

Like Rathfall, but without the flowers and many times the size, the Amigga have nurtured Aspicis into a perfect genetic generator of everything they need. Every one of those vines, behind the thick green skin, holds the nutrient goop that fills the ration crates on every Vincere ship. Other planets have been cultivated to serve as forward-based 'farms', but none reach the production of the Chorus' home.

From this high up, Sax can see a few other patches too, clusters of vines adopting shades other than the dominant emerald. Bluish vines the color of morning skies and purple-red ones, like falling leaves at twilight, appear in blots, and serve as crops for the healing gels and weaponized chemicals proliferating more and more through the Vincere forces.

"They'll cover the whole galaxy, eventually," Bas says, staring through the viewport.

As they plummet, the evac mod grows warmer and warmer, equalizing as the horizons disappear and the gnarled knots of green fill the entire view, to a temperature not far from that of Solis. Sax can't smell anything of the planet, though, as the mod itself stays pressurized. Which, considering how fast they're dropping, is a good thing.

Evac mods carry enough juice for their microjets—provided the escapees aren't surfing the galaxy for too long before their descent—to make it through a bumpy landing even on high gravity planets. Aspicis isn't particularly large, but it's big enough for the evac mod to make a hard lurch when its jets fire up.

"Plake?" Agra-Red says and Sax turns to see the Whelk's using the evac mod's short-range communicator. "You still with us?"

"We're toasty, but here. Don't think they bothered to shoot at us."

"The Oratus think that means they're waiting for us on the ground."

"We don't think," Sax says, loud enough for the intercom to pick him up. "We know."

"I agree with the uglies," Plake replies. "Be ready for company. I've got a set of coordinates for Evva, or at least a safe-house, so if we can get that far without them tagging us . . ."

The rest of her words fade into a burst of static as the evac mod pushes all of its power into the final stages of the fall. If the first minutes seemed to take forever, floating through space on a slow slide into the planet, the last couple pass by like lightning, the vines swarming towards them and, with a half-second warning from Bas, slamming into the mod.

The escape craft is steady, though, and it batters through the vines like a miner's blast through a thin wall. The viewport goes from a small window into the outside world to a useless smudge of purple and green sludge as their crash makes soup of Aspicis' foliage.

At least, until they hit the ground beneath.

It's soft, loamy soil—everything on Aspicis is controlled for optimum conditions—and it catches the evac mod like the pillow Sax wishes he has behind his head, which bangs into the side of the mod as it tilts over and stops.

A hot second later, having confirmed the atmosphere breathable, the evac mod pops its hatch open and lets Aspicis' humidity flood in. A safety feature in case the mod's passengers are incapacitated or it's landed in a sinking lava lake, the quick open lets Sax slice away his small netting and bound out of the craft.

Onto a world he never dreamed he'd see.

Our quarters are little more than a few scraggly nets hanging from the ceiling. One for Viera, one for me, and T'Oli weaves itself through and then uses its Ooblot genes to harden itself around the bands. The room we're in is thin and featureless, with a panel on the outside of the entryway and none on the inside. As soon as Lan shows us in, the Oratus retreats out of the room and the door shuts in a final way that says it's only going to open when someone whose not us tells it too.

"Guess I shouldn't have expected better," Viera sighs as we slip into the netting.

A voice interrupts her, playing through an intercom embedded next to the door, beginning a countdown to the leap.

"Why, because we're on a Vincere ship?" I ask.

"I thought these were the good ones. We fought so hard to escape, and then beat back, the Sevora. Seems like we're owed a break by now."

"Clarity's Dawn survived for a very long time in the depths of Vimelia," T'Oli slaps in. "Every one there deserved a break, a chance to leave and make something of themselves, and we never did."

The mention of the rebel group takes me back. We'd barely

escaped Vimelia because of the large raid the group of freed species staged. Their goal had been to get a signal to the Vincere, to tell them the location of the Sevora's homeworld so the Chorus could use their military might to end the war.

Clarity's Dawn hadn't pitched the thing as a suicide mission.

"No," T'Oli says when I ask it. "But just because you don't come right out and say it doesn't mean it's not true. Few of us expected to live through that day."

"Well, I'm glad you did."

The leap comes hard and fast, a sudden lurch followed by the twisting, bending and almost breaking of reality. My senses go haywire as colors splash across my vision, my stomach heaves and roils, and waves of ice-cold numbness play touch-and-go with extreme heat. It lasts a few seconds and feels like years.

"I'm never going to get used to that," I say when the universe rights itself.

"It's not the easiest method of travel," T'Oli says, "but it is the fastest."

Viera expresses her feelings through the contents of her stomach, which make a splashy entrance on the room's floor. Lan, who opens the door a moment later, doesn't spare the residue a look. As the three of us head back out into the corridor, small cleaning robots, looking like whirring disks, hover into the room.

Lan doesn't speak as we head back to the bridge, even when I ask her a few questions, like where are we, when can I get a meal, and how high rank is Kolas. Her mind is obviously elsewhere, and eventually we all join that soft silence.

When we get to the bridge, I understand why: out that massive windshield is a shape I've seen before. A large, beige sphere, the home of the Sevora is awash with flashing light. Out here, what must be dozens and dozens of ships swirl around each other in deadly dances—shapes that I think would be invisible save for the red and blue outlines the windshield places around all that come into view.

Kolas no longer stands free and clear in the middle of the platform: four struts have risen out of the edges of his station, and the Oratus' head is wrapped in what looks like a half-sphere of pearl.

Lan keeps us well back, letting us take in the constant stream of voices from the pits below, the intercoms around us, and the overhead announcements. Those last sound like orders, demanding this and that group report to this and that section.

"You're attacking their home," Viera manages to say. "Didn't think that'd ever happen."

Now Lan hisses low and slow. "We never knew where it was, until an anonymous signal came through one of our listening beacons not long ago. All it had were these coordinates, and what they were."

"Then we succeeded," T'Oli says, but the Ooblot's slapping voice hardly sounds jubilant. "There were no others?"

"Not that I know of." Lan asks T'Oli what the Ooblot means, and T'Oli goes into Clarity's Dawn.

I tune out their discussion, instead focusing on Vimelia, and how the planet is coming closer as our cruiser approaches it. I've picked out the color scheme now too, and the vast amounts of red indicating the Vincere forces have the blue-tinged Sevora in a slow collapse. A tightening vice around the planet.

"This isn't just a battle," I say to Viera. "This is an extermination."

"The Sevora killed Malo," Viera replies. "Exterminate them."

Without the Sevora, without Ignos, I wouldn't be here. Viera and Avril's people, the Lunare, would have rolled through our jungle and destroyed our tribe. Their weapons would have proved too much for Malo's people, the Charre, as well. Only with Ignos, a Sevora that crashed to Earth, did we put up enough resistance to save ourselves. And yet, all of that pitched against the horrors the Sevora deliver to the galaxy, that they delivered to me . . . I'm not lifting my voice to save them.

We spend a long time watching the slow-moving destruction. However hungry or thirsty I may have felt before, the thought of leaving the bridge and the view of the constant explosions, the burning death by fire, and the inexorable advance of the Vincere, doesn't cross my mind.

Only when Kolas emerges from the sphere, striding its gleaming, scarred rust-colored self up to us do I shake out of the battlefield trance.

"So you see," Kolas says. "At last, we have them trapped. Not a single Sevora ship has escaped the system since we arrived, and not a single one of them will live out this fight."

"How can you know?" I say. "There might be more of them throughout the galaxy."

Kolas gives me a slight nod. "True, and one may create their entire force again someday, but without Vimelia's resources behind them, the Sevora will need many miracles to threaten the Chorus again."

"Are you going to burn every inch of the planet, then?" Viera asks.

Kolas points out the front of the windshield, towards the bottom of the viewing area, where a hint of the golden oval on the cruiser's front peaks through. "Vimelia has a large satellite moon. With this ship, we can break its orbit. When the moon descends into the planet, the impact will do our work for us, and ensure any Sevora buried deep in Vimelia's crust die as well."

Viera's speechless. I'm not so impressed.

"You're claiming they're all guilty," I say. "That they all deserve to die?"

"Of course," Kolas says. "The Sevora are the only advanced species left that is not bound to the Chorus. They have refused to accept our terms and join the galaxy. As such, they are a threat and must be obliterated."

Kolas finishes speaking, inhales as though the Oratus is going to continue listing reasons why the Sevora must die, but a sudden call from one of the Flaum below kills the idea.

"Admiral, we have an incoming message from one of the Sevora factions," the Flaum, a scruffy white-and-tan one, announces from its terminal. "I wouldn't bother sending it to you, but it's a strange one, sir."

"Stage it," Kolas says, nodding towards the windshield.

"For everyone?"

"These are the last gasps of a dying species," Kolas hisses. "We all deserve to know how they would end their lives."

The Flaum argues no further and turns back to its terminal. I'm staring at Kolas, wondering what the Oratus could be thinking—as an Empress, I heard plenty of private messages that would be both interesting and entirely inappropriate for other ears. Apparently the Vincere, or at least Kolas, operates in the open.

There's a flicker across the windshield, and then a large part of Vimelia disappears beneath a wide black rectangle. One that fills in with a vast, crowded chamber. Species sit in rows, pressed in among each other. Flaum, Whelk, Teven, and others I can't name are all staring stiffly back at the window or at the other, miner-armed guards caught on the edges of the frame, aiming at what are apparently prisoners.

"Do you see all of these innocents?" Jel's warbled voice comes through, slightly garbled in the transmission. The creature and its Whelk host lead a faction of the Sevora that wants peace with the rest of the galaxy, but that have never had the power to force it. "If you continue your assault, all of them will die. Their blood will be on your claws. Or, you can negotiate. Work with us to find a solution that does not require genocide!"

As Jel's warble dies away, the window pans to the far end of the lines of species and begins a slow crawl through them. I'm expecting to see anger, fear, on the faces there, but all that shows is a steady resignation to the fate consigned to them. Many of the species look old, with falling clumps of hair, blotches of broken skin or even lost limbs. Hosts rejected and unwanted by the Sevora.

"Kaishi," Viera says.

I know. I see him too.

"Malo," I say his name and it's a ghost coming back to life, a spirit I never thought I'd see again made flesh right there on the windshield.

It's easy to identify the Charre warrior, my friend and leader of my armies, as he stares straight back at us. Always courageous, always defiant, Malo nonetheless looks closer to the edge of death than when we left him. I see cuts running along his skin, bruises along a frame that's thinner than I remember. Still, those eyes pierce across the distance to me.

"Reach out, and help us save the galaxy!" Jel's final plea dies as the window fades and vanishes, putting Vimelia back in its center frame.

The Flaum manning the bridge don't seem to have noticed—they carry on their chittering commands the same as before. Lan, though, has her eyes on me, as does Kolas as soon as the admiral turns around.

"They have a human?" Kolas asks as it approaches.

The question prompts a recapping of our last trip to Vimelia, one I speed through with as little detail as possible, because every passing second, I feel, brings the Vincere closer to their moon-crashing moment.

"Then you would have us save him?" Kolas asks. "You would have us negotiate with the Sevora to save the life of a single human?"

I know what the Oratus is doing. I know Kolas wants to trap me in a terrible argument—one that every ruler must make at some point: how much is a single life worth?

To me, though, Malo is worth whatever it takes.

"You're not going to destroy this planet," I say. "Not with Malo still on it."

I make the gamble. I don't think Kolas will give up on torching Vimelia or eliminating the Sevora entirely, but I might be able to persuade the Oratus on this one life.

Kolas folds its four claws together and gives me the sort of toothy grin I've come to associate with predators who know they've caught their prey.

"Do you know why we brought you here with us, human?" Kolas says.

"I thought it was about witnessing revenge," I reply. "For what the Sevora did to Earth?"

"In part. Yet, we need to see your resolve. The galaxy has no place for species unwilling to make sacrifices for its progress."

"Saving Malo is a sacrifice?"

"The Chorus would say that your ties to a single person make you weak," Kolas says. "However, as an Oratus, bound by the strength of the pairing, I think a single person may be the thing most worth fighting for." The Oratus reaches out with its left foreclaw towards me. "You want to rescue your Malo? Then I give you leave to do so. I cannot, though, risk any Vincere lives in the process, and the Sevora planet will be destroyed, with or without you on it."

The evac mod's crash has punched a hole through the tangled ceiling of vines, a hole which now casts the only light Sax can see into the space. Aspicis orbits a white dwarf star, and its pearl sheen has Sax wincing as he scans for any immediate threats.

If there are any, they've been coated by the dirt thrown up by the crashing mod. Beyond the shower of deep brown—almost black—dirt, there's evidence of what Aspicis looks like when it's not serving as a landing pad; a thick coating of browning, old vines and the mosses intent on consuming them. Even these have probably been constructed by the Amigga to grind dead vines and refresh the soil.

The mosses, though, aren't making the noises Sax hears. Namely, the constant stream of vicious cursing coming from his right. the light, burbling voice of a Vyphen.

"Sounds like the captain made it," Agra-Red says as the Whelk emerges next to Sax, hands guiding the heavy miner embedded in its chest.

The slug-like creature slides out of the mod, its red look turning almost pink in the white light. The Whelk moves by shifting its skin around itself, like a tread, and as Agra-Red hits the soil, the dirt sticks to its body so that by the time the Whelk hits the edge of the clearing, it's a mottled mess

By then, though, Sax and Bas are out of the mod too, carrying a couple of emergency ration packs, along with a pair of small miners holstered by their masks. The masks don't have real belts, but instead form themselves to the handles of anything pressed against them, sealing the item against their body until Sax or Bas decide to reach for it.

"Who wants to lead?" Agra-Red asks, its two large eyes peering out from its new dirt goggles. "Don't pick me. I do better when I get a chance to aim."

Sax lets a hiss loose and steps around the Whelk. Unlike Rathfall, these vines are too thick to cut—not that Sax can't, he just doesn't want to spent the time—so instead he climbs over, through, and between. No thorns, at least, and the vines are soft enough so that Sax can grip them. Bas follows his path, occasionally picking up and lifting the Whelk through any areas Agra-Red can't slime through.

They follow Plake's loud noises for a few minutes until they come to the second evac mod, only, instead of the Vyphen captain and the pair of Teven, all Sax sees is an empty mod and a deserted clearing. A quick hop to the craft confirms Plake's voice is coming out of the intercom, and is looping through a recording.

"She's not here," Sax says.

"Then why?" Bas says behind him. "What's the point of making the noise?"

"To draw them out," the voice matches the continued cursing on the intercom, and Sax looks back towards the edge of the clearing to see Plake perched up on a vine. Now that he's watching, Sax sees the Teven pair as well, opposite Plake. All of them are holding miners.

"They're going to be here soon," Plake says. "I don't want to fight them on the run."

Sax doesn't need to ask who *they* are—it's plenty evident from the rising hum that something's approaching, and odds are low that something's going to be friendly.

"We can't fight them all," Bas calls up to Plake. "We have to run!"

Sax is briefly thankful it's his pair calling for the retreat—he's not sure he has such an order in him.

"Not yet," Plake replies, and Sax catches a sneaking smile on the Vyphen's face, resting on her folded feathered arms up on the vine. "They don't know who we are. There won't be many. We can knock out this force, then disappear before they can call any reinforcements."

"Not a bad plan," Sax says, and anyway they're out of time, so the Oratus breaks for the edge of the clearing.

Bas follows and the two of them climb up to a spot in between Plake and the two Teven, who are nestled together with their miners sticking out like weaponized thorns. Agra-Red, emphatically unable to climb, sludges its way inside the evac mod.

"I think I like the Whelk," Bas hisses as she settles on the vine next to Sax.

"It's deadly," Sax replies, which is the highest praise he can offer.

The hum grows louder, then splits into two. A pair of shuttles. Sax and the others came down in a pair of evac mods, so that makes sense, but it means they won't be fighting the whole Chorus contingent at once. Plake's plan depends on speed—if they take too long to eliminate the Chorus forces, they'll be running away under fire. On a planet run by the enemy, finding a hiding spot in that condition would be difficult.

Sax taps his tail against Bas', and she understands what he's getting at. The two of them break from the clearing, Sax getting one quick nod towards Plake, and dash through the upper layer of vines back towards their own mod.

The Chorus shuttle hovers over their original clearing, a deep blue vessel bearing the orb-and-lines sigil of its owners. Side slats fold out, giving clear view of the armored Flaum squad dropping down towards the ground. Unlike on more industrial planets, these Flaum don't have magnetized boots to catch their fall on metal floors.

Instead, the boots on the scrawny, furry creature's small feet pop as they near the soil.

Kinetic packets—they store up energy with motion, release it when called for to provide just enough thrust to break a fall or give a jump the boost to get the Flaum where it needs to go. Crucial for lesser species to keep up with an Oratus.

Not that it's going to help them here.

Six Flaum, all armed with miners and wearing light vests glittering with reflective coatings meant to disperse laser fire. Better equipped than a casual inspection, yet still hopeless.

Sax flicks his eyes towards the shuttle, then down to the Flaum. Bas makes a slight gesture with her foreclaw towards the sky. Sax grins. His pair always prefers the more interesting challenges. Then again, Sax has gone a while without a good bit of gristle between his teeth.

The sign comes from behind them; chittering shouts and screams as Plake, Agra-Red, Nobaa and Engee get to work blazing away at their team. The noise puts Sax's targets into a frenzy, reaching for various communication devices and then raising their miners in the direction of the noise.

Where they don't look, though, is up.

Sax descends, a hissing missile. All claws, teeth, and talons. The Flaum squad is already in disarray; their encircling of the evac mod disrupted by the chaos with their sister squad. Thus it's not a formation that Sax tears into, but rather a scattered group of furry soldiers that likely haven't seen a real fight in their entire lives.

This, too, doesn't check that box; Sax takes out his first two targets, the only pair near each other, in an opening leap that manages to dedicate a fore-and midclaw to each Flaum, driving them down to the ground with enough of a stab to make sure Sax's victims are more focused on survival than counterattacking.

Using his talons, which get a luxurious grip in the soft, crash-churned ground, Sax bursts to his right, leading the way with his toothy maw to the next Flaum in line. His angle of attack keeps the bulk of the evac mod between Sax and the Flaum he's not ripping into, meaning the first shot that comes his way is courtesy of the fourth Flaum, who's just seen a third comrade tackled and driven into the earth.

As shots go, Sax has seen better. It's a spray of bluish bolts—meaning these forces really were intent on stunning whomever they found—and the shots nail the ground in front of Sax as the Oratus leaps off his latest casualty into the air. He gets high enough for the Flaum's eyes to go wide as they track Sax going up and then, in an unfortunate turn for the soldier, directly down on his reflective vest.

The Flaum's armor offers good protection against an energy assault. It offers nothing more than paper against Sax's claws.

Still, Sax is taking care to avoid mortal wounds. Slaughtering the very forces you want to bring to your cause is a poor way of getting their support. So Sax goes for a light maiming instead, enough to prove that the Flaum's best interests lie in staying down.

Four taken care of still leaves a pair of targets with miners aiming his way, and Sax manages to get his eyes on them as they get around the evac mod. As they raise their weapons, Sax angles to the one on the right, and braces himself to absorb a blast or two.

The blast that comes, though, isn't from a miner. Instead, it's a rain of broken metal and burning terminals pouring from above. A sharp whine cuts between the shouts and shots from both this clearing and where Plake's band is playing its murderous tune as the shuttle's engines struggle with a cockpit that is now nothing more than a shredded, sparking victim of Bas' tearing talons and claws.

Bas leaps clear as the shuttle settles on a crash course into the top of the evac mod, prompting Sax and the two Flaum to perform frantic dives to get clear. Twisting metal shrieks and the gurgling slow-burn of batteries unleashing their pent up energy in fiery gouts works in the background as Sax scrambles along the clearing's outer edge towards the nearest, still-armed Flaum.

This one's barely recovered from its dive by the time Sax hits, and the Oratus tears away the miner with his foreclaws, takes a soft bite out of the Flaum's leg to ensure it won't be moving anywhere fast, then clinches the fight with a head-side smack from Sax's tail as he wheels towards the last one.

Only, when Sax gets around the wreckage, the Flaum's already taken care of.

Bas stands over her prize, breaking the miner into fragments while her right talon presses the Flaum further into the dirt. Sax comes up beside her, gives Bas a quick tail tap acknowledging an assault well-performed, and then they burst off back towards Plake's clearing.

If Sax and Bas fought with some intent on keeping the Flaum alive—Bas even mentions the shuttle she brought down was holding its place on auto-pilot—Plake and the rest of her crew blitzed their enemies with more final means. Sax doesn't need to look more closely at the burned out Flaum to know they won't be getting up again.

"They're never going to join us," Plake says when Bas asks why they didn't go for stuns. "Better to make a statement than play cute with them."

"That's a way to make friends," Sax hisses.

"We're not here for friends," Plake says, then points her miner up towards the second hovering shuttle. "Mind giving me a lift?"

Sax takes the Vyphen in his foreclaws and, with a burst from his legs, gives her a boost up towards the open shuttle. It's a good ten-meter toss, and it gets Plake up to the lip of the open cargo door, which is enough for her to grip and pull herself in.

"Don't start feeling sympathy for these things now," Agra-Red says, slithering up next to Sax and Bas. "If they'd taken us, we'd be stunned then skinned alive in front of the entire galaxy. Guess how many would feel any pity for us."

Zero's a good answer to that question. Sax, though, thinks about Rav and the rest of the Vincere forces back over Solis. If he'd hit those ships like a raging whirlwind and torn as far as he could through their ranks, Sax would never have made it to Bas, would've been gunned down by soldiers who are now allies.

"It's not that simple," the Oratus manages to say.

"For you, maybe not," Agra-Red says.

Any further deep dives into the pros and cons of keeping your enemies alive vanishes as the pair of eager Teven hit the ground from their vines and make their spindly way over to Sax. Nobaa, whose carapace is littered with pegs and hooks holding all manner of small gadgets, is chattering at Engee, whose own lighter carapace is equally adorned with nicks and knacks.

"The plates, see, transmit the neuro-signals through fiber lines I wove into them," Nobaa's saying, and Sax notices the Teven poking at one of the several breaks in the Oratus' scales now occupied by a layered metal seal. "There's no nerve interruption."

The Teven's limbs slip in and out of holes dotting their carapace, eyes on little stalks included, and Nobaa reaches towards a metal plate dotting the back of Sax's leg. The Oratus jerks it away from the fidgety creature.

"Hands-off," Sax says.

"I only want to show Engee how they work!" Nobaa cries, excitement bubbling out. "You're my creation!"

"He's what?" Bas says.

Sax's pink-gold pair stands tall over Nobaa, whom Sax realizes she's never really met. Going by the look on Bas's face, which sits somewhere between amusement and *I'm going to carve this thing up for dinner*, the first real meeting between the two could be going better.

"The Teven saved my life on the frigate," Sax says. He's already told Bas all about the mirrored Oratus, about barely surviving with the help of Nobaa's metal grafts. "He's more useful than annoying. Barely."

"Hey," Nobaa manages to say, but in the face of eight sets of claws, doesn't push the issue.

"Did they work though?" Engee asks. "If they do, that would open a whole new world of—"

Engee's revelations are blessedly cut off by the harsh wind of microjet air as Plake brings the shuttle down. She can't land it—the clearing made by the evac mod doesn't have the room—but the Vyphen brings the craft low enough for the five on land to climb into it. Sax and Bas take turns helping the less-mobile creatures inside, then clamber up themselves.

It's a tight fit—Sax and Bas adopt a permanent hunch, the backs of their necks pressing against the ceiling—and the shuttle is too bare to offer much in the way of other comforts. Instead, Plake takes the narrow cockpit to herself and the rest of them squeeze together in a back bay that gets even more cramped when Plake shuts the sliding exits.

Agra-Red's gooey self is stuck on Sax's right leg, while Engee and Nobaa stake out a central spot in the shelter of the Oratus' large forms, conveniently making it easy for the two Teven to go on about Sax's metallic additions.

"Evva, or someone working with her, dished us the coordinates to a small village," Plake says over intercom. "We aren't exactly close, so get comfortable."

"How long till the Chorus realizes this ship isn't their's anymore?" Sax asks as the shuttle lurches up and forward, gliding out over a sea of swirling vines beneath a very light blue sky.

"I've been ignoring their calls since I took the controls." Plake doesn't seem concerned about it—she's had a fatal bent to her words ever since they leapt out here, as if this whole thing is destined to flame out into disaster and she knows it.

Plake's worries don't play out right away, and they surf the lower skies over Aspicis for what feels like a long time without the slightest alarm. While they're zipping along, Sax notices the daylight staying constant, and so Plake pulls up Aspicis' record on the shuttle's computer. The words spill out on the cockpit terminal, and, with the Vyphen pushing another button, a monotone rendition of the text plays over the shuttle's speakers.

Aspicis turns slow on its axis, but the nearby star is cool, so the side getting drenched in light for such long periods doesn't wind up burning away. The opposite, darker half of the planet gets incredibly cold, which is a process that winds up helping those vines turn their insides to the nutritious jelly feeding the galaxy.

As for the Chorus, their Meridia sits on the planet's northern pole, jutting up and out of the atmosphere as it spins.

Plake isn't taking them anywhere near the day/night border, so when she starts hitting the shuttle's microjet brakes, they're still in as bright a world as the one they landed on. Sax can't see where they're setting down; he only gets a picture of vines as they descend, and he thinks they've found a random jungle hideaway until he notices colored lights shining between the big green tendrils.

"Opening in three," Plake says. "Not picking up any welcome, but let's be ready for one."

After her countdown hits zero, the shuttle's side doors slide open and Sax bursts out, his midclaws reaching around his mask to pull off the pair of miners he's carrying. What he earns for his trouble is one very scared, and very young, Flaum. The small furball scurries back from the shuttle, with what looks like some sort of snack bar in its right hand.

Beyond the child, Sax picks up plenty of eyes looking back at him, and soon enough one of those blinking pairs resolves itself into a frantic parent, wearing not a Chorus uniform but standard dirty, tan civilian robes, dashing out and swooping up the child in her claws.

There's no miners, though. No barked orders to surrender or commands to shoot the new arrivals.

"Clear," Sax hisses, and a moment later Bas does the same.

The Teven, along with Agra-Red and Plake, shift out of the shuttle. They form up around Sax—Bas included—and stand, weapons ready.

"This is all I've got," Plake says as they keep their eyes crawling over the shapes hidden behind the vines around their landing zone. "Evva's supposed to meet us here."

"Maybe she doesn't know we've arrived," Sax says, then he sucks in a deep breath through his vents. "Evva?"

The roar carries, though Sax isn't worried about others overhearing. Anyone loyal to the Chorus probably already knows they're here, and with the stolen shuttle being plenty trackable, this is only going to be a quick stopping point anyway.

"Very subtle," Plake manages to say, but Sax isn't listening to her.

What he's listening for, and not getting, is any sounds of welcome. Any recognition or invitation. Even hostility would show they've at least made it somewhere Evva's known. Instead, there's nothing. At least, not till the the same frazzled parent, her child wrapped tight in her arms, comes back out to the clearing.

"You aren't coming to kill us, then?" she says.

"That's not the plan," Plake replies as the whole group levels stares at the only Flaum brave enough to talk to them.

"Everyone says that, and we died anyway," the Flaum sniffs. "There's only one left for you here, and he's not well."

"He?" Plake's keeping her captain role going.

"If it means you'll leave, I'll show you where he is." The Flaum turns around, walks back towards the vines she came from.

Plake glances at the rest of them, gets no opposition, and they start to follow.

"The Chorus will track that shuttle," Bas says what Sax is already thinking.

"Let them," Plake replies. "We'll just have to be quick. Besides, what can we do about it?"

Bas hisses a laugh. "Wait a moment."

She clambers back into the shuttle, which restarts its microjets a moment later. The craft hovers up and out of the clearing, though its bay doors stay open. Bas reappears, hangs down, then drops right into Sax's arms. A moment later, the shuttle blasts off, rocketing away through the sky.

"It'll keep flying until it runs dry," Bas says.

"They'll just trace it back here," Plake replies. "The last spot it stopped."

"After it goes down, yes, but that won't be for a long time."

Plake nods at last, giving Bas the point. Sax finds the whole thing tedious—Bas shouldn't have to explain herself, especially not to a Vyphen. Instead, he plunges forward past Plake, into the vines and to the village itself.

Beyond the landing zone, it's dim. The white light from the star is blocked by the thick vegetation, but the remedy from the village strikes Sax as beautiful; tear-drop lanterns, painted in arrays of purples, blues, and greens are strung up along the vines. The colors shine together, and give view to the damp streets of a real town beneath the growth.

Single-story buildings rise out of mounds in the earth, or look to be carved from hardened skins of older vines. Doors exist as cotton curtains, which makes Sax wonder how these places survive the long cold that no doubt comes as Aspicis rotates through its slow seasons.

Scurrying through the whole ensemble are families of Flaum. It's been so long since Sax has visited somewhere that's made for actual living and not a military vessel or a place for society's desperate castoffs to find work or refuge that he spends more time than he probably should staring at species just having fun chasing each other or playing with various toy figures.

Aside from the lanterns, there's a decided lack of technology here. Sax can't hear the whines of generators, though the smell of cooking fires lingers. Metal seems absent, with some Flaum carrying clay-formed cups and crates made from the rough skin of dead vines.

"This is different," Sax manages to say as they walk.

"It's weird," Agra-Red grumbles. "Not my kind of place."

The two Teven, though, seem to enjoy it. Now that the threat of immediate death has departed, Nobaa and Engee devolve into jabbering scientists, racing from place to place and asking to poke this, taste that or get some explanation as to what a Flaum's doing.

"Are there only Flaum here?" Bas asks their guide, who pauses long enough to turn back towards them.

"Then you're not with the Chorus?" the Flaum says, and must get her answer from the looks they give her. "The Amigga don't allow other species on the planet without strict permission. Not on the surface, at least."

"Why?"

"Because they think you're dangerous. All of you."

The Flaum doesn't sound like she's joking as she says this, and Sax learns why when they round a particularly large, knotted mound covered in red lanterns. On the other side, nestled against a cluster of vines, is what was another home. Now, though, all that's left are shattered lights, broken chunks of vine and split rock. At the center of it, with a pair of Flaum spreading some purplish gel over his wounds, is a traitor Sax never expected to see again.

Avan both is and is not the Oratus he appears to be. Inside the black-scaled head, covered with more scars and scratches than the last time Sax saw it, is a Sevora. At least, Sax assumes the parasite is still there, still leaching off the life of a Vincere soldier.

Sax realizes he's hissing low and soft when he catches Plake and Agra-Red staring at him. Bas touches his tail with her own, and together the two of them walk past their teammates and have a closer look at the traitor they once rescued from a Sevora seed ship. At the time, Avan had promised he had valuable information, and not long after sending him back to Evva, her resistance had started.

In a way, Sax realizes, the decision to let Avan live, to send him to Evva, is the whole reason they're standing here right now.

He's not sure whether he regrets that move.

Avan, though, probably does; the Oratus is in bad shape, bearing a vibrant assortment of cuts and laser burns. The loser in a fight that started at range, then progressed to get close and deadly. A quick look at the destruction around them confirms the soil and stone building crumpled inward, no doubt succumbing to an onslaught of energy that boiled away its integrity.

"He lives?" Sax asks the pair of Flaum taking nominal care of Avan.

They glance up at Sax, freeze for a moment before one nods and they both make a break for it. Sax doesn't chase—the caretakers aren't the target, and it's not worth trying to thank creatures too afraid to handle an Oratus' direct look. So he turns his attention to the traitor.

Avan's eyes are shut, but they open quick when Sax dabs a bit of Stim—a heady mix of adrenaline and other drugs the two Oratus keep in small vials—into the traitor's mouth.

"Where's Evva?" Sax doesn't bother with niceties. Eventually the Chorus is going to find them again, and when that happens, Avan's opinion of Sax isn't going to matter. "Who did this?"

"You made it." Avan's harsh rasp cuts a flash of memory, a bad one where the traitor tricked Sax out of his mask deep in enemy territory.

The Sax of that day might have taken a talon to Avan's throat as he lies there, but this one, the newer one, holds back. Decides to play a longer game. Besides, there'll be plenty of chances to kill Avan later, when the Sevora's no longer useful.

"Answer the question," Sax says.

Avan blinks. Takes a breath, the pain of it evident in the sudden tightening of the Oratus' razor mouth.

"The Chorus tracked us here, or someone sold us out," Avan says. "An Amigga actually came, along with a pair of mirrored Oratus. They took Evva, probably thought they'd killed me."

"Do you know where they went?"

"You think I was still standing when they left?" Avan tries to laugh—it's a hopeless croak. "Ask them. They'll know."

Sax has a thousand more questions for the traitor, but he holds them back. Evva's the priority. So instead he turns and rifles the questions at the Flaum who brought them here, who's still standing with them, like she's waiting for something.

"They're gone," the Flaum replies.

"Where?"

"Before I show you, I need you to make a promise. The other did, Evva, but in case she does not survive, I want you to make the same one."

"Promises?" Plake interrupts. "You'll tell us where they took Evva, or we'll—"

"Stop," Sax hisses at the Vyphen. "What do you want?"

The Flaum flicks her eyes at the village around them, then down at the child still in her arms. "Promise that you won't destroy this world. Evva said she would not, that destruction was not her goal. If I help you, promise that you will not ruin what we have."

The Amigga run the galaxy, have run it for so long most species can't recall a time when the Chorus wasn't dictating what could and could not happen. Sax isn't so blind to see there isn't a comfort in that, even if the result isn't always good for a species, a city or a planet. Plake, when they first meant, spoke of how the Oratus coming had ruined her life, had forced the Vyphen out of the Vincere and distorted their purpose.

Change is devastating. Sax only has to look at his own claws to see that. Not changing, however, can be equally so. Plake would be dead if she hadn't adapted. Sax would be dead without Nobaa's metal plates holding him together.

"I cannot make that promise," Sax says. "But I *can* promise that we will try. That whatever change comes when the Amigga no longer control our fates will not be made without thinking of what you have."

Bas touches his tail. It's all the acknowledgment he needs, and the Flaum's resigned nod is all the reward.

The Flaum leads their small band through the rest of the village, to another landing site. The fight clearly came this way; numerous buildings, vines, and even people bear scorch marks, holes and worse. Piled robes and sheets cover what Sax assumes are bodies, though none seem large enough to be an Oratus.

"How many?" Sax asks as they walk.

"They killed them all. A dozen maybe," the Flaum says. "They only took Evva. She told us to hide, and the Chorus ignored us."

The second landing site is smaller than the first, and bears the signs of at least one small victory for Evva's force: a wrecked shuttle coats the mossy undergrowth, broken and still smoking from one of the microjets.

"So the Chorus didn't fly away," Agra-Red says.

"They're running," the Flaum replies, and points across the clearing.

There, some of the vines are cut, creating a narrow path.

"Why didn't they just call for help?" it's Engee's voice this time, going for the logical question. "We're on the Chorus' world?"

The Flaum shakes her head. "I don't know. Once they had Evva, they took her, and left."

Which means every second they stand here talking, Evva's getting further away. Sax issues a sharp hiss, cutting off Engee's next question.

"Bas and I are going after her," Sax says. "The rest of you follow if you want."

With a quick touch of their tails, and ignoring Plake's command to wait, the Oratus pair break into a run, barging through the undergrowth in pursuit of their commander, and their friend.

The planning goes quick. Despite Kolas saying no Vincere lives would be risked, Lan volunteers to pilot a shuttle to Vimelia for us. Because the Sevora are holing up within their own atmosphere, the journey down is going to be a dangerous one, and as such, we're stuck with a small, swift craft.

Our crew is five: Lan, her pair Gar, T'Oli, Viera and myself.

The Ooblot, when I tell T'Oli that it doesn't need to come, simply laughs and suggests Viera and I would be dead in a moment without it there to save our hides. I don't bother telling T'Oli that I think the Ooblot's right.

What I do have time for, as we slip on our masks, as we gather up miners and small laser-edged swords to bring down with us, is wondering how Malo survived. I never reached him during our flight out of Vimelia's spaceport. I can see him there, still, lying on the ground by the rock wall, burned, cut and unmoving.

I tried to get to him and failed, and assumed he was dead.

Now I know he's been alive all these weeks I've spent fighting the Sevora, traveling through tunnels, and trying to keep humanity from extinction.

"I don't know," I say when Viera asks me how I'm taking it, as we sit in the shuttle while Lan runs through the pre-flight tests. "I should feel guilty for leaving him here, but what if I had tried to get him and failed?"

"Everyone would be dead." Viera is, as ever, not one to mince words. "You made the right choice, Kaishi. I'm sure Malo would say the same."

"I hope we get to ask him."

Not even the most optimistic of us believes we can simply fly down to Vimelia and, with Viera, T'Oli and I, burn our way into where Jel's keeping Malo and rescue him by ourselves. Kolas has the Vincere establishing a blockade around the planet, content to let the Sevora keep their own atmosphere under control until Kolas decides to smash Vimelia's moon against its surface, something the Sevora apparently don't know the Vincere can do.

I pitched Kolas, there on the bridge, to make a distraction. Just like my Solare tribe would do—keep the boar's attention focused on one hunter while the others prepared the fatal strike. A Vincere raid or bombardment would disguise their coming annihilation attempt, and would give our little shuttle a chance to sneak down to the surface.

Which is why Lan is hissing curses as our shuttle breaks into the atmosphere. Even though Viera and I are strapped in back in the main hold, Lan has the wall screens making it seem like our shuttle is translucent, and Viera and I get a full shot at what a Vincere assault looks like:

Kolas' cruiser is the star of the dozens and dozens of ships, ranging in size from smaller than the shuttle to twice as large as *Nunilite*—a hulking behemoth Lan calls a carrier—and all of them seem to sparkle at once as they unleash their devastation against Vimelia's surface.

Normally a miner's blast comes only as a flash, a moment that passes with deadly results in less than a blink of an eye. The distance these beams travel, and their sheer size, traps the shuttle in what look like long waves of blue, red, and yellow light. Space is washed out by the brightness, and the fringes of the screens glow as the laser's heat brushes against the shuttle's shielding.

"We're going to die now, aren't we?" Viera says, and there's a tight fear in her voice I've not heard before.

"They know what they're doing," I reply. "They won't hit us."

"Always thought I'd die in a fight, or exploring somewhere new," Viera says, and she's not really talking to me anymore, her eyes staring straight out at the cascading light. "Never expected I'd go without control, stuck in something I don't even understand."

"Try to believe you'll *survive* because of something you don't understand," I say.

I realize I'm not afraid, and it's because Ignos, while it took up space inside my head, placed my life, for a long time, on the line of things I didn't understand. Couldn't understand. After a while, I learned to simply let go and trust that I'd make it out the other side. And thus far, more or less, I have.

Vimelia's atmosphere envelopes the shuttle, clear air replacing the black void, the reflected beige of the surface catching the laser light and making the space-black walls of our survival corridor fade. Now those bolts look like glinting flashes, harmless in the cheery daylight. Death all around us and I can't even see it.

Lan, though, who banks the shuttle hard to the left and out of the fiery rain, can. Jel's communication included coordinates for a meeting, and that's where we're going, hoping that it's where the prisoners are being kept. Until we know for sure, Kolas said their bombardment would avoid any buildings matching the profile in the video.

That leaves plenty of targets, though, and the devastation is evident as we swing around, giving Viera and I clear looks through the shuttle's side down towards the planet's surface.

The great cityscape burns. Buildings crumple and fall as laser strikes burrow deep within their sides, while other beams slice through tube transports or hit Sevora ships still buzzing through the skies, erasing them in fiery pops. Black smoke erupts in plumes, as more and more blasts torch the city.

"It's . . . awful," I say. "I don't like the Sevora, but this is wanton. They're not targeting—"

"They're going to erase all of this with the moon anyway," T'Oli interrupts. "All of it will be gone, sooner or later. It's not worth feeling bad about it—the Sevora would have done the same to Marilo and your cities if they had the time."

Not worth feeling bad about the demise of an entire civilization? Then again, the Sevora may have obliterated all of the remaining Solare villages back on Earth. The Charre too. An existential threat uniting all of humanity, just in time for me to pledge it to a greater, deadlier force. One that apparently won't hesitate to squash an uprising with extinction-level assaults.

"You can't fight this one," Viera whispers to me. "We're not strong enough. Yet."

Yet. I suppose there's comfort in the idea that, if we're left alive, we might grow strong enough to avoid the Sevora's fate.

It's something to aim for, anyway.

"Get yourselves tightened up," Gar, Lan's pair and the other Oratus on the shuttle, hisses from the cockpit. "We've got some attention."

The Oratus' warning barely comes in time for me to grab onto the netting before Lan throws the shuttle into a spiraling dive. Outside, I can see we're nearing one of the city's gaps, where the constant carpet of buildings gives way to wider, sparser spaces of sand and the occasional garden. Mountains rise in the distance too, and it looks like Lan's trying to take us closer to their deep brown peaks. Trying, here, being the key; to my right, I can see a trio of black wedges coming straight for us. We're away from the flashing stream of Vincere bombardment now, so the Sevora are free to glide in. At least, they are until red lasers burst from the top of the shuttle, sending burning bolts after our pursuit.

The Sevora pilots begin a weird dance, their ships jerking and swirling around, yet always maintaining their same approach towards us. The fight resembles the clawing, grasping struggle I've seen between jungle birds, where each side swings up and down, trying to get in a strike.

Here, though, we're outnumbered. The Sevora split their trio as they close into the shuttle, breaking up, down, and straight on. Gar, manning the shuttle's defense, unleashes a mighty stream of hissing curses, frantically sending bolts everywhere.

The Sevora, finally, decide to attack.

From three angles, hot energy pours into the shuttle. At first, with blue-white fizzles, the lasers appear to dissipate before striking the hull, though the sudden cascade of bright alarms says the assault wasn't without impact.

"That's just letting us know our shields are gone," T'Oli says. "Every hit takes some energy, and before you know it, you're out."

"I'm guessing that's not a good thing?" I manage to ask.

"Not if you're a fan of being alive."

"Told you we're going to die up here," Viera adds.

This time, I can't really deny her. The Sevora fighters swing back around for another blitz, and suddenly the shuttle lurches and I feel my stomach try to fly up and out of my mouth. We're weightless, free-falling, the rapidly approaching ground flowing up to us outside the shuttle.

I'm screaming too, along with Viera, but our voices disappear into a grand clashing of other alarms.

Just before the shuttle strikes the ground, though, it bounces. The netting strains as it catches us, and when my stomach slams back into position, I let loose my breakfast.

I don't get a chance to recover, as Lan drives the shuttle forward fast, pressing me away from the nets and pushing out what little air's left in my lungs. Bolts pepper the ground around us, super-heating the sand and bursting trees, hedges and other greenery into flame. There's a flash-pop from above and I hear Gar roar, and see why when the cinder wreck of a Sevora ship slams down to our left, breaking into a thousand pieces.

The other two, though, find their zone. It's easy to tell because the hull above us literally burns away as the Sevora lasers pound into it. First the metal glows orange, then it peels back and a single shot gets through, slices the netting between Viera and I. Without the netting's support, we both fall to the shuttle's floor as more shots stitch the interior.

"Take us down!" I shout up ahead, though with smoke filling the shuttle's body, I'm not sure Lan has any other choice.

"Get close together," T'Oli says, the Ooblot sliding off the nets over to us.

Viera and I, as the shuttle rocks towards a swift crash, slip close. T'Oli thins itself out, moves over us and, like a blanket, wraps its cool cream skin around our legs. A moment later the Ooblot hardens, giving us some protection as the shuttle begins crashing through gardens and low walls.

If we'd still been in the city, we would have smashed and burned through a building by now.

As it is, I watch through the cockpit, mouth open in an endless scream, as the shuttle buries itself into dirty ground. Sand and stones spray up around the craft, around us, with plenty falling inside, into my hair and sliding off the mask Kolas gave each of us before we left.

Then silence. Loud, terrible silence.

I run a quick check of my body—I'm breathing, so there's that. My eyes can see the broken and sparking cockpit ahead, though the increasing smoke makes it difficult to know whether Lan and Gar are still alive. A couple twitches confirm my arms and legs made it through the crash intact.

"You all right?" I ask Viera.

"Oh yeah. Completely fine." Viera's brushing dirt off her face, her hand moving automatically. "Let's do that again."

"I'd say our odds of surviving another crash like this are very, very low," T'Oli adds.

"Joking, T'Oli," I say. "She's joking. Can you get off of us now?"

The Ooblot complies, softening and sliding away. "What a strange time to tell a joke."

I stand slow, my muscles still freaking out. "Humans are strange, T'Oli." I try to wave away some of the smoke, realizing we probably don't want to stay in the downed shuttle any longer than necessary. "Lan? Gar?"

There's a soft hiss, and then Gar bursts through the smoke, Lan held in his four claws. Lan's emerald skin is burned black all over the place, but I see her vents still open and close.

"Leave, now," Gar hisses, and then he clomps over to the shuttle's side and slaps at the wall panel.

The door doesn't open.

"Of course," Viera says as she stands next to me. "That'd mean something would have to go right on this mission."

T'Oli flows up my side, along my arm and to the edge of my hand. I feel part of the Ooblot harden to latch itself to my wrist, its eye stalks poking out to the sides. The rest of its body extends from my hand, adjusting its shape to have very fine, very sharp edge.

Guess we're getting out of here the messy way.

"Move," I tell Gar, and the big, deep blue Oratus steps aside as I make for the door. "Hope you're sharp enough for this."

"Easily," T'Oli replies.

I swing the Ooblot, slashing into the side of the shuttle. Every cut peels apart the metal like I'm cutting grass, and in moments we have a makeshift exit. Which is good, because small fires are springing up— at least our attackers did us the favor of burning an exit for the smoke —and I feel another minute inside would leave us burned and baked.

Instead we make it out into a burning field of what looks like some form of stalk-grown crop. Thanks to our laser-filled crash, though, I'm in the middle of an array of candles. Gar, with Lan, and Viera follow me out, and gradually our eyes are drawn to the approaching whistle of the two Sevora ships.

"They're lining up a run," Gar says. "We have to leave now."

Both of the black shapes look like slivers against the sky as they curl around towards us, and for a moment I wonder if I can pull the miner from my mask and start shooting.

"Don't bother," Viera says to me. "You won't hit them."

I don't get a chance to reply, because Viera pulls me, with T'Oli's now-dulled self still wrapped around my wrist, away from the burning shuttle and after Gar's loping form. The Oratus, even carrying another of his kind, outruns us easily, dashing away into the thicker plants.

"Isn't he going to wait?" Viera huffs as we move.

"Why?" T'Oli replies. "Does Gar owe you something?"

"Is this entire galaxy full of greedy murderers?" Viera replies.

"I'll submit myself as evidence that it is not," T'Oli says.

"What's that?" I say, as much to cut into their aimless conversation as to point out the slim, soft-yellow building rising up ahead of us.

Before anyone replies, there's a skittering boom from behind us, and a quick look confirms that what's left of our shuttle has been sent to whatever afterlife awaits spacecraft. The Sevora fighters tilt up, then their aft jets turn a white-blue and they rocket off back towards the city.

"I think it's what we came for," T'Oli says, its eyestalks angling towards the building. "Kolas had the communication traced, and Lan tried to get us as close as she could."

"Do you really think they didn't see us?" Viera's still watching the plume trails left by the speeding fighters. "These stalks aren't that tall."

"Either they did and don't care, or they didn't see us at all," I reply. "We shouldn't stand here, though. Let's go."

What none of us say as we walk through the tall stalks towards the building, though, is that we're trapped here now. Stuck on a planet that, whenever Kolas decides our time's up, is going to get very hot, very fast.

As we get close to the building, I notice that its roof keeps changing color. It's not just yellow, but a swirling mix of shades that dart and dash around each other. Jel, and her Sevora faction, had paintings like this on the walls of their base that we saw on our first trip to Vimelia.

"At least it looks like Lan took us to one of Jel's bases," I say.

The word 'base' oversells the building. It's not much larger than the shuttle, and spouts adorn the outside, linked to hoses that are, in turn, stretched to floating drones spraying water over the crops. They don't seem to care that half their field is burning up from our shuttle's explosion.

"There's no door," Viera says a couple of minutes later as we circle the structure. "What's the point of a building if you can't get into it?"

"Maybe we don't have the right key?" T'Oli says.

"Can you make your sword again?" I say. "Then I'll just cut a hole."

"That only works on thin metal, like the shuttle's hull," T'Oli replies. "I'll break if you try to slash rock with me."

I stare at the squat structure. There has to be something we're missing. I'd ask Gar or Lan, but the two Oratus have disappeared. Instead, I run my hands along the soft gray surface. It's cool to touch, and the building as a whole vibrates with the amount of water rushing through it.

"Lan tried to fly us here for a reason," I say. "There's got to be a way in."

"Maybe we need to see the way out first," Viera says, and I see her looking at T'Oli.

"I don't like those eyes," T'Oli says.

"When's the last time you had a bath?" Viera replies, smiling for the first time in a long while.

Using one of the energy blades, we cut a hole in one of the hoses leading to one of the watering drones. The hoses themselves are half as wide as I am, and the amount of water they're spewing is immense, but it's also not constant. The drones shut off their spray if they have to shift across a wide spread of watered crops. It's during one of these short moments when we stuff T'Oli, or as much of the Ooblot as we can, into the tube.

"You're both terrible people," T'Oli says, its voice coming back up in an irritated patter.

"Can you block it?" I ask.

"Already did," T'Oli says. "I went a ways down the hose too—if this works, you'll see a big pop in that corner there."

The drone doesn't seem to notice there's an issue and makes its way to a section of merrily burning crops. There's a burst of rushing pressure, and then the building shudders.

"You both owe me for this one," T'Oli says.

"Whatever you want," Viera replies.

"You don't even have any money."

"We'll get you something better," I say. "A title. Empress's Ooblot."

"Stop it."

The blocked water makes itself known first by the rapid rattling of the spout attached to the building, the spout that T'Oli's blocking with its Ooblot body. Then metal starts to fly as holding rings pop, seams break, and the entire corner of the building, like T'Oli predicted, crumbles away as the pipe bursts.

Water explodes around us and, as the tube forces its way wide around T'Oli, the Ooblot goes rocketing away too. T'Oli lands a dozen meters away. Viera and I, though, have our miners out and are already walking through the expanding puddle, past Vimelia's newest geyser, into the leaning building.

In the middle of the floor is the reason there's no door—there's a platform, big and metal, with a panel on a stand about the height of my head. It's clearly meant to go down.

"Guess we found our way in," Viera says.

"Question is, to where?"

T'Oli catches up with us as we play with the panel. It's not that hard to parse—there's a big arrow pointing down wrapped in a green square—but every time I try to press it, the panel gives an annoyed beep and the whole screen flashes red.

"You know how to work one of these?" I ask the Ooblot as T'Oli slimes its way onto the platform.

After I show T'Oli what's going on, the Ooblot swivels its eyes to me and blinks, then turns its gaze to the back part of the platform, behind where Viera and I are standing. There, wedged into the narrow gap between the platform and the rest of the building's floor is a piece of one of the spout's binding rings.

I glance at Viera and she takes a step over to the piece, reaches and, with a bit of effort, pulls it out of the gap. She throws it away as I press the panel again. This time it flashes green and the lift's motors start revving up.

"Sometimes it's the obvious solutions," T'Oli says.

"More often than not," I reply.

The platform sinks below the surface, into a shaft not much larger than the platform itself. White lights speckle a deep blue-painted wall. Apparently this lift doesn't warrant the kind of spectacular paint job provided to the building's roof, but it's plenty pretty anyway. If I make it back to Earth, I'll advocate more for this kind of thing—life's hard enough, it may as well be pleasant to look at.

"Oh no," Viera says suddenly, and I follow her eyes up to see a pair of massive forms falling towards us.

Gar and Lan land on the platform, their huge bodies causing the lift to rattle, the motors to whine, but apparently the Sevora design their elevators well, because it doesn't stop. I look at Lan, mouth slightly ajar at the sheer scope of the injuries running along her body; burns, broken scales, and a long, dark scar running down her neck.

"A close shot," Lan says as she sees me noticing. Other injuries have clear creams spread across them, stuff that seems to be wriggling. "Nanobots, performing miracles. My mask kept me from dying, and these will keep me useful."

"Why did you run?" I ask Gar, because I don't know what

nanobots are, and I'd rather figure out if we can still trust the living weapons that just landed in our midst.

"I needed space to help her," Gar hisses. "You were a good distraction."

Viera has her miner up and aimed as Gar finishes. "Say what we are again, you overgrown lizard."

For once, I agree with my friend, even though I'm sure the two Oratus could kill us without a second thought. Gar, though, just falls into a fit of hissing laughter.

"Overgrown lizard?" Lan says. "I've never heard that description before." The Oratus turns to Viera, who swivels her miner to track Lan. "I don't think you can be picky about your allies here, human. If we leave you, who's going to fly you off this planet?"

"T'Oli and I can fly," I say. "Viera's right. If we can't trust that you'll stick with us, then you should leave. We're in this together, or not at all."

Gar stops his hissing for a moment, and both Oratus look over at me.

"This human is brave," Gar says. "She thinks she can survive on her own."

"But she won't have to," Lan hisses. "Kolas asked if we wanted to help, and we volunteered. We will see your friend returned, or we will die trying."

When Lan says the words, a weight I didn't know was there lifts off my chest. Deep down, I know that Viera, T'Oli and I won't be able to rescue Malo alone—there'll be too many Sevora, and too little time. But with two Oratus?

There might be a chance.

It's been a while since Sax has chased anyone, and running through the thick vines of Aspicis makes for an exhilarating rush. He operates on instinct and the tiny shafts of light that manage to poke down from the sky. Each one is a signpost, pointing Sax towards the next bend, the next spot to sink in his talons as he and Bas rocket along the carved trail.

The two Oratus hold their silence during the run, saving their breath for breathing. There's no telling how long it might take to catch up to Evva's captors, or how far the Amigga and its Oratus guards need to get before they'll find another way to fly.

As if sensing the magnitude of the moment, Aspicis itself is quiet. Aside from the *scritching* sounds their talons make as they dig into the ground, there's little other noise; no bird calls, none of a jungle's hiss and growls, nor the heavy mechanical shunts of technology. The Amigga have constructed their homeworld to their own desires, and Sax finds the result boring.

The smells, too, are bland. The vines don't flower, and the only scent they bring is a lukewarm nuzzle; a soft, ill-defined layer in the air that tastes of dried grass. The Amigga have embarked on a quest to make the least interesting mix of sensations possible.

That thought ends when Sax reaches the trail's conclusion. It's not clear how far they've run, but they've arrived at another village. Or, no, something else.

What sits in front of Sax is a large cylindrical dome, made from vines that still look alive, but directed to grow like this. The dome itself is huge, several times Sax's own height and long enough to be a space station wing. At the far end, where the dome looks to have been chopped off, sits the greatest concession to mechanical necessity Sax has seen on the planet.

A mag-lev rail.

It's a single shimmering silver bar, and it's raised almost a meter off the ground. The track extends back from the dome away from Sax and Bas, vanishing into the dark jungle.

The dome and the area around it dazzles with brightness, as the overhead vines have been cleared. Sax can make out other trails leading away from the dome too, and these are occupied with groups of Flaum making their way to and from the station. Some wheel cases behind them, others pull long carts stacked with crates and floating on microjets.

"So Aspicis isn't always obsolete," Bas hisses as she stands next to Sax.

"The war. I bet they couldn't keep the planet sacred anymore, not if they needed supplies."

Regardless, what they don't see as they look around is Evva and her captors. The Amigga and its bodyguards aren't anywhere here. At least, not in sight.

"Hiding in there?" Bas says, guessing what Sax is thinking.

"If they are, they'll know we're coming," Sax gestures towards some of the moving Flaum. Plenty of the furry creatures have thrown looks their way, their faces twisting into shock or confusion, then retreating into fear and a quickened step. "Not that it matters. If we can't save Evva, then this is all worthless."

Bas doesn't argue, so together the two Oratus stride across the clearing towards the dome. The entrance to the station is, apparently, on the other side from their approach, so their first sight of the Amigga comes when it rounds the near, slope-sided end of the station.

Unlike Dalachite, the last Amigga Sax's seen, which had grown itself literally into the space station built under its direction, this one has a more typical arrangement: encasing its round, flesh-colored form is a clear shell, with a pair of white-metal bars sticking out from either side. Each bar splits into a variety of appendages, with one jutting straight down and ending in a low-powered microjet that keeps the Amigga off the ground.

What's really important, though, is how many of this Amigga's 'arms' end in miners or edged blades. Sax counts a half-dozen weapons, all of them angling towards the Oratus. Two of the miners, one on each side of the Amigga, loom larger; high-energy models made to devastate and destroy. The ensemble makes clear how the Flaum village wound up a flattened mess of broken homes and burnt bodies.

"You're not cleared to be here," the Amigga announces, with plenty of slime in the words. The voice comes translated and piped through its speakers, so there's no mouth for the Amigga to pull into a caustic grin. "In fact, you're no longer cleared to be anywhere, traitors."

The Amigga doesn't wait for a response—as soon as it finishes the sentence, those big miners on either side start spraying molten energy at Sax and Bas. The two Oratus, though, weren't expecting a friendly chat and manage to dive out of the initial blast. As he jumps to the side, Sax uses his right midclaw to grab one of the miners off his mask and, when he lands, snap-aims the weapon and fires.

His shot strikes home, melting the front of the Amigga's right-side miner, as Bas does the same to the cannon on the creature's opposite. The Amigga's only reply is to laugh and bring its set of four smaller miners to bear.

These don't even get shots off. Apparently the Amigga's not used to facing Vincere-trained, three-letter Oratus, because every time one of its miners takes aim, Sax and Bas blow it to red-hot pieces. Sax has miners in both midclaws now, and they don't stop shooting until the Amigga's left without a single weapon on its rig.

"Where's Evva?" Bas rasps at the Amigga when it realizes it's weaponless and finally stops trying to spin to an armed end.

"Inside," the Amigga says. "Waiting for the train. You can join her if you like. We're happy to take all of you."

The Amigga wouldn't leave Evva alone in the station, which means the mirrored Oratus must be in there, so that's where Sax goes. Or rather, tries. He gets one long stride towards the Amigga, meaning to go around the harmless blob, when something slams into his side and drives Sax to the ground. Then lifts him up and throws him back towards Bas.

"Kah, you didn't need to come out here," the Amigga says as Sax shakes his head to clear away the blurriness. "I had them."

Bas is by him now, helping Sax stand up, and together with his pair, they turn to see the Amigga's broken and sparking defenses complemented by a massive mirrored Oratus. Sax can't tell much of Kah's features, exactly, as the reflective scales only give a rough outline where the light seems to bend.

"This is what you fought on the frigate?" Bas whispers. "I didn't think they existed."

"They do, and they hurt."

"Traitors!" the Amigga calls. "I ask again—surrender, and perhaps your deaths will come swiftly!"

Doesn't the Amigga understand that a Vincere Oratus will never surrender? That they've been trained to do everything except give themselves to an enemy? A list of things that, as it happens, includes fighting back.

"Finish the Amigga," Sax hisses. "Then help me."

Sax digs his talons into the dirt, fakes a burst forward towards the mirrored Oratus, firing both miners as he moves. Kah doesn't stand still and take the fire, but leaps up and forward, lunging towards Sax just above his aim, biting on Sax's move. So Sax digs in hard, leans back and brings up the miners as Kah's leap doesn't meet the charge the mirrored Oratus is expecting.

To his right, Sax catches a passing pink blur as Bas heads for the Amigga. Without its weapons, the monster shouldn't be much more than a snack for his pair.

Kah, too, isn't much more than a target for a hot moment as his momentum carries the mirrored Oratus right into Sax's fire. Blistering burns light up on the mirrored Oratus' chest, melting vents and scoring gashes in the creature's reflective skin.

Then Kah's ramming hard into Sax, pushing him back and tearing away the two miners. It's an aggressive call for any Oratus, particularly one that should have been able to engage Sax with something other than its claws. Now, though, they're in a clenched duel of slashing talons, biting teeth, and raking attacks from all four arms.

On Rav's frigate, Sax hadn't been enough. The mirrored Oratus had overpowered him, gashed and sliced Sax to pieces. Here, though, Nobaa's additions prove their worth; the metal plates provide protection, and Sax maneuvers himself to catch the mirrored Oratus' attacks on those pieces while his own claws rake at a body whose whole advantage comes from being hard to see at distance.

Kah realizes quick that this isn't a fight he wants to have, and with a tail sweep, the mirrored Oratus forces Sax back. Bleeding and burned, Kah's having a hard time standing straight, while Sax bears his scratches with an open, hissing mouth.

Ready for more.

At least until he sees a second shadow crash into Bas and knock her away. The Flaum back at the village had mentioned two mirrored Oratus, and the second one begins to thrash Bas, pinning her to the ground and going for a mortal strike with its talons. The Amigga, behind it all, crows again for the impossible surrender.

Sax reacts. He falls into the bloodlust, that instinctual do-or-die state Oratus enter when survival leaves no other options. He charges Kah, then feints right, as if he's going to run by the mirrored Oratus towards the cackling Amigga. When Kah goes for it—apparently

Kah's not used to tricky fighters— Sax plants his right talon and jumps.

It's a tactic that wouldn't work against a fresh adversary, against one that could leap up to meet him or grab Sax's tail and sling the Oratus back to the ground, but Kah's hurt and tired and misses his chance. Sax lands beyond Kah and, with a hard shoulder charge, bowls the mirrored Oratus off of Bas.

And Bas doesn't burn the moment, getting herself up and pulling free her two miners. Aims one at Kah and the second at the mirrored Oratus Sax has just pushed away from her.

"You said it," Sax hisses towards the Amigga in the suddenly still moment. "Surrender."

"We will not," Kah rasps, moving in slow, unsteady steps towards the Amigga. "Either kill us, or let us go, traitors."

"That's an easy choice," Sax says. "End them, Bas."

"Wait!" the Amigga says, and its voice, for once, isn't drenched in haughty superiority. "You're after us for the Oratus, right?"

"She's inside the station," Bas says. "We'll take her back after we take care of you."

Not that he's deviating from the conflict at hand, but Sax is picking up some rustling in the air. Vibrations in the ground. Paying slight attention to his peripheral, Sax notices that the Flaum moving around the station have all disappeared—not entirely surprising given that miners were firing constantly moments ago, but to have not a single one venturing to and from the station?

"You won't find her there," the Amigga says. "Not yet, anyway."

Amigga have no facial expressions. No tells, especially when their limbs are grown into their exoskeletons. Sax has no idea if this one's lying, but the way the mirrored Oratus stay still mean it's not trying to give them cover for a surprise attack.

"Give me a reason not to fire." Bas gives a slight shake to her miners.

"Now," the Amigga begins. "There's a conversation—"

Bas presses in on the trigger and her left miner fires, scores a deep blast into the lower abdomen of the left, less wounded Oratus. Neither one, to their credit and Sax's respect, move.

"She's in the station," the Amigga blurts. "I was lying. We stunned her and left her there once we saw you coming. Let us go!"

There it is. The cowardice Sax believes sits at the core of the Chorus, of the entire Amigga species. Why else build someone to fight your battles for you? Why else try to remove anything that threatens your power rather than work with them to find a mutual solution?

Bas nods at Sax, who hesitates. He doesn't want to leave Bas out here with these three. She takes away the choice, though, with a simple touch of her tail, a promise that she'll be fine.

Though he doesn't say it, Sax makes a promise of his own—he'll find and end all three of these monsters if they touch any part of his pair. And with that, he makes a break for the station, looping around the outside of the vine structure towards the entry, which isn't a door so much as a wide arch without a seal of any kind.

Inside, with cold electric globes providing the light, there's a large platform for the mag-lev train. Lying on the ground, unconscious, is Evva. Bunches of Flaum occupy the walls, pressing back to get away from Sax as he moves forward, picks Evva up in his claws, and carries her outside.

As he leaves the dome, the rumble he's been feeling grows, and now it's accompanied by a shrill whistle. Turning his head, Sax can see the bright purple and blue front of the mag-lev train swing into view. It's moving fast, and mostly silent, that rumble coming, Sax realizes, from the pumping of power from somewhere deep beneath him up towards the track.

"Let us on that train," the Amigga's saying as Sax rejoins Bas, who's still holding her miners and her targets dead. "It's the least you can do."

"They tried to kill us," Sax hisses. "Do the same to them."

"Go," Bas announces. "Get on the train, and get out of here."

The Amigga and its escorts don't wait, moving slow and gingerly as Bas guides them towards the train with her miners. The train cars open wide, their entire sides swinging up and letting Flaum come and go, though Sax sees more than a few elect to stay seated rather than get off on the same platform as a quartet of bloodied Oratus and one Amigga who's looking in dire need of a new suit.

Still, space is made. The mirrored Oratus board and help the Amigga join them. The train cars shut, and with another hissing rumble, the mag-lev shunts into reverse and vanishes down the track.

"Why?" Sax asks, finally. "Why let them go?"

"Because I don't know if I could have killed them all before they got to me," Bas says, her eyes tracking the departing train. "You're holding Evva. We achieved the objective. Why risk it?"

His pair makes sense, and yet . . .

Sax would've taken the shots.

The platform ends its descent by stopping next to a copy of itself. The two platforms sit flush, the second one angling along a straight tunnel that follows the white globed lights into the distance.

"Guess the ride doesn't end here?" Viera says.

We transfer over to the new platform, which is a tricky process when you've got a pair of three-meter tall Oratus maneuvering all their limbs in the small space. Apparently the Sevora never expected to use hosts like Gar and Lan for the kind of maintenance work these plain transports are meant for.

The second platform has a panel like the first, and soon we're whooshing along the tunnel towards a dark ending that eventually turns into a massive space. It's as big as the spaceports I saw earlier on Vimelia, but rather than ships buzzing in and out, the giant rectangle populates itself with streams of fresh crops funneling in from one of many openings. Other tunnels with other platforms echo the one we're on, and all of them connect to a grated catwalk that circles the upper section of the chamber.

"Every time I think we've done something right, I see it's being done bigger," I say, thinking back to Damantum's granaries. I thought our storerooms were huge, with enough space to keep our entire city fed for a season. This place, and the amount of food getting shunted into the chamber's lower level, divided by steel walls to sort the crops, makes our best efforts look feeble. "We have so far to go."

"Don't compare yourselves to this place," Gar says. "It will be erased before too long."

It's almost sad, because the sounds of so much plenty pouring in, the sight of so much food that could end so much hunger, shows the Sevora aren't entirely evil. They clearly care enough to keep their own fed, to invest in constructs that support their civilization.

If you're going to keep billions prisoner, I suppose you have to feed them somehow.

There's nothing to our right except more portals to more platforms, and none of them look any different from ours. To our left, the walkway continues a long ways to what looks like a more permanent dividing wall, with an outline of a door. Platforms line the outside this way too, but at least there's something different at the end.

"As much as I'd like to take more rides," I say, nodding to the left. "Let's head that way."

We make it all of a dozen steps before the door we're heading towards slides open. A pair of Whelk, both a sickly blue, slither out, miners raised. I'm about to ask them where the prisoners are when they open fire.

Viera dives into one of the open platform tunnels, with Lan following, while Gar takes a leap to the right, using his claws to grip the catwalk railing and scramble towards the Whelk. Before I can move, T'Oli wraps itself around my chest and hardens to its impenetrable self—just in time, too, as a bolt blitzes into the Ooblot a second later, leaving a hard black scar.

"Any time you want to fire back!" T'Oli says.

I'm on it; I yank my main miner from my mask, raise the weapon and pull the trigger. Bright red bolts lance out, stitching a line well above the short Whelks.

"Sorry!" I say, diving towards the left wall, trying to get inside Viera's tunnel. "I don't really know how to shoot!"

Bows, yes. Miners? No.

"That's what I'm here for," Viera says, reaching out and pulling me into the tunnel.

I'm surprised the Whelk didn't get me with more than one shot, but after peeking back outside, I suppose I shouldn't be; Gar not only drew their attention, the Oratus took care of both Whelk entirely, spreading the sloppy remnants of their bodies all over the catwalk. With a couple of bites, the Oratus snaps their miners into junk.

"It's what he's good at," Lan says as we look at the destruction.

"Apparently," I say.

Gar didn't get through the encounter free from harm—his mask is splintered on his legs and in the middle of his chest, where direct miner shots disintegrated the armor, but the Oratus doesn't seem to care.

We join Gar at the dividing wall, and I take the lead in looking through the door the Whelks opened. On the other side is the reason why those guards were here in the first place; the prisoners we saw on the video are all clustered on the bottom floor of this half. The crop walls have been removed, allowing all of the prisoners to sit on the ground in a giant crowd, along with the dozen guards watching them, miners ready.

There's another quartet up here, on our level, and they're watching our doorway. I have to jerk my head back as a couple Flaum send fiery shots at me.

"Prisoners and guards," I say and describe the setup. "Lan, Gar, you've got the most experience with this. What do you think?"

"Attack and devour?" Gar hisses.

"Yeah, except we don't want to get shot doing it," Viera says.

"Capture the top level, and the guards below won't have posi-tion." Lan takes over. "They'll either surrender or, without cover, we'll finish them fast. As for how to beat the four guards up here, we'll need a distraction, and then some sharp shooting."

Lan finishes the plan with a look at Viera, who nods. "I'll hit them, don't worry."

"Then what's the distraction?" I ask.

The Oratus points her scaled green foreclaw at T'Oli, still wrapped around me. "The Ooblot should be able to draw fire without risking itself."

"Just what I like hearing," T'Oli slaps. "Send the Ooblot out—it's basically a puddle anyway!"

Lan's expression doesn't change. Neither does Gar's. I glance at Viera and she shrugs.

"T'Oli?" I say.

The Ooblot slithers off of me onto the catwalk, slithers over to the door. Its eyestalks swivel back towards us as we cling to the sides, out of sight.

"If I die for this, I'm holding it against all of you." T'Oli says, then the Ooblot slithers over and out of sight through the door.

"Now!" Lan hisses at Viera, and my friend quick-steps over to the door.

Watching Viera work is mesmerizing—the Lunare grips a miner in each hand, spins with her shoulder against the dividing wall to look through the doorway, and even though I only see her ash-white hair and the edge of her set face, I know every bolt that leaves her miners hits its target.

After the flashing cascade, Viera steps through the doorway and we follow. The results of her handiwork are the smoking ruins of the four guards, in addition to the sporadic and rapidly dwindling return fire from down below as Viera continues her cleanup. By the time I reach the railing, my own miner and lack of ability in hand, the five remaining Flaum guards have tossed their weapons to the floor.

"Nice work," I tell her.

"I know." Viera doesn't look over at me, keeps her focus on those guards.

I'm a lucky Empress to have friends like her.

On the far side, against the end wall, there's another platform that takes us down to the floor level. Viera elects to remain up top and provide cover, so T'Oli—thankfully fine after its decoy duty—and the two Oratus accompany me.

What I see are thirty or forty prisoners, mostly Flaum and Whelk, lined up against the wall to my left. They're packed against one another, and they all look broken and miserable. Like the remnants I'd met who served in Clarity's Dawn, but without any spark of hope. Center among them, though, is who we came here to find.

"Malo," I say his name and there's more than a bit of disbelief as I do. "You're alive."

He looks up slow as I approach, and the damage I noticed during the video is worse up close. Malo's thin, with cuts and bruises across his body, and he's clothed in the same rags as the rest of the prisoners. His eyes are red, and though his mouth forms a half-smile at me, I can barely keep myself from crying.

"Hi, Empress," Malo says, his voice a whisper.

"What did they do to you?" I ask, and I stretch out my hand, run it along the side of his scruff-covered face.

"Tried to break me," Malo says.

I shake my head. What would be the point of breaking Malo? He's not with the Vincere, he wouldn't know anything useful.

"Humans, we must leave," Lan hisses from behind me. "These Sevora say they're the dregs, that all the rest of Jel's forces are trying to get on the only good ship left on this planet. The ship we need."

I glance back at the Oratus. "They never expected to trade the prisoners for their lives?"

"I don't think they believed," Malo whispers behind me. "They hoped the Vincere might care, but they didn't believe they would."

I close my eyes for a second. This might not be the time for politics, for morals. We have to escape the planet. Now. And we're taking all of them with us. "The prisoners are coming too. As long as we made this journey, we may as well save who we can."

Gar hisses something I don't catch before Lan cuts her pair off with a twitch from her tail. She doesn't object, though, and instead points a foreclaw at the five remaining guards, lined up and looking defeated.

"Can one of them lead us?" I ask Lan.

"They will," Lan says.

"Even though they're Sevora?"

Lan bares her teeth. "If they get us to that ship, we'll take them. Ask Kolas to, perhaps, give them a chance." Lan's looking at me, so the guards behind her can't see those yellow eyes, those black slits in her pupils. None of those Sevora are getting off this planet, regardless of what they do.

And I don't care.

I thought they took Malo from me. I thought he died in that cavern as T'Oli flew us away. Now he's standing behind me, and if he's not dead, he's plenty close to it. Turning away from Malo turns my sadness, the pity and blighted hope at seeing him alive into anger, rage. The bleak force that comes when you failed to save someone you care about.

I walk past Lan to the row of five Sevora guards, all of them Flaum, and all of them wearing the dark blue armor of Jel's faction, whose name I don't even remember. I meet each of their eyes, and their beady blacks stare back at me. Of course they don't know. Of course they weren't responsible for what happened to Malo that day.

"Viera?" I call, not breaking eye contact with the Sevora.

"Empress?" Viera answers from above.

"If any of these five do anything without my permission, I want you to end them. Don't wait. They get no second chances."

"You got it."

I nod towards the Sevora, to let them know I'm talking to them now. "You heard the Oratus. Take us to the ship, so we can leave this miserable world."

. . .

I march at the front, with Viera, T'Oli, and Lan. Gar volunteers to hold the back, hissing that he'll enjoy eating anyone that falls behind. The Sevora guards point us to a secondary chamber off of the large one, a space packed with terminals monitoring the crop flows and water supply, and that has a single transport tube.

Moving such a large group on one of these seems like it'll be a problem, until the Sevora use the panel on the side of the tube—at my order—to request a larger transport. We watch as the single pearl platform, which can mold its surface to match our seating needs, is joined by ten more. They don't sit as separate platforms, but instead form two-meter long white links from one to the next.

"Climb on?" I ask the Sevora, and, in particular, a red-brown furred Flaum that's taken position as their leader.

"They'll all stay together," the Sevora says. "We should go to the front."

Viera, with her miners out and aimed, follows me as we climb ahead. The five Sevora cluster with us on the lead platform, with Lan on the one immediately behind, along with the first set of prisoners. I let Malo, who seems increasingly tired, stay with Lan, and he leans on the Oratus like she's the only reason he's standing.

I want to talk to him. Want to tell Malo how sorry I am, but there's no time, so I bite back the words, and focus on the Sevora, on the platform, on getting us to the ship.

The platforms lurch forward, then pick up speed faster and faster until we're shuttling underneath the ground at a blinding speed. Overhead lights blink by so quick they look like a single white stream amid the gray-black tunnel sides. The stream, though, vanishes in a moment as we shoot out from beneath the ground and into a clear tube that soars through a scorched sky.

The two Oratus stand just outside the station with a third, unconscious, Oratus settled on the ground by their feet. Rescue was the plan, and now that they've done that, Sax isn't sure where to go. The Flaum certainly aren't helping—most have outright fled, and the ones who haven't shrink back every time Sax looks towards them as they cling to each other in the station's corners.

"I don't think we thought this through," Bas says.

Sax looks at her and suppresses a smile. She still looks radiant, even after the scuffle with the mirrored Oratus and the Amigga, even after dashing through a dark and grimy jungle. Here, while they court disaster, he's with her. Bas, and the mission. Nothing else matters.

The mission, though, is currently stunned, and Sax guesses it won't be long before that Amigga returns with a larger force to reclaim its prize.

"Look at these two uglies," the voice comes from the right, the slimy one of Agra-Red. "They found themselves an Oratus, too!"

The crimson Whelk nudges its way fully around the station, aiming its embedded miner with its left hand while holding a smaller shooter in its right. Ready to blast anything Agra-Red doesn't like into molecular oblivion. Behind it, armed and ready, are Plake and the two Teven.

"She's stunned," Sax offers when Plake gives Evva a concerned glance, and the Vyphen holds both her feathered hands over Evva's chest until she feels the Oratus' vents sucking in air.

"Then we have to get her out of here," Plake says.

"You say that as if we haven't been thinking of a way to do that," Bas replies.

"Have you?" Plake rounds on her. "Thought of a way? Or is standing here the best you've got?"

"I was thinking we'd carve you up, disguise Evva in your feathers," Sax offers, coupling the words with his toothy mug.

Engee, the Teven, steps between the group. "While you were all chasing after them, Nobaa and I talked with Avan some more. Evva's force had to get to that village somehow, and he says they have skiffs back there. Ones we can use."

Everyone, Sax included, stares at the Teven.

"You couldn't have mentioned this earlier?" the Whelk says.

"There wasn't a reason for it, earlier," Engee replies.

"Skiffs aren't safe!" Nobaa adds.

"Neither is staying here," Plake says. "Let's go."

There's no question who gets the joy of carrying Evva's paralyzed self. Sax starts with her, then hands Evva off to Bas when his arms go numb from the weight. Together, the two play a weird passing game with Evva until they make it back to the Flaum village.

Avan's there to meet them, looking better, if still on the wrong end of recovery.

What Avan can do, though is point them in the direction of the vine-runners, small skiffs barely enough for a single Oratus, and that look like sleds coated in microjets. A small windshield curls up from the front, with a pair of microjets on its top to help with sudden drops.

"I suppose that none of you know how to drive one of these?"

Avan says as they stand in front of the ten skiffs Evva's crew used to get to the town.

The Oratus leader is leaning against Sax now, coming into coherence but unable, yet, to stand on her own power or do more than slur a few words at a time. They must have zapped her with a strong blast to keep Evva, a large, red Oratus, stunned for this long. Then again, why take chances with the most wanted creature in the galaxy?

"I can figure it out," Plake announces.

Engee and Nobaa say the same—and proceed to climb into one of the skiffs, laying down side by side and slotting their small limbs against the edges of the sled. On the sled's edges sit small sticks which go either up or down, allowing for an ascent or a dive as needed. Nobaa takes one, Engee takes the other.

"It's fine," Avan hisses when Agra-Red wonders if the Teven will keep themselves in sync. "The two levers are tied to each other. They'll go wherever the push or pull is strongest."

That leaves a skiff for each of them, plus a few left over that Avan has no trouble donating to the village. A small repayment for the damage they've caused, but Sax agrees it's better than nothing.

Thinking so much about how others see their actions is frustrating; far easier to carry out the mission with eyes on the results and nothing else.

"Who's taking Evva?" Sax asks as Avan mounts his own skiff.

"I'll take her," Plake says. "I'm the only one small enough."

The Whelk's not large either, but Agra-Red's still carrying that monstrous miner, and together the two would make for a tight fit. Sax and Bas definitely can't fit a second Oratus on either of their skiffs. So the choice gets made without a struggle, and the group loads up.

The skiff makes for a weird fit, as Sax has to drape his midclaws over the side and then essentially hug the sled with the rest of him. He follows Avan's example and tucks his tail in by his side, its tip up near his head. A glance at Plake confirms she's in the worst spot, though; Evva's bulk is pressing Plake's feathered limbs hard into the craft, and the Vyphen's stretching out her neck as far as it can go to keep her eyes where they can see.

"The skiffs are set to follow mine," Avan announces, his hissing still light from the wounds. "You'll just need to hang on for the ride."

Sax is happy to hear that—they don't train Oratus to be pilots, especially not small skiffs. Bas has spent some time with shuttles and the like, but Sax prefers his knowledge focused on weapons and the ways to use them.

With a synchronized hum, all six skiffs start up with a bit of levitation, rising a meter over the ground. Sax hunkers down on his, peering through the glass windshield at the glowing purple village lamps as the microjets spool up.

"Take a deep breath!" Avan shouts above the whine.

A deep breath? Sax opens his vents, sucks in air on instinct, and it's a good thing he does, because the skiff lurches forward into a blindingly fast launch a moment later. The windshield keeps the air from blowing Sax clean off, but he clamps his claws tight anyway as the vines blow by beneath him.

The warm light of Aspicis' star proves ideal once Sax gets comfortable with the skiff's hurtling speed, giving him an easy view across the vast emerald expanse of huge, curling vines. Puffy pearl clouds and drifting fog break up the cerulean horizon. It's beautiful, though Sax finds the sheer lack of landscape disorienting; there's not a single hill or mountain pushing the vines up above each other, no valleys or plateaus. Just a relatively even canopy forming where the vines get too heavy to keep pushing themselves up.

It's a world tamed entirely to suit the species that owns it.

The skiffs stick true to their programming and they all fly in formation behind Avan for what seems like a long time before the traitor begins to slow. Then, Avan leans his skiff forward and dives towards what looks like a thick cluster of vines. Sax isn't expecting the shift and thinks about jumping free from the suicide course, until they get near and he realizes it's light playing tricks on his eyes.

The vines aren't quite as close as they looked, and Sax, along with the others, shoots through a series of tight gaps, eventually coming through into a burrow lit by the same dangling, colored globes as the Flaum village.

While that place held families and all the pieces of a real, civilized life, this one has the makeup of a military camp. The skiffs settle down in the middle—where plenty of other skiffs rest on the ground —and Sax sees tables carved from vines and random debris covered with weapons, tools, and spare Caches, those all-encompassing bracelets of knowledge.

Terminals are strewn around the place, hanging from slap-dash connections bored into vines. Sax traces the wires and they all slide through to a circular plate—the only true metal section on the ground —which glows ever-so-slightly orange.

Staring at the new arrivals are an assortment of Flaum, of course, but also a variety of other species. None of these wear any Chorus uniforms, and most look like they've spent a long time living on the edges of society; patched fur, scars or even missing appendages, mismatched clothes that go hard for function over fashion.

And no fear.

Evva's found herself a hardened crew, and Sax's hope for success rises high as he untangles himself from the skiff and takes his first few steps around. Something more delicious than nutrient goop is cooking on a rack of grills off to one side, a lime-green Whelk covered in a dirty brown apron standing guard over what's presumably dinner.

"Welcome to Quell," Avan says once the group's off their skiffs. "It's as close as you'll come to a home on this planet." The traitor— Avan will never be anything else in Sax's mind—points around the circle, giving basic names to places like the kitchen, showers, and various spaces for mission planning, engineering, and more.

Quell is well organized, which is exactly what Sax would expect from Evva's camp. What it's not, though, is exciting enough to keep exhaustion from rolling over him. They've been on a non-stop rush since leaping away from Solis what seems like an eternity ago.

Evva still needs to recover, and they don't seem under any imminent threat, so Sax gets directions from Avan, then he and Bas wind their way along a short trail through more vines to a hammock cluster. They come in all sizes, and they're made out of stiff, woven vine-skin.

"Think they'll hold our weight?" Bas hisses.

"I'm willing to try," Sax says. "Or I'll sleep right on the ground."

They choose the largest ones that happen to be close to each other, then climb inside and fall asleep—claws touching in the space between—to the slow breeze and steady sounds of a camp moving into its evening meal.

Morning finds Quell and the people within it the same as when Sax vanished to sleep. There's no change in the light, the temperature, but the smells are different; namely, there's no hint of cooking food, no ozone-stinging scent of batteries being repaired or plugged into miners. When Sax enters the main clearing—Bas is catching a few more moments of rest—there's a small cluster of fighters, all of them armed and all of them standing silent.

Evva's there too, and she raises a single foreclaw to her mouth. It's a universal signal and one Sax respects, slinking back under the cover of a nearby vine and holding his questions. A moment later there's a loud buzzing that comes from above, whining like a giant bee and then passing almost as quickly as it arrives. Only when the sound vanishes do the fighters relax, does Quell return to its normal quirks.

"They comb the planet constantly," Evva says as she meets Sax in the middle of the clearing.

The great red Oratus, all four letters of strength, leadership, and poise looks not too worse for her long stay in the unconscious. Still, Sax notes some of the luster is gone, Evva's no longer quite as clean, as polished as she was when she stood commander of a Vincere cruiser. Her scales are often scratched, her neck bears a long, puckering gash from her face to the top of her torso, something that could have been healed on a Vincere ship but has instead hardened to a scar.

"They?" Sax says.

"We call them buzzers," Evva replies, and at Sax's questioning look, she goes on. "I've not seen them used outside of Aspicis. They hunt for irregularities in the vines, in the villages, and catalog anything that stands out."

Makes sense that the Amigga would devote paranoid resources to keeping their planet as they like it.

"They can't detect your machines? The power?"

"If they have, we don't know it," Evva says, then nods over at a metal plate embedded in the ground. "Power, here, isn't drawn from a generator. We steal it, like the Amigga do, from Aspicis' core. This taps into a through-line, and we siphon off what we need."

"It doesn't look like you need much," Sax replies, then gives Evva a hard stare. There's a question he's been waiting to ask for a long time. "What did Avan tell you that changed your mind?"

Evva sniffs at the question, then sweeps her claws across the Quell members doing their work. "You understand, now, that the Amigga have no interest in keeping this alive. Us alive. As soon as we've played out our usefulness, they'll replace us with the next creation. You found them already, I believe?"

"The humans?"

"Avan told me the Sevora had sent one of their few remaining seed ships to that space just for Earth. The mind he took had notions of a species made there, one that failed, but came too close to abandon entirely," Evva says. "One meant to deliver a fatal blow to the Sevora, but also keep the Amigga from our lethal claws should we ever turn against them. I needed to see if Avan was right."

"So you sent us."

"I sent the two Oratus I thought I could trust." Evva says. "When you shared what you discovered of the species, I dug further. Found the order to eliminate the humans, and the analysis recommending a new version, with changes. The Chorus isn't going to stop, Sax, until we're all pacified or dead. The Amigga aren't interested in a shared galaxy—they want it for themselves."

One of the Quell members, the lime green Whelk who hovers around the stoves like they're its most treasured possessions, approaches with a pair of browned, thick green circles. It hands one to Sax, and Sax stares at it.

"Vine cakes," the Whelk burbles. "Get used to'em."

The creatures slithers away after Evva takes her share, and Sax takes a bite. It's crunchy, the browning adding some flavor, but otherwise bland filler. Marginally better than nutrient goop, but Sax had hoped for better. Nowhere in this galaxy actually has good food anymore.

"What happens if we win, Evva?" Sax says. "When we take apart the Chorus, destroy the Meridia?"

"First, we convince the Vincere to back us. Then, we push for representatives from every species to come together and draft bylaws, like the Vincere itself uses. Hopefully, from there, we can find some common ground to begin a new civilization."

"I've been to places governed by themselves," Sax says. "They barely survive, Evva. Their people fight for daily food, they destroy each other for the smallest gain. There's no higher cause, no grand vision to strive for."

*Scrapper Station* and its tangled webs of power, and Rathfall's delusional blend of hunting, profits, and castes of gas miners and executives stick tough in Sax's mind.

"At least, this way, we make that choice," Evva says. "It might not be better than now. It may be worse, but at least it will be ours."

A ruined city stretches before us across the horizon. Towers that rose once as sparkling diamonds or sharp spears to the sky are broken and burning as the Vincere continue their long bombardment from space. Strikes hit like lightning, breaking into buildings or immolating streets in flash-fires.

Except for one huge structure that stands above the others, a sphere whose bottom vanishes into the ground. We're speeding towards it now, past interchanges with other tubes where the platforms can twist and swerve to other corners of the city or beyond.

The whole time we're moving so fast that speech is impossible— aside from the roaring wind, the only thing I can hear are my own thoughts. Around me, the Sevora guards stand straight, the platform molding around our feet to lock us in despite the speed. Their eyes are locked ahead, their arms loose, as if the Sevora have resigned themselves to their fate.

I risk a look back to see how the prisoners are doing, and they're the opposite of the guards. They're not composed, but rather squeezing back from the edges as much as the platforms will allow. They're hugging and holding each other, like mothers and children, even across different species. I suppose the end of the world would be frightening, even if the only world you've ever known has been a horrifying one.

Up ahead we're approaching the edge of the city itself, and those flashes are getting brighter. This close, I can see that the huge sphere isn't standing because Kolas hasn't tried to bring it down, but rather because the flashes that do hit it fizzle out against what looks like an invisible bubble; a shield, like what our shuttle used, before the Sevora fighters overwhelmed it.

The thought has me look around for more of those fighters, and while there's plenty of craft blitzing through the sky, none seem to be on patrol, but rather zipping towards one destination or another. Even as I look, a pair of ships slam into each other as they try to avoid an orbital shot, their debris sprinkling down to the avenues of the city in shrapnel rain.

The platform shudders as we cross into the urban landscape, and I jerk my eyes ahead. It's a straight shot from here to the sphere, and I realize that huge building must be Nasiya's own headquarters, and what better place to keep your last escape than your home?

I'm ready for it too. Ready for the fight. My mask has two miners on it, two razor swords I'm far more comfortable with, and I have Viera's sharpshooting and a pair of very deadly Oratus ready to spill some more blood.

What I'm not ready for is a second, longer shudder. One that pushes me from side to side and makes the whole tube shake before it stabilizes. A building already damaged by blasts ahead and to our right tilts to the side and crumbles. At first, I think it must be an earthquake—something we had from time to time back home—but a shape in the corner of my eye draws a longer look.

Vimelia's moon is a large, gray blob. My first time to this planet, I noticed its circle resembled our own, but now it's a stretched thing, as if someone's pulling on its right side, causing it to warp. And it's stretching towards Vimelia, the distorted part expanding into a ghostly white slate as the moon comes closer to the planet.

Our time is running out.

A bright flash breaks the ice-fear of what a crashing moon means, and the platform's sudden jerk has me twisting forward, catching myself on the alabaster-white railing as our speed slows. The tube in front of us is ablaze, split apart by a blast from above that's rent it in two. The platform's not stopping fast enough either—we're getting closer and we're a dozen meters above the ground.

"Viera!" I shout as the roaring wind from our travel dies along with our velocity. "Get off the platform!"

"It would be a good idea if we moved too," T'Oli says, the Ooblot sealed tight to my back.

But our feet are sealed in. I try to move, try to scramble away as the platform skids along the glassy tunnel towards the jagged opening. I'm looking at my feet, trying to pick them up, when a green-scaled claw slashes down and carves me free.

"Go!" Lan hisses as she continues hacking away at the others on our platform, even the Sevora.

I press back, trying to get away, when things shift beneath my feet, when my stomach lurches as gravity takes hold of me.

I'm falling.

The platform drops away beneath me and I jump, reaching for Malo, locked to the second platform, and my warrior, my general, manages to catch my hand with his. I hang for a moment, feeling his warm fingers on mine, his eyes tired and red, mouth creased with the effort of holding me, and then we plummet.

And land in a burning, milky mess. I hit, and my back explodes into bruising pain, but I'm cushioned, as if hitting a heavy mass of water. Then I bounce off, rolling onto the hard street amid fiery ash and flickering flames, the end state of Kolas' bombardment. Malo's beside me, and I dive on him immediately, brushing away burning flakes from his skin. He doesn't have a mask, has no protection.

Only when I've cleared the warrior do I look around at the cascading clumps of people and platforms falling around us. The glance provides the reason I'm alive—the platforms, when they hit the ground after the fall, lose their form, becoming instead soft, blob-like pillows. The cushion is wide enough to keep most from landing on each other, though the clumps of prisoners aren't so lucky. Most are rolling on the ground, or lying still.

"You survived," Viera says as she limps over towards Malo and I.

"One of the few, apparently," I say, looking past the Lunare.

Both of the Oratus look fine, as if the large drop was nothing more than a normal jump for them. Which, maybe it is. The first few Sevora guards seem all right too, standing clumped to the side, though their furry faces are tight with pain.

"Guess our rescue isn't going so well," Viera joins me in the survey.

"We gave them a chance," T'Oli states. "It's better than they had."

The Ooblot's not wrong, and I'm not going to ruin what little chance the rest of us have by waiting in the avenue.

"Let's go!" I shout, getting the attention of those able to hear me. "We don't have much time!" I help Malo up from the ground, notice the warrior's breathing hard. "Come on, Malo. It's just another day for us, right?"

"Just another day," the warrior echoes, giving me a slight smile. "I missed you, Kaishi."

I toss him a scratched, exhausted smile back. "Missed you too."

The wreckage around us makes for a bad spot to share a moment, though, as aside from the soft platforms, the intersection that's become our landing spot is full of the burning casualties from Kolas' bombardment. Looming over and around us are further remnants of the transport tube and the bare lattices of buildings with the glass blown or melted out of their windows.

The sky, I notice, is getting ever more orange, and while I can't see the moon from where I stand, my guess is that our time is close to being out.

Those still alive and able form a shambling group walking beneath the tube transport and towards the great sphere. Before, on my first trip to Vimelia, most of the streets were deserted, with the crowds choosing to cluster in transport tubes or ships shuttling around the surface. Walking isn't efficient enough for the Sevora, apparently. Now, though, with all normalcy blown to shreds, panicking Sevora join our motley assortment of recovering wounded, Sevora guards, humans and Oratus. Many, with their hosts, take one glance at Lan and Gar and assume we're a raiding party and run the other way—screaming out warnings to the wind. Others hope that the Vincere won't fire on their own and trust their lives to our band, joining as stragglers behind, where Gar keeps a toothy eye on them.

"Have to say, this is like a dream coming true," T'Oli says as we walk down the devastated street. "I've wanted to see Vimelia burn for a long time."

"With you still on it?"

"Can't let perfect get in the way of good, Kaishi."

"The Ooblot's losing it," Viera says behind me. "Surprised a living puddle kept it together this long, really."

"I'm far saner than any human," T'Oli replies.

"You're both crazy as far as I'm concerned," I say, ducking beneath a broad metal beam that's fallen, crossing the entire street from one side to the next.

I want to move faster, but forcing the Sevora into a run would mean abandoning the prisoners, and someone would have to carry Malo. Glances at the moon when ruins allow seem to show our doom progressing slowly, but then, I've never seen a planetary annihilation before.

"Malo, what'd they do to you?" Viera asks our rescued warrior friend.

"Everything, and nothing," Malo replies. "Little food, a lot of questions. Attempts to infect me."

"Did it work?"

Malo does some combination of a laugh and a cough. "I'm here, but every time they failed, they tried again. Until the Vincere came."

I clench my hands. I remember that—when the familiars on the space station *Cobalt* sucked the Sevora out of my head, then let it back in after I'd taken a good long look. To say that experience was unpleasant would be underselling it. To say I'd had more nightmares than I can count . . .

"We're here," one of the Sevora guards announces, and I look up enough to realize that yes, we're nearly at the foot of the sphere.

This close, it's larger than I thought, and appears to be covered in row after row of dark slats that shimmer in the daylight. At the ground level, the circle curve melds into the landscape like a mountain, a smooth transition to a patchwork stone pattern beneath. Poles adorned with banners showing Nasiya and its Oratus host stand in the courtyard, though most are at some degree of bent and burned by this point, even if the sphere itself looks untouched.

As we watch, another bolt from above strikes the sphere and sparks the shield, the slight blue wave cascading around the structure and fizzling away to nothing.

"Does the front door work?" Viera asks, gesturing with her miner towards a line of ground-level slats angled vertical instead of to the side.

Each one of these has a peppered line of green lights around the outside. It seems friendly enough, but when none of the Sevora guards respond to Viera's question, I repeat it.

"We don't know," the one that's been talking, with its red and brown Flaum fur singed from the crash, responds. "Nasiya and its faction have never been our friends, we've never been here."

"You're invited now," Viera says. "Get to it."

I nod, seconding the command. The guards glance at each other, hesitating, until Viera raises up her miners at all of them. Lan seconds the threat with a hiss.

If Nasiya's base has some sort of defense, better to have the Sevora trigger it than one of us.

But there's no explosion, no scattering of Sevora and Flaum parts as the quintet approach the slats. Rather, when they get close, those green lights flash and all of the slats slide to the side, open and free.

"Well, that's disappointing," Viera says next to me.

"We still might need them," I reply.

"They said they've never been inside," T'Oli interjects. "Their usefulness to the mission is likely minimal at this point. It would be safer to eliminate them."

All five of the guards have their backs turned towards us, at least until their lead looks around to see if we're coming. I'm standing with Viera and Malo to my left, Lan to my right, a couple dozen random prisoners, Gar and his trail of Sevora hangers-on. Viera could burn down all five guards, I have no doubt.

"Not yet," I say. "We can still use them as bait."

Why am I keeping the Sevora alive? Maybe it's because we're surrounded by so much death that I can't bring myself to order more right now. Maybe it's because these five are probably going to die later, anyway, by Lan's claws.

And if I wait until then, I won't be responsible.

"Whatever you say, Empress." Viera lowers her miners. "Guess that means we're going in?"

"Yes," I reply. "Weapons ready. We have no idea what's going on inside."

When we go through the slats, though, it's clear that we've missed the main event. Nasiya's headquarters opens with a monstrous lobby that rises taller than our Tiers at home, higher than the tube transport. It's full of color too—though these murals don't shift and are, rather than scattered paints, picture-perfect images of various planets. The lobby itself arranges like a miniature version of the building its inside of—curved walls conclude in an arched ceiling, from which those images hang like banners.

Along the walls, too, flow glass-sealed rivers of the ink-purple liquid I remember well from the very first night I found the Sevora crashed into my jungle home. The rivers are spaced and come together into pools on either side of the silver center, a space that might be beautiful if not for all the bodies.

Every species I can name is represented among the casualties, from the charred, colored sludge of Whelks to the broken carapaces of Teven. Flaum fur is plentiful, and some bits of the stuff still burn.

"This was a big fight," T'Oli says.

I wait for Viera's cutting remark, but for once she doesn't say anything as we walk through the graveyard. Even the Lunare is silenced by the sight.

"One I'm glad we missed," I say finally, then turn to Lan. "Where do you think Nasiya's keeping its ship?"

"At the very top," Lan hisses. "Where Nasiya itself spends the most time."

The idea makes sense—keep the escape where you're going to be.

"There's a lift back here," says Viera, who's kept walking as I talk to the Oratus. "Going to be a tight fit for everyone though."

"Then we send the most important first," Lan says to me, and I know what she's suggesting.

This is the point we ditch away the riders, the leeches and the Sevora. I look over at the prisoners. The ones that've made it this far seem to only have eyes for the corpses, and I'm sure they're imagining themselves in that role.

"Then we send the lift back down," I say. "For the rest of them."

Lan nods, and in another few seconds we've assembled the star strike team; Malo, Viera, myself and T'Oli, and the two Oratus. Nobody questions the arrangement, because we're the only ones with weapons.

Viera's right; the lift isn't meant for a bunch of Oratus, but we solve the puzzle and manage to squeeze everyone onto the white platform. As we're getting in, another quake rattles the ground, this one longer and deeper than the others, prompting a few sharp squeals from the huddled prisoners in the lobby.

"Better hope they built this place well," Viera says.

"It's the strongest building on the planet," T'Oli replies. "Clarity's Dawn tried to crack it many times, even tried using explosives around the base. Nothing, and we lost some good souls on that one."

We might lose some good souls on this one too, but the platform isn't going to be where that happens. After we're all on—Malo adopts a truly weary pose, crumpling down onto the platform's floor—T'Oli and I set the destination on the lift's panel. All the way to the top.

"What do you think those guards will do now that we're gone?" Viera asks as the lift starts its ascent. "Take those species prisoner again?"

"They don't have weapons," I reply. "What does it matter? Nothing here is going to last long anyway."

"I hope they fight each other," Gar hisses. "That would be a better way to die than by moonfall."

"Moonfall?" I catch the word. "You have a term for this?"

"While this technology is new," Lan hisses. "More gradual planetary destruction has been attempted. Conducting a moonfall can help break apart an icy world, add land to a smaller planet, or grant access to difficult minerals."

I shake my head. Again, this galaxy is proving itself a place far beyond what I thought possible.

For now, though, the lift's slowing and the panel's beeping that we're about to reach our destination, which means it's time to see if this fight's still happening, or if Nasiya's already gone.

Which means we're dead.

The true surprise comes later, after Sax and Bas have had their meals and accustomed themselves to Quell and how it works. There's not a lot to the base, though Nobaa and Engee immediately find themselves fascinated with the terminals and the core lines that Quell has managed to tap into.

"So we have access to their logistics data?" Sax hears Nobaa exclaim at one point.

Sax isn't so dour as to believe that such knowledge isn't useful, but Evva's Quell isn't built to last through a long war of attrition. There's not enough fighters here, for one, and, according to Evva, they only have a few other safe houses. Meaning, if the Chorus finds this base, the whole initiative is doomed before it ever really starts.

So when another skiff lowers its way into the base with a familiar Flaum piloting it, Sax feels the first real tug of hope he's had since arriving on Aspicis.

Coorvin, with his ash-black fur looking better than Sax has ever seen it, gets off the skiff and is mobbed by a bevy of Quell members asking for information on this and that. Sax, though, turns to Plake with a different question.

"How'd you get him here?" Sax assumes the Vyphen's responsible for it somehow, and Plake's shrug confirms he's not wrong.

"Wasn't hard," Plake says. "Coorvin has a reason to be here—he was on *Cobalt* when it blew up, and the Chorus wanted to talk to him about it. He's also Flaum, which, if you haven't noticed, is kind of a requirement to get onto this planet. So he reached out to the Vincere on Rathfall, said he'd been kidnapped and needed an extraction. They came and got him, brought him here."

"And he escaped?"

"If they even tried to hold him," Plake gives Sax a skeptical look. "You think *you'd* devote a lot of effort to keeping a Flaum jailed if there's no evidence against him?"

Sax thinks he'd probably eviscerate the creature if there's a chance it could do him harm, but that's probably not appropriate to say, so he agrees with Plake.

Coorvin, though, makes the Chorus pay for their ignorance; while in the Meridia, the vast construct rising from the surface of Aspicis up into near-space above, the Flaum took careful notes of just how the Chorus keep their security running. It's a spicy setup: plenty of guards, passcodes and timed accesses, more the higher you go. To even get in the front entrance, they would have to get past an Amigga-only bio scanner.

With every observation of the Meridia's impenetrable security, Sax sees the morale deflate among the people present. It's one thing to believe in a cause when there's a chance, a whole other thing to keep believing when failure's a certainty.

Coorvin, though, keeps them hanging till the end, where he gives them a bit of hope: even though the lifts are staggered, so no one can shuttle all the way to the top, even though the security measures are vast, once inside the Meridia an insurgent force would be hard to take down. The key is getting into the tower's base.

"The levels themselves are crowded, with easy points to defend," Coorvin concludes. "You'll have to find ways to work the lifts, but once you're inside, you should be able to get up to higher levels. The hardest point is the entrance. You have to be an Amigga to get in, or with one. And unless something's changed, we don't have an Amigga on our side."

"We don't need one," Engee pops in here. "Bio-scans can be defeated. If we can get access to the scanner, or to the control . . ."

Coorvin nods. "Thought of that too, but I couldn't start asking questions about that without looking suspicious."

"I can take a guess," Evva says, her eyes ordering the rest of the Quell forces back to their work. "The Vincere has a protocol for sensitive securities, one I would guess the Chorus follows: never keep the control next to its target."

Yes. Sax knows this one—it's why every Vincere ship has its bridge as far away from its most vulnerable parts, the engines. It's why the power source governing those same engines is housed in a different part of the ship, meant to force a strike team to traverse all across a cruiser before it can get full access to its systems.

"You think the control for the Meridia's security lives outside of the Meridia itself?" Coorvin says.

"The Meridia is a giant target for anyone looking to attack Aspicis." Evva says. "The Chorus has the Vincere, the strongest military force in the galaxy on their side, which means any attack would have a short time to succeed. Would you take a chance that a single, focused raid could break your system and get to the top, just because you housed your own keys in the same place?"

"If the controls for the bio-scan are somewhere else," Bas says. "Then where?"

"The place least likely to break!" Nobaa says. "Your vital systems ought to be where there's the least chance they'll get interrupted, and that means power."

All eyes turn to the metal slat. Energy from the planet's core: unceasing and un-interruptible.

The plan flows quickly from there; Nobaa and Engee take charge of designing a defeat program, one that should swap the bio-scan to see any species as the right one, not just Amigga. Sax and the others use Quell's terminals to get a good idea of the target.

Cavignum: Aspicis' largest power plant, the one closest to the Meridia. A massive thing that is, essentially, built around a giant hole bored deep into the planet. The construct saps the heat pouring out of Aspicis' core and uses it to generate the energy that powers the Meridia, that charges up a quarter of the entire world.

For that reason, Cavignum is plenty well defended. The few images they can pull up make it clear there's surface and air turrets, plenty of guards, and all the usual security measures like locked doors, sections that can be sealed off, and more. All of that gets coupled with the fact that moments after an attack starts, an endless stream of deadly reinforcements are only moments away.

Short of an orbital bomb, Sax isn't sure how they're going to get in. Especially when Nobaa and Engee say that they'll need to get to the right terminal in the power station itself.

"It's not as simple as just running the program," Nobaa says. "We need to get access to the bio-scanning system. Literally get into how it operates and change what it does. That can't be done remotely, not that we can see."

"So we have to get the two of you into the power station," Evva says. "And leave you there long enough to run your program, then get you out?"

"That would do it. Of course, there's no sure telling how long this might take. The system might be easy to crack, and we'll be ready to go in a few minutes. Or, it might be a day."

"That's not going to work."

The discussion ebbs and flows from there, eventually driving Sax close to insanity. There's too many variables on hand, too many unknowns to make a plan capable of success. What they need, really, is more information. What they don't have is time to gather it.

That desperation forces a compromise: Nobaa and Engee, along with their program, will try to get as close to Cavignum as possible so that when Sax, Bas, Plake and Agra-Red figure out a way to crack it open, the two Teven can take advantage. Evva, Avan and the rest of Quell will work on creating diversions and, if possible, get ready to hit the Meridia once the two Teven open up the front door.

It's a loose, fractured plan with plenty of holes. It's also the only plan they've got.

So Sax, Bas, and Plake board the skiffs not long after. Coorvin has a contact for them, someone who should be able to get them close to, if not inside, the power station. The problem, as Coorvin states, is that this contact operates on greed and greed alone.

They'll have to convince it that bringing down the Chorus is going to bring up its profits.

Coorvin delivers the coordinates and Sax, Bas, Plake and Agra-Red drop the numbers into their skiffs. Their miners have been charging all night, they're stocked with arms and provisions, and both Sax and Bas have their masks on and ready to go.

It's as prepared as Sax has been in a long time and his claws are itching to take advantage.

Plake offers to take the lead, and they link their skiff to the Vyphen's so that when she starts her ascent, Sax's ride lifts up with hers. He sneaks a glance back down to the Quell base and notices not a single soul is busy watching them—they're all getting geared up for their own assignments.

As it should be.

Their target is a city, one of the few on the planet not directly linked to the Meridia. Called Terrodyne, it's the planet's manufacturing center. Powering all of those factories is Cavignum, built around a hole burrowed into the planet's core. Set far north of their current location, it's going to be a long ride.

As the skiffs accelerate, Sax gets his head beneath the windshield, where the noise of rushing air dies down and it's possible—barely—to speak. Plake's out in front as they blitz across the vines, leading a diamond formation with Agra-Red as the rear point. Across from Sax, he can see Bas, hunkered down like him, looking beautifully pink in the bright light.

It's a peaceful ride. There's no sign of storms, and the endless vines beneath them break up occasionally to show mag-lev train tracks or signs of small habitations. Sax would almost call it pleasant, except that it grows boring. There's nothing to do except sit and take in the same view as the minutes pass.

"Eyes up," Plake's voice warbles through the skiff's small intercom. "We've got skiffs coming in from the left, and it looks like they're on an intercept."

Sax tries to look that way, but Bas cuts between him and the view. Raising his head up high might blow Sax off the craft, so he has to trust what the Vyphen can see.

"They're armed," Bas hisses. "Do we have any weapons on these things?"

"Not seeing any," Agra-Red says, and Sax hisses in agreement.

There's nothing on his skiff except the pair of levers to control the craft's pitch, the right one with a trigger for acceleration and the left for braking. A small display on the windshield gives coordinates against a geographic map of the world, highlighting the path to their destination. No sign of a weapons system, of shields, or anything of combat relevance.

"We'll have to out-fly them, then," Plake says. "I'm unlinking us. If something goes wrong, meet up at the target however you're able to."

"Don't lead the enemy there," Sax says. "The mission above yourself."

He wouldn't have said the words if only he and Bas were here, but Plake and Agra-Red are mercenaries. They can't be trusted to make the sacrifice.

"Unlinked!" Plake says and Sax immediately feels loose in the skiff.

He's fading to the right, because Sax is leaning that way. The Oratus stabilizes himself, the skiff helping ever-so-slightly to keep Sax level. He nudges himself left, then back right again, getting a feel for how much he has to move to get the skiff turning. Then he pulls back on the levers, sending the skiff angling up, above the other three.

Now Sax gets a clear view of the pursuit—a half dozen skiffs coming closer by the second. They're in two uneven lines, a W spread, and they're homing in on Plake's lead. Sax's ascent puts him behind his own party, which gives the Oratus a chance to take the initiative.

Sax leans left and pushes the levers down, turning the skiff into a dive towards the approaching group.

"What're you doing, Sax?" Agra-Red asks. "Getting yourself killed?"

"Maybe," is all Sax bothers to reply.

He plunges towards the oncoming skiffs, and Sax sees they're all piloted by Flaum wearing the same deep blue Chorus uniforms, including thick, visored helmets. Not elite, then. Not expecting resistance like this. Each skiff, though, looks like it has a pair of assault miners strapped to the front of it, sticking out like needles.

They're not caught off-guard, though. As Sax gets close, the Chorus skiffs scatter, some heading up, others right to dash beneath Sax, and the last pair cut their acceleration hard to try and keep Sax from hitting them.

A tactic that would work, if not for Sax's tail. The Oratus boosts his speed to the maximum, leans hard left, pulls back on the levers to sweep his skiff over the two braking hard. The Flaum glance up at Sax, just in time to see the Oratus, his skiff flipped on its left side, slap down with his tail and nail the first Flaum across the face.

The impact ripples pain along Sax's body and throws the skiff into a wobble that has Sax spinning over his second target. Apparently going that fast and striking another object isn't what Oratus tails are made for. Sax, though, manages to pull left again and swing around in time to see the results of his strike blooming into an orange fireball below.

"Juke right!" Plake cries through the intercom and Sax flips his weight as blue-white fire streams where he would've been.

There's two options here—Sax can either focus on evading the pursuit, or finding a target and, in attacking it, hope he loses that pursuit. Sax, of course, takes the second one.

As he's already juking right, Sax leans into the turn, wrapping himself around and coming into a collision course with the second skiff he missed during his first tail-whipping assault. That skiff is just accelerating, and the Flaum has no time to react as Sax's skiff shoots towards it. Sax himself only manages to jerk the levers back on his ride, slanting up the nose just as it strikes the Chorus skiff.

Sax's harder hull crashes through the windshield of the other skiff, including the Flaum behind it. The impact makes an expected end of Sax's enemy, but a pair of bleeping red lights and a constant shower of sparks from the front of Sax's skiff indicate he didn't exactly make it out unscathed. In fact, his skiff seems to be in a constant, gradual decline, and those vines aren't too far away.

"Going to need a new lift," Sax hisses, though at least the enemy fire is gone.

Apparently everyone can see Sax isn't a threat; the Oratus sends his skiff left, corkscrewing his decline, and catches a swirling mess of a fight; Agra-Red dives and twists frantically as a pair of skiffs cling to its tail, filling the air with lasers. Bas seems to have a momentary advantage on her opponent, beating the Flaum through a tight loop and getting behind it, though Sax isn't sure what she'll do, seeing as their skiffs don't have weapons.

Plake, though, has her target in her sights, and has a miner held tight in her right hand. She's taking pot shots over her windshield, though every time she raises the weapon, the wind seems to knock her aim off course.

All told, Sax's two-for-one victory is the best the group has going for them right now. It's also bought Sax some isolation, so he uses it. Rather than keep the forward thrust, which forces the skiff into a dive, Sax pulls the air-brakes and locks the levers into their hovering position. The skiff isn't perfect here—those dead front jets mean Sax is still sinking at an angle—but now he's stable enough to pull out his miners.

"Line'em up for me!" Sax calls through the comm.

Agra-Red takes first advantage, swinging its now-smoking and sparking skiff into a line above Sax's firing angle. Because Sax is low, the Chorus Flaum don't see him, continuing their straight pursuit after the Whelk. Sax holds down his triggers, lets the miner's energy fly free, and delivers a staccato set of shots to the closest skiff, skittering the bolts into the underside of the craft.

The shots melt away the microjets, leaving the Flaum in a skiff that has no upward thrust. The creature's smart enough to realize it's not surviving here and takes a hard tack out of the fight, leaving Sax to aim for the second one.

Only this Flaum isn't oblivious to what's happened to its friend, and it's looping up and over, turning down into a dive at Sax. The Oratus raises his miners to greet the descending skiff and its two heavy cannons. There's not a hope of winning this firefight, but Sax pulls the triggers anyway.

The Flaum's bolks spray around Sax, belting into the skiff. Sax's own shots burrow into the front of his target, and then Sax leaps, because to stay would mean death. As Sax flies, he twists, keeps his miners focuses, and pours laser into the descending enemy. His own skiff explodes, superheated into a mini-nova, followed moments later by a smoking, burning second skiff as Sax melts his target past the point of control.

The Oratus, though, is now in free fall, plummeting the rest of the distance into the vines. Sax has long enough to take a breath, to speak one name.

There's a bite of pain, then, and the world goes dark.

The lift opens into a top level entryway that may have been beautiful at some point, but that is now a wreck of shredded furniture, with a great, broken hole where I think a door once stood. The colored walls—bright blues and yellows—of the rounded atrium are pocked with scorch marks, and the light above, a bronzed flavor coming from a full, somehow whole sphere dangling from the ceiling, washes the scene in a hazy cast, as though we're stepping into a memory and not the full, deadly now.

"Looks like we're a little late to this party," Viera says as we leave the lift.

"Unfortunately," Gar adds.

"I prefer not getting shot," I say. As soon as we're all out of the lift, its doors shut behind us and the thing starts its descent. Soon we'll have prisoners and more Sevora arriving up here. "Let's keep moving, before this gets complicated. Viera, Gar, you two take point."

Which leaves me with Malo, and Lan bringing up the rear guard. I figure an Oratus on either side is going to keep us safest, especially as we move on from the atrium into a wide hallway—big enough for the four-clawed lizards—with plenty of side rooms. There's more evidence here of a crawling battle, with miner burns etching staccato patterns into the sides, floor, and ceiling around us.

Something larger detonated not far ahead either; its orange plasma burns marking a halo around our path and leaving a once-molten groove across the ground.

"Jel's forces came with firepower," Lan hisses as we go, slowly. "Be cautious. One explosive thrown back our way could kill us all."

"They're fighting for their lives," I reply. "They'll use everything they have."

I know I would. I know, if I was fighting for the last bit of human-ity, I would throw every weapon, every soul I had into the battle even if there was no hope of winning.

The hallway ends in a full-width door, one that's also been forced open. Apparently Nasiya's forces weren't able to use the tight quar-ters to finish the fight. We stalk up close, bunch up and look through into the vast space on the other side.

Big enough to be the other half of the sphere, with the neat translucent wall effect going on through the entire ceiling and along the downward sloping side away from us, Nasiya's private docking bay has plenty of size. And plenty of bodies.

We're too late to see most of the action; like the lobby, smoking corpses litter the ground both directly in front of our doorway and at the boarding ramp of the ship, a great diamond of a thing with a hull that shifts colors even as we stare at it. At first I think the changing is random, but then I realize that it's playing to the surroundings, and the yellow-orange streaks appearing are the result of the ship catching the flashes of the Vincere bombardment outside.

"Beautiful," Malo says softly.

"Sure," Viera replies. "If you want to call it that. What I'm worried about, though, is that there's nothing left alive in here."

She's right. There's racks of batteries and canisters of things I don't know littered around the docking bay, along with crates of what must be emergency supplies, but nothing's moving, and there's no sound. At least not out here.

The ship's boarding ramp, though, is down. It, too, is wide enough for an Oratus. Apparently Nasiya's had its host for a long enough time to have this built with its size in mind.

"If the fight is over, then whomever won will try to leave," Lan says. "We have to hurry."

Obeying her own command, Gar and Lan break into a clacking run across the docking bay towards the ship. I pull Malo with me, while Viera shrugs her way into a rear guard, watching the bodies with her miners drawn.

"Don't get too far ahead!" I try to say to the Oratus, but they ignore me, hitting the ramp at a run and vanishing up.

"They were never really yours to command," Malo says.

"Oratus only belong to the Chorus," T'Oli states from my shoulders. "Anyone else is an ally of convenience."

"Then let's make sure we keep it that way," I say and pick up the pace.

The ramp is a silver, slotted thing, the gaps providing grip for talons like those I don't have. When we get to the base, I let Viera take the lead, as now there's plenty of noise coming from inside the ship; hisses, bangs and snarls. Something's alive in there.

"Can you stand on your own?" I ask Malo, and the warrior nods. "Then cover us."

I hand the warrior one of my miners and take up the other—I might not be accurate, but in the close confines of the ship, I bet I can hit something. Besides, with T'Oli sliming down to my left hand and sharpening itself into a needle-sword, I think I'm well-covered.

Even so, Viera takes point, and together we clomp up the ramp. Nasiya's ship is several times the size of the shuttle, and so when we get to the top, we walk into a large space, the fat end of the teardrop ship's shape. Here, at least, Nasiya's concessions to luxury are still apparent; those color-shifting paintings are everywhere, and jewels line them, providing glinting divides between the changing scenes.

Rather than netting, the floor of the ship is the same alabaster as the tube's platforms, and it changes at our touch, firming up to catch our feet and, I'm sure, ready to mold over and keep us stable should the ship decide to launch. Light doesn't seem to come from anywhere, but rather a soft illumination reflects off of everything, as though we're walking into a morning glade.

The noises come from our right, so Viera takes a turn that way, tossing her eyes at me for quick confirmation. There's a shut circular door to the left, across the alabaster room and towards what I assume is the rear of the ship, where, by now, I've learned the engines are likely to be. There's no sounds from there, though, and no signs of struggle, so I let Viera lead and keep my miner ready as we head towards the bridge.

Nasiya's craft splits itself in the same way as the underground crop granary—big dividing walls split the main room off from the next section of the ship, with domed doors serving as the ways between. The one closest to us, leading towards the front, is open, and as we near, words begin to pour out.

"No Sevora can match an Oratus," Gar's hissing voice says. "No matter how long you've been in there, you're nothing."

There's a rasping laugh at that. "Nothing? I defeated an entire army. Me! Almost alone!"

"And you're still nothing, and now you *are* alone," Lan replies.

I nod at Viera, and we both pass through the door, into the second, and final, chamber of Nasiya's ship.

Nasiya's bridge isn't designed for a full crew—towards the front of the ship, everything inside the space narrows down to a single point; a swath of netting towards the very end, with two long screens sliding across the crystal-blue windshield on either side. The very apex, where I can just see around Nasiya's huge body as it leans to the side, houses the flight stick.

Lan and Gar have Nasiya cornered, though on first glance it looks like the Sevora isn't putting up any fight. Nasiya bears more burns than I've ever seen on a single body, so that its yellow-gold scales are more a mash-up of ash-black and bubbling pink blisters. Its left foreclaw is simply gone, and Nasiya's tail lies limp on the floor, with some deep cuts around where it joins to Nasiya's body.

None of the damage has stopped Gar from putting his right foreclaw up to Nasiya's throat, and his midclaws into a lethal pressure position around Nasiya's abdomen. If the Sevora tries anything more than a twitch, I have no doubt Gar would destroy the Sevora leader, and that Gar would love every moment of it.

"You're alone?" is the first thing I say. I'd been expecting some sort of shootout, a ragged struggle against Nasiya's most battle-hardened troops, but apart from the bodies outside the ship, there's nobody here. "Lan, Gar, you didn't find anyone else?"

"Who would still be here?" Nasiya hisses in reply, and plenty of wet flows up with the words. "Every Sevora that can fight is already dead, or is flying what few fighters we have left. If my species is dying, what's the value in protecting me?"

I can concede that point.

"So you were going to fly out of here alone?" I reply. "Leave the rest of your species to die?"

"I was waiting," Nasiya says. "Some of us know about my ship, I thought they would come. As you can see, they did not make it."

Lan glances at me. "Human, we need to go."

I want to ask Nasiya more questions. I want to understand how the Sevora leader came to this, and who did such damage to its host body. But I also want to avoid a moon slamming into me.

"Fine." I nod at Gar. "Get rid of it. Outside."

Gar might slaughter Nasiya right here if I don't specify, and the last thing I want in our small bridge is the remnants of Gar's favorite pastime. Nasiya, for its part, doesn't struggle as Gar drags the Sevora out, doesn't say anything beyond its low hisses. I hear the weight of the bodies on the entrance ramp as Lan goes forward to take the ship's controls.

"Can I take off?" Lan asks me.

Malo and Viera are in the shuttle. Gar's going to be coming back soon. Lan could leave now, and we'd ditch all the prisoners and the Sevora guards behind. We would be safe.

Outside the windshield, as if hearing my thoughts, the first set of prisoners bursts into the docking bay, running towards the ship. There's another rattling shake, harder and longer than any of the others, and I'm forced to catch myself on the side of the bridge's back wall as my knees buckle. T'Oli catches the struggle, slides down and forms itself around my feet, keeping me in place. Viera, with no such luck, holsters her miners and braces herself against the wall.

"Can we scan them?" I ask Lan. "To see if any are infected?"

Lan blinks at me. "Not here. On one of the cruisers, yes. But going that far is a risk, human. One Kolas would not have us take."

"Kolas isn't here."

There's a roar from the boarding ramp, and Lan taps at the left monitor, and it shifts from its clear view of the docking bay to a feed of the ramp's base. Gar's standing there, his claws wide. I don't see Nasiya, but the prisoners and Sevora guards are surrounding the Oratus, chittering and yelling for a spot on Nasiya's ship.

"You must think of the galaxy, human," Lan replies. "These few dozen are not worth risking everything."

I look down at T'Oli, but the Ooblot only blinks its eyes at me. Malo's back in the passenger section of the ship, so I look to Viera.

"Make the call, Empress," Viera says to me. "But do it fast."

Do I accept the cost of innocent lives as necessary, or do I fight for every single one? Before, back in the intersection, I'd made the call to leave behind the wounded, those who couldn't keep up. In the moment, I felt we didn't have a choice. If we hadn't made it here, all of us would have died.

Now we do.

"We're taking them," I say.

Lan shakes her head, hisses low, then begins to tap away on the two screens. A gentle whine fills the craft, and, in the feed, the ramp beneath Gar begins to recede back into the ship.

"Apologies, Human. I cannot allow that." Lan says.

I raise my miner, point it at the back of Lan's sizeable head. "Lower the ramp, Lan."

Threatening an Oratus. I might be making the worst, and last choice of my life. Yet as I hold the miner steady, aimed directly at Lan, I don't regret it. I don't question it.

Father let Malo and his Charre warriors take me away from my tribe in order to save it from what might have been a bloody extinction. He took the easier way, let me go rather than risk a greater loss.

I am not my father. I will not make his mistake.

"Don't make me say it again, Lan."

The Oratus makes no move to tap the terminal and stop the ramp. "Human, these are the creatures that tried to destroy your entire race. You wish to save them?"

"They're not all Sevora." I flick my eyes to T'Oli, who's got its eyestalks split between Lan and I. "T'Oli, stop the ramp."

"Think she might eat me if I try," T'Oli replies.

"I'll shoot her if she does."

The Oratus stands up from the net, though she has to bend her green neck to keep her head beneath the ship's low sloping ceiling. As she rises, Lan's left midclaw taps at the monitor and the ramp pauses, leaving Gar standing just above the shouting crowd. Lan turns all the way towards me, takes a single step my way. T'Oli's binding keeps me from retreating, but Viera, with her right hand still keeping her stable, aims a miner with her left, backing up my threat with her sharpshooting.

"One more step, Lan," I say, and I'm impressed at my own voice for being this steady.

"Trillions," Lan hisses. "Trillions have died due to their efforts. They devour species, they steal freedom. You're willing to risk their return for a paltry few?"

"I am."

Lan opens her mouth slightly, the sharp teeth glinting. I know that if she decides I'm not worth keeping alive, I'll never get more than a shot off. Viera's probably wouldn't kill the Oratus either.

"We head straight for the *Nunilite*, for Kolas," Lan says finally. "Nobody leaves the ship without a scan. Any with a Sevora inside die. You must tell them. They must agree. Then we must leave."

I can tell that's as far as I'm going to get with the Oratus. Lan's already staring—and breathing—pure disgust at me, so I nudge around her and, with T'Oli guiding me, activate the ship's external speaker.

"Prisoners and Sevora," I begin. I've never made a speech asking a group to decide which of them ought to live and die, but I don't have a choice, so I plunge ahead. "We cannot allow any Sevora-hosted species to leave on our craft. If you are free of infection, board. If you are a Sevora, you will be found out and eliminated, so I advise you to seek your survival elsewhere."

As I say the words, Lan lowers the boarding ramp, so that by the time I finish, Gar's back on the ground dealing with a flood of bodies. The Oratus steps aside at the push and lets the crowd up the ramp. The tired prisoners manage to move fast, and help those couple that fall making their way up. The only ones that don't try to board, the ones that turn and run back towards the lift, are the five Sevora guards that came with us all the way from the compound.

"They're not even trying," I say as I watch them run on the monitor.

"A sure death at Gar's claws is more frightening than an unknown chance at life," Lan says. "They may not yet understand their moon is crashing down on them."

Once the crush of prisoners finds their way inside, Lan retracts the ramp for a final time, with Gar taking up supervising duty with Viera over the cluster of prisoners clogging up the ship's main bay.

With the engines primed, her claws on the flight stick, Lan lifts the ship up from the ground. T'Oli locks me into place by the back wall, where I brace myself as we start to move.

"Thanks," I tell the hard, ceramic-looking mass beneath me.

T'Oli blinks its eyes my way. "Brave thing you did. They'll thank you. Clarity's Dawn would be proud."

"Even Sapphrite?"

The Amigga had lead the rogue faction of un-hosted species beneath Vimelia's surface. Neither T'Oli nor I have heard anything about their survival after our escape from the planet the first time, which I take to mean Clarity's Dawn died in doing their final mission.

"Sapphrite would have said it wanted revenge above all else," T'Oli replies. "But it did all it could to nurture our band, and give us a mission. I think it would be proud of you."

T'Oli's words, delivered through the strange slapping of smooth skin against itself, and with all the emotional feeling of a clacking branch, don't puff me up with happiness, but they do calm the buzz of nauseating fear that I've made a terrible mistake.

Lan taps away at the monitors at her sides and, ahead of us, a gap slides open in the sphere building's wall, showing a different world from the one we were in moments before. Where a vast city once stood, smoking ruins now exist. As we leave the cover of the docking bay, I see that the fires are only partially caused by Kolas' bombardment; the now-constant quakes from the moon's approach makes the ground beneath us appear to ripple. Cracks split open the streets, and break apart batteries, pipes, and whole buildings burst into flame, explode or just collapse into great ash clouds.

Up above, what had been a great white streak of stretched moon has expanded to fill most of the sky. The moon's shape is still distorted, and plenty of fissures line its surface too, breaking the big ball into different fragments, which drift apart from one another slowly, but nevertheless in motion as I watch. The first, a pointed crescent, begins to make initial contact with Vimelia's upper atmosphere, igniting in a blue-orange flame across the entirety of its shape.

"Hold on," Lan says, and I hear the Oratus' voice echo from behind us as the order gets relayed to our passengers.

The ship bursts forward and up. The acceleration is so hard, so sudden that the air leaves my lungs as my body presses back into the dividing wall behind me. Even though there's no wind in the ship, my eyes start to water as the force compresses my head.

Beneath us, the city ruins dwindle. I realize we're not making any evasive maneuvers around Kolas' big lasers and manage, once I get a breath, to pose the question to Lan.

"They needed to get out of the way," Lan says. "The moon could damage the fleet as well as the planet. Now they're watching for anyone trying to escape."

"Like us?"

"I hope so." Lan's voice sounds tight, so I stop my questions and let the Oratus concentrate.

Above us, the cracking moon fragments even further as the fire burns its way through the gray-white surface. Bits and pieces scatter off and begin to tumble towards us as we climb to meet them. Flames burn around the meteors, and smoke trails mark their scars as they slice Vimelia's dying sky.

"Now we see if the Oratus can really fly," T'Oli says to me.

I only nod—any words might distract Lan.

The Oratus, though, looks to be in total concentration. She sends Nasiya's ship to the left around the first fragment, a tower-sized block of rock breaking up into smaller chunks as it slides by. Then Lan swoops the ship up and around, tracing the outline of a larger piece, using the big rock to block faster, smaller boulders blasting through around us. With a quick right cut, Lan pushes us around the outside of the big one, leaving us in the path of a hill-sized ball careening our way.

I can't help it—I shout. It doesn't help, but it's all I can do.

A bright red stream fires out from the point of our ship, striking the ball with pure energy and super-heating it. Coupled with the burn from the atmosphere, the rock melts and bursts, and instead of flying through solid matter, the outside of the ship crackles as thousands of pieces fry in its shield.

"A point for me!" Gar's hissing laugh comes over the intercom.

On the other side of the debris field—as I gasp for breath—there's another series of boulders that, thankfully, keep themselves well-spaced enough for Lan to loop her way around. Then we're in the upper atmosphere, its fires licking at the sides of the ship. Around us, instead of the blue-black of space touching the sky, floats an endless descending minefield of moon rock. Like fruit from a tree, the moon's fragments take turns succumbing to Vimelia's pull, dipping out of their gradual decline into sudden bombing.

"We're going to make it," Lan says, and the Oratus' words are the first clue I've had that she didn't think success was assured.

"Thanks to you," I say.

"This is a good ship," Lan replies. "The shuttle we flew down here would not have survived that ascent."

We coast our way through the rest of the moon, until at last we break to the other side. The Vincere fleet, even larger than when we left it, shows itself through the occasional blast and explosion of a Sevora ship attempting a futile, last ditch attempt to get away.

"They have to get far enough away to leap," T'Oli says as we watch a species go extinct in little pops before our eyes. "Or else, when they try, they could fold part of the planet, or the moon, into their leaping space with them. A very fatal mistake."

T'Oli explains this matter-of-fact, and I take it in, but what I'm thinking, really, is that we survived. We did it. We made it down to Vimelia's surface, found Malo, and got off alive.

Flashes; blinks and moments come and go. Sax gets the impression he's lying on the ground, the light above carved apart by thick black lines. He breathes, but the rest of him lies at a distance, untouchable, apart, so Sax sleeps.

Oratus dreams are like any other species—fragments of life and wishes spun into visions of futures past. There are endless hours spent with Bas in frenetic missions against Sevora scum, odysseys through jungles of Sax's distant memory, the neon-lit caves of Earth where the humans lead him to the den of an angry horde of Fassoth.

When the last one fades, Sax opens his eyes again to see a familiar face staring at him, rose-gold and wonderful.

"Found you," Bas hisses lightly.

"You did," Sax manages to say. His throat is dry from too little water, his head throbs—no, his entire body aches. "How long?"

"It's still light, if that helps," Bas says. "It's been over thirty hours."

The announcement prompts a dire laugh from Sax. "Thirty hours? It took you that long to shake the skiffs?"

Bas sighs. "I was overruled."

Sax, though, is finding his connections to his muscles are still intact. It's a slow process, standing, but with time and effort Sax gets there. Notices, as he looks up, that there are a number of deep indents on the vines above, marking the passage of his fall.

"Plake?" Sax says.

"The mission," Bas replies.

"You chose the mission over me?"

"I didn't want to, my pair," Bas says, and she uses her claws to help Sax stay upright. "But we couldn't know if you survived. Agra-Red and Plake drove away the last skiffs, but more were coming. Even if you lived, we had no way to carry you."

The reasoning makes sense, and it's impossible for Sax to be angry with Bas. That would be like becoming angry with himself.

"Yet, you came back?"

Bas beckons towards a pathway obviously cut with her own claws. The vines there are torn asunder, their pieces littering the ground as they walk towards a small clearing similarly sliced open, though the charred ends here show a miner's handiwork.

Sitting in it is a small shuttle, barely larger than the evac mod they took down to Aspicis. Plake and Agra-Red wait outside of it.

"Managed to survive?" Agra-Red says as Sax walks into view.

"Looks like you owe me," Plake says to the Whelk.

"When don't I?"

"One of these days I'll collect."

"And that's the day you'll find out I have nothing to give you," Agra-Red warbles a wet laugh. "All I've got is this miner and a bit of loyalty."

Plake shakes her head, takes a harder look at Sax. "You still able to go on this?"

"The mask shaped most of the fall and the vines did the rest," Sax says. "I'll be sore, but still better than you."

The Whelk laughs again, and Plake just points to the open shuttle bay. Sax creaks in first, expecting cramped quarters and finds it's even worse than he thought. There's no actual cockpit inside—there's only cargo space and it's already filled with what looks like racks and racks of dead power cells. As it is, squeezing in requires Sax to reassess his flexibility and bend himself into a mess of limbs.

Bas doesn't get any better treatment, generally placing herself on top of the path Sax defined between the racks of dark batteries. Plake and Agra-Red get the small open area directly around the bays, the Whelk settling its assault miner so the point aims right out the door.

"Where's the pilot?" Sax asks once they're inside.

"Don't have one," Plake replies. "Apparently Cavignum has such tight security they don't let much manned cargo in. Our contact says our only chance is going in by drone shuttle."

As if to emphasize the point, Plake pulls out a small device and taps a couple of signals on it. The drone begins to power up, rising from the ground on the strength of its microjets.

"How'd you convince them to take us?" Sax asks.

"I used my claws," Bas replies. "And, we promised the Flaum a position heading all of the power on Aspicis."

Sax hisses a laugh. "I thought the point of this was to remove corruption?"

"Nah," Agra-Red says. "We just want to change from corruption that destroys galaxies to the usual, grifting sort."

There's not much to say to that, though Sax feels a bit of sadness worm its way into his body as the shuttle flies along. Evva certainly had more noble aspirations than replacing the Chorus with a wheeling-and-dealing set of greedy paws, but what does Sax know about governing? He couldn't run a planet, couldn't even run a ship.

So instead he focuses on things he knows; namely, rehearsing the plan of attack. Their mission's pretty simple, now that they're on the way to Cavignum. Once they land, the group needs to break in and cause a diversion large enough for Nobaa and Engee to find a way inside. Then, of course, get out alive and, if possible, reconnect with Evva at the Spire.

Simple.

"Have you two ever done anything like this?" Sax asks after

they've run through the plan twice. "An actual assault on an enemy position?"

"You're talking to a merchant and her thug," Plake replies. "We've assaulted plenty of enemies, but not like this."

"Usually it's one or two, up real close," Agra-Red adds.

"Then let Bas and I do most of the work," Sax hisses. "Cover us. Keep your eyes open for anything we miss, and clean up anything we leave behind."

"You're making it sound real glamorous."

"This has nothing to do with pride," Bas says. "The only thing that matters is the mission."

"Then I think we have a problem," Plake says, her voice running up high with concern. "Because we're not going to the right place."

Lan sets the course towards Kolas' cruiser, the *Nunilite*, as we clear the last bits of the moon. Beyond Vimelia's atmosphere, the gravity in our ship drops to zero, letting my black hair float around while T'Oli does work keeping me gripped to the floor.

"So we glide on home?" I ask the Oratus. "Then what?"

"Kolas will have the ship scanned for any Sevora before we're allowed to leave it," Lan replies. "Then, after some time to rest, I imagine you will be sent to Aspicis, to present your species to the Chorus."

I suppose that was the original purpose of Lan's mission.

To my left, the door splitting the bridge from the crowded rear of the ship slides open and I'm surprised to see Malo glide in, followed by Viera. The Charre warrior still looks ill, but he manages to give me a weak smile.

"Sorry," Malo says. "It's really crowded back there, and once everyone started floating . . . "

"And the vomit," Viera adds. "If you think humans getting sick is bad, try a bunch of Flaum. It's disgusting. All in their fur, and—"

"I guess I'll stay up here then," I cut off Viera before her descriptions send my own stomach tumbling and the two of them settle in against the side opposite me.

Viera nods towards Lan, sitting in the netting. "How's the pilot doing?"

"Fine," Lan hisses.

"She did well," I say. "Didn't panic at all."

"It helps when you don't fear death," Malo says, and the warrior coughs out a half-hearted laugh.

"What?"

"Them. The Oratus. You're not afraid of anything, are you?" Malo says to Lan. "Not like us, like humans."

Lan turns a yellow-black eye towards Malo. "The only thing we fear, if you want to call it that, is losing our pair."

Outside, we're heading into the outskirts of the Vincere fleet. Open space fills in with smaller ships buzzing around, larger freighters and what must be battle-ready cruisers move past us, heading towards the ruin of Vimelia. Probably to make sure nothing survives Kolas' plan.

"Humans are like that too," I say. "With those we love."

"I love these miners." Viera gestures with the weapons in each of her hands. "Wouldn't want to lose them, either. Can't say I'm afraid about it though."

"You're terrible at these conversations," Malo says to her.

"I choose to be terrible, Malo, because it's funny. That's how I cope with this madness."

Lan, at least, gives Viera a slight hissing laugh for her trouble. The conversation ebbs and flows from there, with Malo giving us a rundown of his time on Vimelia after we jetted off-world and left him collapsed in the docking bay cavern.

At first, Malo woke without any idea of where he was, only that things were dark and the air smelled thick and rotting. His whole body was sore, and Malo couldn't really move, so he sat there in the dark until he realized the smell was the same as the sewers we'd all been running through not long before. Malo figured if he was back there, then maybe he'd been taken by one of the Clarity's Dawn members, and started trying to make noise.

"It's tough to scream when your throat is dry and your lungs burn," Malo says. "But I kind of growled out a call for help, and someone came."

That someone turned out to be Rackt, a Vyphen member of Clarity's Dawn, and Rackt said he was surprised that Malo still lived. Nobody knew how a human's body worked. All they had were experiments, medical cream meant for scales or furry Flaum skin. But humans aren't so special after all—or so Malo found out when he didn't die.

"I stayed in the dark for a while, getting better," Malo says. "I thought we'd won at first—Rackt said that you had made it away, and I was happy about that."

The Sevora, though weren't as thrilled with Malo and the rest of Clarity's Dawn. They struck on what Malo thinks was the third day, hitting Clarity's Dawn's headquarters beneath the surface. They took some prisoners, the ones that didn't fight back too hard, the ones who might still be useful as hosts. Others, like Rackt and Sapphrite, vanished in a hail of burning laserfire.

"By the time I realized what was happening, it was already too late," Malo says. "I managed to get out of my chamber, and that was the end of it. They stunned me, and I've spent every day since then with these prisoners, waiting to see what the Sevora were going to do."

By the time Malo finishes his story, Lan announces that we're closing in on Kolas' cruiser and the back edge of the fleet. With T'Oli loosening its grip on my feet, I manage to float my way over to Malo and wrap the warrior in a tight hug.

"We're not leaving you behind again," I say. "Promise."

"Shouldn't promise things you can't control, Empress," Malo says, but I think he's joking, even if his eyes have a wary look to them.

He's still recovering, still putting himself back together. I would be cautious too.

Gar's roar surprises everyone. We're in the final approach, and the crashing, hissing, pained noise comes out of still air. I jerk apart from Malo, just in time for Lan to push me out of the way as the Oratus streaks away from the net to the call of her pair. I try to look through the door, but Lan blocks it and when she's through, the only thing I see is a roiling mass of chaos as the prisoners throw, cut, and bite at the Oratus.

"Are they insane?" I say. "What are they doing?"

"A case of the space crazies?" Viera says, and she pulls up her miners.

Speaking of, a pair of flashes blitz through the door, followed by another hissing roar, this time from Lan. More surprise, more pain.

"Viera, go," I tell her. "Help them. I'll hold the bridge with T'Oli and Malo."

"You want me in that mess?" Viera eyes me. "I don't know . . ."

"If Lan and Gar get hurt, Kolas might not let us back on board," I reply.

Viera takes the hint, pushes off from the floor and heads through the entryway back into the ship's main area. I tell T'Oli to follow her and keep a barrier between the bridge and the rest of the ship—the last thing we need is whoever's causing the problem back there to get their claws or whatever they have on the flight stick.

"Empress," Malo says, and I turn to see him drifting into the cockpit's netting. "You might want to hold on to something."

"What?"

Malo reaches, grabs the flight stick, and shoves it forward. The ship lurches down, away from our landing path with the *Nunilite*. The new velocity pushes me back against the wall, and I hear more frustrated hissing and a single, angry yelp from Viera.

"What are you doing?" I yell as Malo boosts the ship's speed, faster and faster as we launch out beyond the end of the Vincere fleet.

"Saving my species, Kaishi," Malo says. "What I tried to do on Earth. What I won't fail to do now."

"Sevora." T'Oli slaps the word as I put it together.

"Ignos?" I say a name that I thought dead and gone. "You're alive?"

"Barely," Malo, no, Ignos says. The Sevora is sending Malo's hands tapping away at a feverish pace. "Like your warrior here, I nearly died in your escape."

"You crashed the transport shuttle yourself!" I shout. "You chose to come after us!"

"No, Kaishi," Ignos replies. "I chose nothing—everything I've done has been forced upon me by the Vincere, by your Oratus friends. Do you think we wanted to escape our home like this?"

The prisoners. We never had a scan to search them for Sevora. Jel or Nasiya could have infected all of them. The thought makes me sick, but I push the nausea away. No time for that now. Instead, I press my legs against the wall, and push forward, flying towards the pilot's netting.

"How many?" I ask as I head towards Malo, towards Ignos. "How many of them are Sevora?"

"Every last one," Ignos says, and the Sevora doesn't turn his head until I catch the netting. Then Malo's face, twisted in a sad, steady stare, looks at me. "It's the only time Nasiya and Jel ever agreed on a plan. One that would have failed utterly if you hadn't come through for us."

I try to get around the netting, but Ignos shakes Malo's head. "Don't try it, Kaishi. Touch me, and I'll kill you." With Malo's right hand, Ignos brandishes a small, shining knife from beneath the ragged folds of his clothes. "I'm going to leap in a moment, before those Vincere fighters decide we're not worth the risk. Find some-where to strap yourself down."

Ignos glances back at the monitors, and his right hand lets go of the knife, leaving it to float in space, to punch in a command. I start to let go, to drop back to the wall where I'd rode out the acceleration, then I pull myself around the netting, this time to Ignos' right, reaching for the knife.

And catch an elbow in my stomach. It's a hard hit, one that blows the air from my lungs and, with nothing to hold me, sends me floating back along the same way I'd been faking a moment earlier.

"The human body is not a bad one," Ignos says, and now, outside, I can see the barest few flashes as the Vincere start shooting. I hope they hit us. "It takes some time to get hold of the nerves, but with Malo stuck in our facilities, and with my experience from your own body, we had that time."

"You stole him."

"Kaishi, don't be naive. You are fighting for the survival of your species, like us." Ignos taps one more green-outlined box on the right monitor and the ship's alarms go off, announcing a short leap count-down. "Just because we've won, doesn't mean you're any better than we are."

The hissing and roaring from behind us has died down, and I don't hear any sarcastic remarks from Viera. T'Oli has its eyestalks split, one back into the mess, one towards us.

"They're all stunned," T'Oli says when I look its way. "They kept small, microstunners beneath their rags. Ingenious, really."

No. A desperate attempt that only succeeded because I ignored all advice. Lan, Kolas, even Viera tried to warn me. I tried to do what Father would not, and because of that, I've lost everything.

The leap is both instant and long, a warping of everything I am that goes handily with the mind-wipe I'm going through. The back of Malo's head, covered in scraggy black hair, seems to split into a dozen copies of itself that spill around a prism. I look left and instead of that side of the bridge, I see T'Oli spread out across the cosmos; an infinite expanse of cream blending with the stars.

Then the universe snaps back to itself and I'm there again, trapped with a bunch of my worst enemies. Outside, dead center in front of us, I can see a ship that's definitely not part of the Vincere fleet: it's huge, for one. Larger than *Cobalt*, though they share their round exterior.

"A seed ship," T'Oli says from its spread position across the bridge's sole doorway, though whether the Ooblot is telling me or whistling its own surprise I'm not sure.

"Where did you take us?" I ask Malo, pushing myself off the wall.

Part of me wants to go to the door, to check on Lan, Gar, and Viera. T'Oli says they're stunned, a fate I think I'd share if I went that way. So instead, with Malo and Ignos still staring towards the front, out the windshield, I wave to T'Oli, tell the Ooblot, with my hand, to come over, and T'Oli complies.

"Deep space," Ignos says. "Well off any charted course, near no habitable planets or points of interest. An ideal place to park the last sanctuary for our species."

T'Oli wraps its cream self around my left arm, sharpening its edge into a blade. I glide towards Malo, a warrior that I'd given everything to save, one that I wanted desperately to be alive, and that desperation blinded me.

Time to fix that mistake.

"Kaishi," Ignos says as I get close. "Don't—"

The Sevora doesn't finish. I stab forward with T'Oli, drive the diamond-hard point of the Ooblot towards my friend. But it's hard getting momentum without weight, and instead of the decisive slice I'm hoping for, my stab barely gets through the net. Malo has plenty of time to wheel out of the way, to press his back against the windshield as my swing falls short.

"Put it down," Ignos says, raising Malo's hands, palms up, to me.

"No." I slice the netting away. "You've betrayed me at every turn. Used me, like you're using Malo now. I'll never do what you say again."

"Your friends will die if you kill me," Ignos says, and there's not an ounce of fear in its voice, even as I draw my arm back for another strike.

Ignos has no room to move this time, nowhere to send Malo's body to get away from my Ooblot sword. Yet, I know why it's not afraid. I know why it's simply staring at me now, taking a slow, deep breath.

I can't. I can't kill Ignos if it means the rest of my friends will die.

"What happens now?" I say, keeping T'Oli level, ready. "What are you going to do?"

Ignos points towards the huge seed ship, towards the docking bay that's opened up for our approach. "We're going to begin again. The Sevora will grow, we will find a new home, and we will spread."

"Until the Chorus finds you, and this whole process repeats itself."

Ignos laughs. "As it has before, so it may again. We are learning, though, and the Amigga, I think, are beginning to lose their grip on the galaxy."

"What do you mean?" T'Oli asks the question, pattering away from a patch between the eyestalks, up near my elbow. "The Chorus is as strong as ever."

"Ooblot, you've been buried under Vimelia's rock for too long. There's a rot within your civilization, one that's growing too fast for the Chorus to contain. Even if the Amigga survive this revolt, they won't be strong enough to fight us."

Seeing Ignos turn Malo into a gloating clown only makes me angry, and I push the sharp tip against Malo's body, pinning Ignos to the windshield. Nowhere in Ignos' plans was there anything for us, which means the only way out we have is the same way Malo's taken; through the mind of a Sevora.

I'd rather die than let another one of those creatures into my head. Viera, Lan and Gar would too.

"Wait," Ignos says, and now, at least, there's a leak of fear in that voice. "Kaishi. We can make a deal here. A good one."

"Make it, then."

Outside, our ship drifts into a wide, blue-lit docking bay. It's huge, and there's a smattering of other craft around, but unlike every other bay I've been to, not a soul moves in it. There are no robots, no scurrying Flaum or any sign of life.

"I'm sure Nasiya and Jel will agree with me," Ignos says, "if we promise you your lives. You, Viera, and this one. Malo. I will give him back to you."

"What about me?" T'Oli says.

Ignos shrugs. "Go with them."

"Gar and Lan?" I ask.

Now there's hesitation as the vessel settles to the ground, the whine of microjets coming in clear. As we land on the seed ship, I feel some slight gravity return, pressing my feet to the floor. If I had to swing now, the cut would be quick. Deadly.

"We can't risk them getting away," Ignos finally says. "They'll head back to the Vincere and tell them what we've done."

"I could do that too."

"But you won't," Ignos replies. "Before you managed to figure out where, who to speak to, we'll be gone. And if you betray us, then before too long, your precious Earth will see another Sevora seed, and another tribe will find their god. Only this time, I'll have full control."

My species for the Sevora. A trade.

There's only one thing to do. One way to go.

"I agree."

The drone shuttle's bay doors are shut and there's no windows to speak of, so the first glimpse Sax gets of where they're going is after the ship lands with a thud on something distinctly metallic. The shuttle's doors open with a whoosh. There's a lot of loud shouting, orders for Plake and Agra-Red to drop their weapons.

From his squashed corner, Sax can only see a little, but what he gets is a deep blue metal enclosure, far different from the vine-wrapped spaces he's seen elsewhere on this planet. He can't make out the enemies, but they must be dangerous, as Plake drops her miner and Agra-Red ejects the power pack from its own fixed weapon. Both items are swept up by furry Flaum fingers as soon as they hit the floor.

Chances at surprise are few, so Sax and Bas wait, with the latter positioning herself so that she can curl off of Sax towards the shuttle's doors, claws out and at the ready.

"Either you two leave now, slowly, or we melt the shuttle where it sits," the voice is the mechanical whine of an Amigga. "We scanned the ship for heat sources on the way in. We know you're in there."

"This is the last time I trust anyone other than you," Sax hisses to his pair.

"It's just another adventure, Sax," Bas says lightly, then climbs off of Sax and heads outside.

His muscles are still sore, so Sax takes a bit of time extricating himself from the shuttle's cramped confines, but when the Oratus manages to get himself out into the chilly, northern air, the first view tells him why it's dark: the camp's on the very edge of Aspicis' night line, with the white dwarf setting oh-so-slowly on the far horizon.

Around them rise daunting metal walls, above and over which bits of tangled vine drape. None of the greenery, however, makes its way far inside the enclosure, which, Sax notices, is covered by a wispy laser shield, the kind of screen not visible except for the small insects and occasional bits of dust that strike and, in turn, are immolated by it.

Plake and Agra-Red have already been hustled away from the shuttle, where a quartet of Flaum watch over them. Another dozen or so of the furry creatures aim miners of their own at Sax and Bas, while an Amigga bearing a taller, treaded and apparently weaponless exoskeleton stands over them all.

"Plake, when this is done, I'm going to find your contact and eat them," Sax says across the yard to the Vyphen.

"I'll serve them up to you," Plake snaps back.

"Stop," the Amigga commands, and Sax resists the urge to take a running leap over to the thing and destroy it right then and there.

The Oratus is wearing a mask—albeit a damaged one—and with Bas there, the two of them stand a decent chance of taking out all the Flaum. However, Plake and Agra-Red have no such defense, and sacrificing their companions for a risky move seems like a poor choice.

"You've arrived at Fenebris, and it will be your new home until the Chorus decides what they would like to do with you," the Amigga says. "First, of course, we will gather your names. Then, we will submit them for your fates to be decided. My guess is that you will all die horribly within the next twenty-four hours. Any resistance will only confirm that fate."

Flaum step up to Sax and Bas, reach for their masks and for the equipment hung therein. Sax catches his pair's eye—do they fight back? She shakes her head slightly, and the decision is made. No resistance for now.

"You can take away my miners," Sax says to the Flaum as they pull the weapons away. "I'll still have my claws, and that's more than enough for you."

The furry creatures glance at each other, and Sax enjoys their quick steps away from him a second later. A little fear goes a long way.

The escort from the landing area is a short one—Sax is expecting cells, some form of detention center, but what they get instead is a shift from the wide area of the landing pad to a wider and far more sloppy yard where the ground, instead of paved stone, is mostly muddy dirt. Sticking up from the earth every so often are four-meter high heat sticks with glowing-orange bulbs throughout their length and soft fans on top to blow the heat down, and clustered around those sticks is the saddest collection of creatures Sax has seen since *Scrapper Station*. Flaum, Whelk, Teven and more huddle around each other, talking quietly or just seeming to sleep on the ground.

In the middle of the space is a large, circular trough. A few species linger there, picking at what looks like a flood of nutrient goop moving slow through the container, flowing up from one end and down on the other.

At the far end of the space, set against another large wall, stands a gate slightly taller than Sax, and aside from the way they came in—a similar gate—looks like the only way to go in or out of this space.

Altogether, the vibe Sax gets is a depressing one.

"The best part of being here," the Amigga's saying when Sax tunes back into its endless haranguing. "Is that you'll never have to worry about leaving. There's no more dreams to have, no more problems to solve. It's just this space, the nutrient goop, and the glimmer worms."

Glimmer worms?

Sax isn't the only one with questions, as he catches a shrug from Plake and similar cocked-head confusion from Bas. The Amigga, though, doesn't seem interested in going further; the creature, along with the Flaum guards, retreats with miners out and ready back through the gate, which trundles down and settles heavy on the ground.

"Can't say this is what I was expecting," Agra-Red announces in a huff. "Always thought I'd die in a firefight, not crumbling to dust in a labor camp."

"I didn't think the Chorus had these?" Bas says. "The Vincere never mentioned them."

"I guess if you break the law on Aspicis, they're not much for due process." Plake sweeps a winged arm across the space. "Look at all these miserable things."

The Vyphen's not wrong. Sax would normally see a bunch of defenseless creatures as food to have, prey to hunt, but nothing here gets his hunter's instinct going. The nutrient goop means none of the species he sees are shriveled or malnourished, but they're dead in spirit. There's no fire here.

If Plake's right, though, and these are criminals, then they must not be grievous ones. The Chorus tried to kill all of them in the skiffs not long ago, but now they're content with leaving dangerous captives in a labor camp?

"Your contact," Sax says. "They didn't tell the Chorus who we were."

At Plake's look, Sax goes over his reasoning. Namely, that the four of them should have been shot on sight, or stunned and used as an example. Why leave a dangerous quartet with outside friends alive?

"So they didn't completely screw us," Agra-Red burbles. "I'm still going to disintegrate them."

"And I'll eat whatever's left," Sax hisses. "What I'm saying, though, is that we might have a chance to get out of this. If they don't know who we are, then we might have time."

"Until they decide to look," Plake replies. "I'm not trusting for a moment the Amigga here won't run our images and see what it gets. I say we find a way to breach these walls now."

Which is how they spend the next few hours. Sax and Bas, Agra-Red and Plake split and circle the wide walls of the camp, drawing wandering looks every now and then as they brush up to the barriers. They're hard rock, though Sax feels his claws could pierce them.

"If we climbed over, then what?" Bas says when she notices Sax run his metallic claws across part of the stone, leaving a white-chipped line. "They either shoot us, or Plake and Agra-Red."

"Then what, we wait?" Sax asks, and he can't keep the derision from his voice. There's nothing worse than waiting, especially when you don't know how long. "I prefer doing something over nothing."

Their conversation—the heated tones, more likely—attracts the attention of an older Teven, its mud-brown carapace chipped and cracked, that Sax didn't even notice until the stick-like creature rises up from the ground near their feet.

"You ever hear of sleep?" the Teven announces. "It's a practice where those of us who've worked our hides all day get back a scrap of energy so we can do it all again."

Sax bares his teeth at the creature. Wants to take a swipe with his claws because Aspicis, on the whole, has been a giant crap pile for him, but Plake moves in front and talks straight to the Teven.

"Hear what we were saying?" Plake asks.

"How could I not? You're all talkin' like there's some big thing you're missing cause you're here."

"You know much about this place?"

The Teven laughs, always a strange thing, as Sax can't see their mouths, so their flute-chuckles pop out from their carapaces at a seeming distance from the creature itself. Like hearing an echo.

"I've been here almost my whole life," the Teven replies. "Tried to fix a way off this world, got nabbed for it, now I've caught so many glimmer worms it's all I see when I sleep."

"So there's no way out?"

"Didn't say that," the Teven replies. "Just no ways for an old Teven all alone. Crew like yours, there might be options. These folks aren't used to resistance. Push back, maybe you'll find they break. Or maybe you'll find yourselves fried and dead on the ground."

"One of those options sounds good," Agra-Red says.

Sax, though, is done listening to the Teven. Done standing around here. There's not a single Oratus in this yard, which means it's plausible this prison isn't designed to hold a creature like him.

"Watch," Sax hisses to Bas, and then he breaks into a long-loping run towards the nearest wall, one of the long side ones without a gate.

The sparse light makes it hard to make out anything other than smooth stone rising six or seven meters before ending in a rippling series of what look like small spikes. Sax jumps before he gets to the wall, his leap carrying him nearly halfway up before his metal claws punch into the stone. His fore- and midclaws cut right through, and Sax scurries up towards the top without hesitation.

He'll have to thank Nobaa for the claws next time he sees the Teven.

Sax hits the wall's top and there's no alarm, no streaking bolts from one miner after the next. Over the edge, Sax sees plenty of the vines, sure, but there's something else. Something huge, glowing orange that spans half the horizon and rises up into the sky. Lights glow in the long purple twilight as dozens of skiffs and other transports flit into and out of the structure, the departing ones vanishing in all directions.

Cavignum.

Sax places his left foreclaw in between the nubs, glances back down towards his crew to tell them what he's seeing, when his foreclaw goes numb. The icy blankness spreads along his arm, into Sax's torso and all along every part of him, until even his eyes go limp and his lids close halfway.

Then, with no strength holding him back up, Sax plummets back to the ground.

At my words, Ignos nods behind me, and I whirl to see a red-patched Flaum standing in the doorway, a pair of miners in its clawed hands pointing at me.

"She won't be trouble," Ignos says to the Flaum.

"That's what you told us the first time," the Flaum replies. "I'm inclined to destroy her right now."

"You can try," I reply. T'Oli takes my tone, broadens and hardens its shell so that I have what amounts to a shield on my left arm.

"Nasiya," I get the sense that Ignos says the name for my benefit as much as the Sevora leader's. "This isn't the place, and you don't have your Oratus host any longer. You're not a weapon. She could kill you easily."

Nasiya's body keeps the miners steady for another heartbeat, then drops them to the Flaum's sides. "You made a deal, Ignos. I will honor it."

We disembark the ship in silence. Not even T'Oli has words for the still forms of Gar, Lan, and Viera as the Sevora Flaum and Whelk carry them from the ship. I can see Viera's chest rise and fall as she breathes, but her eyes are closed. Her hands empty, dangling from her sides as she's carried down the ramp I, back on Vimelia, ordered lowered for these monsters.

Like a ramshackle ceremonial procession, Nasiya leads us out through the docking bay and into a strange, huge section full of windowed buildings that rise from floor to ceiling. They're smaller than the towering heights of the structures on Vimelia, but they make every other ship I've been inside feel tiny. Yet, unlike Vimelia and the underground dwellings in Marilo, home of the Lunare back on Earth, all of these windows are dark.

The avenues splitting the buildings are dim too, with only the occasional glow coming from tall poles dotted with hooks and branches. I'm not sure what those are for, but Ignos and Nasiya, who walk near me at the head of the group, each spend a few footfalls looking at the empty roosts.

What is clear, though, is that this seed ship is meant for far more than the few of us that are here. Thousands and thousands could fit in these spaces, and that docking bay had the resources for dozens of ships.

"A last resort should be empty," Ignos says to me as we walk. "Still, these streets should throng with Sevora. This ship should hum with the possibilities of our species."

"Isn't that the plan?" I reply. "If the Vincere don't blow you up again?"

Ignos ignores my jab. "It is the plan, but first we need to decide who to sacrifice."

"Sacrifice?"

"Sevora do not breed like you," Ignos says as we near a large half-moon door that Nasiya calls a *gateway*. "One of us will need to mature, and from them, we can spawn a million more."

"That doesn't sound like a sacrifice."

"At the center of this ship is a prison. It is couched in glory, but it is a prison nonetheless. The Sevora that takes residence there will never leave it. They will control the seed ship, and nothing else."

The next area we enter is again filled with buildings, but rather than the block-like utility of the last section, these are laid out in vibrant, twisting designs. As if someone had shrunk and transplanted a part of Vimelia's great city to the ship. Except this great city is empty. It's one thing to stare at the dark windows of unoccupied homes, it's another to look at a grand square, with a curling crystal spear sticking out of a dry fountain. Benches sit alone, pristine and never used. Terminals aligned in banks against the walls look back at us with blank screens.

All of us, even the Sevora, hurry through the section.

The next area grips my chest like a vice. I haven't seen a literal seed since finding Ignos so long ago on that jungle night, but here they're hanging row after row around a great ring. Their sharp noses point down, towards a gray metal floor far beneath us.

"It will open," Ignos says when it catches me looking. "When it's time for us to spread, this is how. A single seed can carry a Sevora for many, many light years until it hits its target."

"How long did you travel to get to Earth?"

"Comparatively short," Ignos replies, gesturing for me to keep walking with them as they circle the ring. "We already knew of Earth, that the Amigga were conducting some sort of test there. I was sent to see about the results, to corrupt them if I could."

"You succeeded."

Ignos laughs. "Succeeded? Here you are, despite my every effort to turn your species into slaves for mine. If anything, Kaishi, I helped your people achieve technological prowess sooner than they should have."

"But if you hadn't, you and all of your kind would be dead now."

"Maybe, maybe not," Ignos says, then the Sevora gestures with Malo's left hand towards a thin metal bridge going over the gap beneath the seeds to a squat square door. "That's what we're looking for. The final bridge. The Sevora that crosses over will never come back."

I'm expecting Ignos to explain why, but it falls quiet after saying the words, and I realize Ignos itself is thinking about making that choice. The Sevora walks Malo forward, joining Nasiya's Flaum host and a third, a small lime-skinned Whelk at the foot of the final bridge.

"They're choosing," T'Oli says.

"I gathered." I look around at the other Sevora. Most are watching the trio discuss, and those that aren't are hovering over Viera, Lan and Gar. The carriers have set the Oratus and the human down, and they rest on the floor, stiff and still. " T'Oli, we have to find a way out of this."

"I don't think the two of us can beat all of them."

"If we can't, they'll take us too," I reply. "I don't trust Ignos at all."

"Right. That seems logical. That Sevora has betrayed you at every opportunity."

"Thanks for the reminder." I shift, with T'Oli around my wrist, closer to the stunned bodies. If any of them are close to waking up, I might be able to distract the Sevora long enough to get an ally . . .

"I will claim the honor!" Nasiya's voice is high, skittering, and, beneath the bravado, trembling. "I will walk the final bridge, and become the founder of our new beginning."

The words seem ceremonial, but the buzz, and even angry replies Nasiya gets from the rest of the Sevora show the proclamation isn't a certainty. The entire pack of Sevora, even the ones watching the Oratus and Viera, descend on the trio, pushing and shouting at each other.

"I suppose the factions haven't ended their fight after all," T'Oli says.

"They're giving us a chance." I look at the bodies. The seed ship's gravity isn't as high as a planet—an aggressive run and I feel like I'll float off the ground—but I don't think I can carry an Oratus alone.

Viera, though, is much smaller.

While the Sevora struggle with each other, T'Oli slips off of my wrist as I squat down and slide my arms beneath Viera's back. With my legs, I try to lift my friend. I strain, pull hard, expecting resistance and I don't get much. Viera doesn't float, exactly, but I'm able to tilt her upright and forward, where, as she begins to fall with her face destined to smash into the ground. I catch her, bringing up my arm to keep Viera's chest pressed against my own shoulder.

It's probably not comfortable for her, but as Viera's in stunned oblivion at the moment, I'm not too worried.

"They're noticing," T'Oli says.

"Then distract them," I reply, starting to run around the ring.

Viera's feet and ankles drag on the floor as we go—she's taller than I am—but my floaty jog gets us some momentum. Some of the Sevora yell, but no miner shoots at my back, no weapon strikes me down.

I wonder if they don't want to damage their last ship.

After a few steps, with the seeds hanging like spikes up above me and the shining outer walls of the central ring to my right, I hazard a glance back. T'Oli's taken control. The Ooblot's swimming around a quintet of Flaum chasing after me, using its liquid and solid changing to trip and irritate the pursuit. Every time one of the Sevora tries to pull a miner, T'Oli liquefies its way up their body and slurps itself into the crannies of the weapon, then solidifies to burst it into pieces.

Still, T'Oli is only one Ooblot, and eventually a couple of the Flaum break past it and come after me. It's a foot race I'm not going to win, but I'm close enough now to the open door of my destination; the empty entertainment quarter.

"Stop!"

Ignos yells the word. I keep moving.

"Kaishi stop!"

The doorway's there, Viera's in my arms. All that's left is one foot in front of the other.

"We'll shoot!"

I reach the ramp heading up to the gateway. Risk a quick look behind me and see the two Flaum scrabbling my way, with T'Oli close to them. See Ignos with several more well back, with miners raised in my direction.

"I trusted you!" I shout back to Malo, to the Sevora inside his head.

And I run. Carry Viera through the gateway and back into the dark, empty mess of the entertainment section. No miner bolts blaze through the spot I leave behind. The two Sevora Flaum don't even crest the gateway.

Which means I'm free to carry Viera through the dark, running between buildings, trying to find a place to hide.


The place must be a restaurant. The only clues to that are the large pieces of equipment in a separated room on the lower level, bulky metal pieces that look well-suited to cooking. Staying on the ground floor is a poor plan, though, so I drag Viera—whose starting to feel awful heavy even in the low gravity—to what looks like a lift.

It doesn't move.

Of course not. The Sevora won't turn this section on, not till there's a reason to, and my needs definitely aren't a reason. I chose the restaurant because the outside lacked the flair of the other buildings, only a nameplate in curling white on a black banner labeling the place 'Verdant'. I figure they'll search all the buildings eventually, so I might as well be caught somewhere with a name I like.

If I don't get this lift moving, though, I'm going to be found way too soon. The idea is to get some weapons, defend myself and give humanity one last good showing before the Sevora devour my species or the Chorus grinds them into galactic dust.

"Having problems?" T'Oli's slapping voice is a relief in the lonely dark, and I look over towards the entrance to see the Ooblot slime in.

"How did you get away?"

"The thing about Ooblots, they're very hard to kill," T'Oli replies. "I managed to slime a miner away from one of them, this beauty here, and your friend Ignos decided to let me go rather than get in a firefight."

"I guess we take that. Any ideas?" I sigh, glance at the platform around me. "I want to get up to the second level, but I can't get Viera there."

T'Oli oozes up the side of the wall next to me, gets a little over my head, and then solidifies part of itself. "A new handhold. One of my many talents."

"Nice. Viera goes first."

Together, the Ooblot and I lift Viera higher and higher up the lift shaft, with me using my legs and all the energy I've got left to push Viera up one meter at a time. T'Oli wraps itself around Viera's body, stabilizing her for my next push. Until, with one more jumping shove, I get Viera's shoulders level with the next floor's gap.

Just like in the sewer depths of Vimelia, T'Oli forms itself into a lever, pulling Viera up and over the edge.

"Have another jump in you?" T'Oli asks me a moment later.

I nod. Gather my legs, and leap. Doing this in low gravity is a freeing sensation that brings a momentary belief that I might never come back down. With T'Oli catching me, I never actually do. Climbing with the Ooblot isn't at all like climbing a tree—it's more like sticking your limbs into an immovable vice, then using that vice as leverage to pull yourself up and reach out with the other hand into T'Oli's stretched out body, and repeat.

"Do you ever get tired of being used?" I ask T'Oli when we're up on the largely-empty second level. Whereas Verdant's ground floor was full of tables and cooking appliances, this space appears dedicated to a different type of gathering—long, wide tables split the area, and each one is surrounded by cushioned couches.

"Are you asking if I dream of doing more?" T'Oli says. "Don't you think I should enjoy being useful?"

"Well, I . . ." I start, but T'Oli's right. My idle question gets to a deeper point—what does T'Oli want? Why is this Ooblot tagging along with me?

"If I said I wanted to see the Sevora dead, would that work?"

"No." I lift Viera onto one of the cushions, then step over to the broad windows on the second floor. The dim yellow lights in the section's ceiling provide the little light we have, and all I see on the street are static shadows. Bent building corners, rounded sidewalks aligning streets meant for bustling crowds. "You're too calm for that. I've seen things driven by hate before."

Sax, as the Oratus went after the Amigga on *Cobalt*. The Fassoth that tried to devour me in the caverns beneath Earth's surface. Even the assassins after the Emperor's death, who believed I would be the end of their entire civilization.

"What if I just live?"

"I don't understand?"

"I don't dream, Kaishi," T'Oli says this like it says everything—without sorrow, without emotion, just as a fact. "I spent so long underneath the ground on Vimelia, seeing so many drive themselves to death chasing impossible goals, that I lost my own need for them. Instead, I do what I believe is best, and help those I choose to."

"You're choosing to help me?"

"It's quite entertaining," T'Oli says, the Ooblot sidling up near me. "I don't have any grand motives. You're here, you're kind, and helping you has brought me to places I would never have seen otherwise. That's quite enough for me."

Bas kicks him awake, laughter in her eyes as Sax blinks himself alert. He's lying in the muddy filth beneath the wall, and the rest of their group stands around him. What's clear, too, is that he's been out for longer than a few seconds.

"It's time to go," Bas says. "I would've let you sleep longer, but . . . " His pair nods over to the far gate and Sax stands up to see a phalanx of armed Flaum standing outside of its open portal. "Apparently we need to gather glimmer worms."

This seems to be the purpose of the prisoners here, as all the ones previously lying about the courtyard are now shuffling towards the open gate, with no excitement whatsoever.

As Sax gets up, he notices a few new aches joining in with the bruises from his earlier plummet through the vines. He's putting the mask through its paces, and even with its protection, Sax makes a note to avoid far falls in the near future—he's not averse to pain, but dealing with it every second gets tiresome.

"Does anyone even know what glimmer worms are?" Agra-Red asks.

"My guess?" Plake says. "The Amigga made everything on this planet, so they have to serve a purpose."

Before any of them can follow up on the idea, a loose, low musical blast pours out of the speakers embedded in the corners of the prison walls. It's loud enough to stifle any conversation, and the prisoners around them pick up their pace heading towards the gates.

"Come on, my friends!" the Amigga's voice rings out in its synthetic glory. "It's another opportunity to earn my respect, another opportunity to power the galaxy whose gifts you so ignorantly spat upon. Hurry, now, to the Glimmer mines—as you know, any laggards will be melted once the final trumpet sounds!"

Sax winces as the Amigga's booming voice makes his head hurt even more. The point, though, is made and they tromp beneath dark clouds in the dim light towards the open gate. They're the last bunch through, and the Flaum guards don't hesitate to toss Sax and the others sneers beneath their visored helmets.

"Should I eviscerate them?" Sax hisses to Bas. "There's only a few."

Two dozen, actually. All armed and skittish. Sax wouldn't stand much of a chance, but that's not what he's going for; when the Flaum slip to slight panic, when they back away and a few squeak and raise their miners, Sax gets his laugh.

"You're going to get us all killed," Agra-Red grumbles. "Don't want to die so you can have your fun, Oratus."

"I don't care what you want, Whelk," Sax replies.

Then they're through the gate, which opens into a wide tunnel slanting immediately down. Like the prison yard, the Glimmer Tunnel, as Sax decides to call it, sports the bare minimum of supports holding the slick, black rock walls up. The tunnel's floor is made of mixed rock patches and slippery sand, and with every breath, Sax's vents pick up the stale scent of hundreds of unwashed, sweating species.

So far, as experiences go, this isn't a pleasant one.

The tunnels spiderweb quickly, breaking off into larger corridors and tiny cracks. The pair of Oratus, three meters tall, find themselves with very limited options. Plake and Agra-Red, in the interest of following the trails of the other prisoners who, presumably, know more about where these glimmer worms are hiding, split off and leave Sax and Bas alone.

They have two options in front of them—one, lit by the usual glow lights jammed into the ceiling, seems the more traveled route. The other, with a few light spikes driven into the walls, jerks and twists out of their view a few steps along.

"Neither of these paths are going to take us out of here," Sax says. He's delaying partly because this crossroads is the only spot he's been able to stand up straight for a while, and his sore back is luxuriating in the stretch.

"Sax, my pair, have the falls broken your mind so much that you only state the obvious?" Bas hisses in reply. She cloaks the words in a soft smile, though, so Sax doesn't feel the cut. "We're not escaping while we're down here, so we may as well try and find one of these creatures."

"You mean, a hunt?"

"It's been a long time."

Since a real hunt, of an animal and not a criminal, or a Sevora. Yes. Every so often with the Vincere they'd been lucky, been sent on a mission to a wild world that, after the objective had been secured, offered the chance to revel in their instincts. If being imprisoned by the Amigga is going to offer them anything, Sax will take the chance to fall inside his true self and delight in the hunting that follows.

First, Sax opens his vents and catches another deep whiff of the cave's many smells. There's the already-mentioned stink, and beneath that the loam of growing plants, the dripping twinge of wet dust, but under all of those things, there's something else. A jolt hanging at every breath's end.

The scent comes from his right, down the twisting tunnel. Sax turns that way as Bas takes a step in the same direction. Their tails touch—no words necessary here.

As they set off, Nobaa again makes his modifications worth their efforts. Sax's talons and, when he places them against the rock walls, claws pick up vibrations. Like scents, each tiny shake carries a pattern that Sax sorts through to find what he's looking for. There's the steady footfalls caused by the many pounding feet under the ground here, and in between those, a wriggling, a constant shiver in the earth.

"I can't read it," Bas says, her claws next to Sax's own. "There's too much clutter."

"These can," Sax says, pulling his metal claws away. "A snake lies over here."

Sax takes the lead then, stepping through the tight tunnel. They bend around corners, duck beneath leering rocks and jump across small streams. The further they go, the less frequent the light, until the glow-sticks disappear entirely and the two Oratus use their masks to cloak their eyes in low-light vision. What was black and brown shifts to green grades, allowing the two of them to keep making their way.

Every so often, Sax touches the wall again and confirms he's on the right track. Every time, the vibrations are there, only more pronounced as the extra noise from the other species fades. Bas catches it too, now.

Not a word's spoken until the tunnel hits a new, wide chamber whose walls are perfectly visible to Sax because of the wriggling thing hanging down in the center. That the neon-blue-lit creature is a glimmer worm is obvious—not just because of the blue-white light the thing emits, but because it's carved a hole through the ceiling and is now in the process of munching its way through a large, sparkling geode resting on the cavern's floor.

With a blink, Sax gets rid of the blinding night-vision and takes in the glimmer worm, which appears to be taller than Sax, if thin. Its skin, pulsing with light, is covered in tiny hairs, each one occasionally launching sparks to another. The worm doesn't have any feet, and the head devouring the geode is the only dark space, where small blue tongues lance out and take tiny chunks from its meal.

"Found it," Sax says.

"Remember what I said about the obvious?"

"Not at all," Sax says the words as he moves into the cavern, slowly making his way to the opposite side of the chamber.

Most prey can run. Best to cut off any escape before the battle starts.

Sax, though, doesn't get halfway across the room before the glimmer worm pauses its crunching meal. The creature turns its rock-black face, with the tips of its blue tongues barely visible in the worm's own light, towards Sax. They both hesitate, then Sax flicks his tail ever-so-slightly.

Alive. That's how they're supposed to deliver the glimmer worms. Dead, they're worth nothing. So when Bas reacts to Sax's signal, she leaps at the glimmer worm with every intention of tackling and driving the thing to the ground.

Instead, the worm sucks itself back up towards its hole, causing Bas to blow by beneath it. Sax takes his leaping turn as soon as the glimmer worm retracts, aiming to grab the thing's head, and manages to snag it. The glimmer worm's face is just as rock-like to the touch as it is to the eyes, and Sax's heavy weight pulls the worm from its hole, the blinking body piling out and onto Sax as the Oratus lands on his back.

Any thought of victory goes up in a bright flash as the glimmer worm takes its sparkling blue light and flares. The cavern washes out in white, and Sax closes his eyes, yanks his claws back to cover them, and by the time the glow fades, the worm's wriggling away further down the tunnel.

"That, that was terrible," Sax manages to say.

"We don't know anything about these creatures," Bas hisses. "These Amigga are playing with us, sending us after prey without preparation."

"They'll die for it," Sax says. "But now I want this worm. Set the masks."

Sax flips his vision to infrared, a spectrum that runs on heat. He doesn't leave it there—chasing the worm through the tunnels is going to be impossible if they can't see any of the twists and turns—but now the mask will flip between the low-light vision and the infrared with barely a twitch of Sax's eyes.

Then, with talons scratching on the rocks, the Oratus give chase. Running down prey is exhilarating—every step, every breath in pursuit of something using its every moment to get away. There's no more pure comparing of strength, skill, and intelligence than a hunt.

Unfortunately for the glimmer worm, the Oratus are great hunters, and the caves don't give the creature many options to get away. As Sax and Bas catch up they begin to pace the worm.

"It must be going somewhere," Sax says as he and Bas settle for keeping the worm's blue-lit tail end in view.

"Or it's just running from us."

"On Rathfall, I found a nest that let me survive," Sax replies as they vault over a spiky set of rocks and splash through a stream on the other side. "If this worm has its own lair . . ."

"We couldn't grab one of them, and you're already thinking of more?"

"Planning ahead, Bas."

"This new you is strange."

Bas, though, doesn't sound all that upset.

The clue they're waiting for comes soon after in the form of a rising glow further ahead. Going from night-vision dark to the green warning that it's too bright is jarring, but Sax blinks over to infrared just in time to see a boiling mass of pinks, blues, and oranges.

There must be a dozen worms or more here.

The one they're chasing dives into the pile, but the wriggling mass doesn't make any moves to get away. The worms could be flaring constantly, for all Sax knows—it's not going to help them here.

"Take the closest?" Sax says.

Bas touches her tail to his in agreement, and they take a few steps forward, reach out with their claws, and grip the first worm. It struggles, but once Sax and Bas get it free from the rest of its group, the worm seems to realize it's captured and falls limp.

"Playing dead?" Sax says, holding the flopping body in his midclaws.

"This is an Amigga creature," Bas replies. "Any instincts it has are programmed into it. If they truly want these worms, then my guess is they're primed to become passive once caught."

"Then why would they flare?"

"Because you don't want just anyone taking your glimmer worms. Only those who know, with your permission, how to do it."

As fun as the hunt was, an ending without a fight, without blood and carnage, fades the excitement from Sax's two hard-beating hearts.

Still, at least they caught one.

They don't get to hold on to the worm for long—after Sax and Bas carry the thing back up to the tunnel entrance, they're directed to deposit the worm into the back of a large cargo skiff, where a Flaum pilot sits in front of a rectangular bin. As the worm slides in, joining three others, the skiff powers up and a soft purple sheen appears over the top—one that would no doubt give a nasty shock to anyone trying to breach it.

The Flaum guards watching Sax and Bas drop off their catch give the Oratus plenty of space, more than before, to which Sax attributes his constant claw flexing and teeth baring. Keeping Flaum on edge is too much fun to stop.

"Batteries," Plake says later when they've reformed in the crowded yard. "That's what the glimmer worms are for."

This time, Sax and the others have their own heat lamp. Nobody wants to tangle with a pair of Oratus, so they're given plenty of space. With their masks, Sax and Bas aren't cold, but Agra-Red's skin is dull with chill and Plake has her feathers held in tight. If it's going to take their entire crew to get out of here, Sax might as well help keep them comfortable.

"Why don't they just use normal batteries?" Agra-Red replies. "Like everyone else?"

Plake shakes her head. Sax doesn't know either, but Bas gives a low hiss and they turn her way.

"It's all vanity. The Amigga built species to solve other problems, so why not this one too?"

"That's a lot of trouble to go through for pride," Agra-Red says.

No one disputes that, and nobody knows otherwise, so Sax turns the conversation to ribbing the Whelk and Vyphen for failing to catch a worm of their own.

"We can help you with that tomorrow," Sax finally says, once he's earned steady glares. "We found a whole nest. Even you two should be able to catch one there."

"A whole nest?" Plake asks, and the way she turns her head towards Agra-Red has Sax reading layers into the words.

"Might be enough," Agra-Red replies. "I've never tried with a glimmer worm. Might just explode."

"What?" Bas and Sax hiss at the same time.

Agra-Red jiggles its loose, gel-like skin. "I'm a Whelk. What I've got for organs float around in mostly water. If we can get a glimmer worm out of the tunnel without them collecting it, I should be able to pass its current along into the gate, short it out."

"Couldn't any one of us do that?" Bas asks. "We're all organic."

"Yeah, if you want to dilute the current. I've done it before, to help jump start machines on the *Mobius*."

"And it doesn't kill you?" Sax says.

"Stings a bit," Agra-Red laughs. "There's a theory Whelks came around because of lightning strikes hit the wrong puddle. Stick us into a power source and we'll pass the energy through like a wire."

The Whelk's plan, though, requires them to get a glimmer worm out of the caverns without getting detected. Given the worms are well over a meter long, that's going to be a trick in and of itself.

"We'll cause a diversion," Sax hisses. "They're already scared of me—they won't look away if I start showing some claw."

Nobody objects, though Bas gives Sax an eye roll. She knows as well as he does that Sax wants the chance to slice, bite a bit.

He knows she wants the same, even if she won't admit it.

I need you to stay here," I tell T'Oli as I turn back from the windows.

The Ooblot's twin stalks look back at me. It's unnerving that there's no expression, no face to read on the slime creature, so after a second I start the walk towards the other side of the room, towards the lift shaft leading down.

"You're going to need weapons, you know," the Ooblot says to my back.

"I'll find some."

The Sevora took the gear I had on Vimelia, and while I'm still in my mask, I'm not foolish enough to think I can do what needs doing with my hands.

"Why don't we start with these?" T'Oli oozes over to me, goes up along my arm and hardens itself into a blade again, and points with its eyestalks towards one of the tables.

With three quick slashes, I cut apart one of the legs and slice the rounded end to turn it into a jagged point. I make a second one, and then set the pair of makeshift short spears into my mask, where they hang as though I'd set them into glue.

"You'll keep her safe?" I say to T'Oli as I head to the shaft, armed and slightly dangerous.

"An Ooblot's not going to stop much by itself," T'Oli replies.

"Keep her alive till she wakes up, then come find me."

"What are you going to do?"

"Lan and Gar are the only things on this ship that can stop the Sevora," I reply. "I'm going to rescue them."

"A suicide mission? Clarity's Dawn had plenty of martyrs. They never accomplished what they wanted."

I quirk a smile. "It's my fault we're in this. I told Lan to let the Sevora on the shuttle. I have to try."

"Or we could try and make it back to the shuttle."

"You and I both know that's where they'll think we're going."

Ooblots can't sigh—that I know of—but the puttering pops that come from T'Oli then seem awfully close to it. "Then do yourself a favor and stay alive. The galaxy is much more fun with you humans in it."

Going down the shaft is easier than climbing up—I hang from the edge, then push off into a roll, just like dropping from a jungle tree, though the floor here is harder than the leafy dirt I'm used to. My haphazard spears scratch against the tiles too, something to note if I'm trying to be quiet.

From there it's back into the dim dark entertainment section, where I spend my time slinking back towards the ring gateway. There's still no sign of the Sevora in here, and I'm surprised that Ignos and the others think I'm so little threat as to not warrant even a couple Flaum.

But then, Ignos has been around humans. It's been inside my head. If anything can judge how dangerous I am, it's the Sevora.

So I try not to take the lack of interest personally as I make it to the gateway, which is shut. I try to do what Ignos did and walk over to a black nub. Ignos had stared into it from Malo's eye, and I try to do the same, but get no response. There's no panel in sight either, which means I'm stuck.

No, it means I have to look for another way in.

I retrace my steps quick—behind me, there's the entertainment district. Then the empty and even creepier residential area. Following both of those is the docking bay. That last is the only place I'm sure the Sevora won't leave me alone—if I get to the shuttle and toss a message out to Kolas and the Vincere, their new civilization is going to end quick.

Now, I've never sent a message through space, but Ignos wouldn't know that.

I backtrack, my boots treading soft on the metal. Alone, the entertainment district goes from being a curiosity to a cavern of shadows. The emptiness takes on an ominous tone, and the faint whir of electronics bustling beneath the surface permeates everything, a continual whine that sets me on edge. What I wouldn't give for a singing bird or a rippling breeze through some trees.

What I wouldn't give for a bite of food too—I haven't had anything to eat since before our assault on Vimelia, and my stomach's considering that an emergency on par with being a solo insurgent on a seed ship.

The gateway on the other side of the entertainment district is open. There's a black nub here, on the right side, so I don't think it's a different setup than the ring-ward door. Both of them opened when I came through with the Sevora, so if only one is open now . . .

The Sevora are setting a trap.

I quickstep to the side of the gateway and peer through back into the residential district. While it's not a bright oasis, there's been a change since I was last here: the lights along the avenues and in some of the buildings are glowing, and they're casting a green-blue glow through the space. Doorways into those same buildings, dark and closed when we first went through here, now stand open, beckoning to soft-lit interiors full of screens.

What I don't see are any threats—no Flaum, no Whelk, nothing. So I take a cautious step through. The glow of a building to my immediate right, a five-story sloping affair that looks like a mountainside turned domicile, draws me towards its orange fluorescence. It's not the flickering fires of home I'm seeing through its jagged, curled entrance, but the similarity is enough that I can't resist going closer, holding my short spears at the ready.

There's a whistling bang from behind and I whirl, jabbing at air. Nothing there. Except, I notice, the gateway. It's shut.

I have no way back.

For the gateway to close now seems too suspicious to be coincidence. I turn back to the gravelly building, but instead of fascination, I hunt for traps, tricks, eyes in the dark. A vice holds every nerve.

Breathe, Kaishi. You'd be dead already if they wanted you that way. You've made it this far—beyond the skies of your own home, on a ship of an alien species, one of whom has taken over the mind of the man who took you on this journey to begin with, a man you're realizing you . . .

It's all too impossible to be scared.

But I can't let that distract me.

The deep breath does help. As does my grip on the spears, the light feel of the mask on my skin. I'm way beyond what I know, but I'm an Empress. I've survived this long.

When I walk through the archway into the building's entrance, I see the imitation fires burning in glass cages dangling from a close ceiling. Their source, rather than dried wood or brush, are little discs set in the bottom of the cages, and their gouts of sporadic orange and red glint through the enclosing prisms to dance along the walls.

I say walls, but as soon as I recognize them as such, as soon as I step into the middle of the entrance, they shift, fading from the rocky brown to a deep blue that draws in the fake-fire light. In large, block letters, a question appears:

*What is your name?*

I stare at the image. What is my name? What kind of question is that?

"Are you going to answer it?"

Ignos' words have the telltale verve of a transmission, a wired tone that says the sound isn't entirely natural. It's a twisted version of Malo's voice and I hate it. There's nobody in the room, though. Ignos must be watching me—from outside my mind this time.

"Kaishi, you have to play along."

There's no nub to look at. No direction I ought to stare. Only the screen. Only those words.

"I will not *play*."

The screen doesn't change. Ignos doesn't appear out of some hidden door. But there's a hint, a whisper of a sigh making its way through the magical channels that tie Ignos' voice to my ears.

"Kaishi, we are closing in around you at this very moment. Even if Malo or those Oratus gave you enough training to evade us, I'll seal you in this section. This ship is huge. You'll starve before we need to think about opening it up."

The door I came through is still shut, so if those Sevora are coming, they're not here yet. There's no other way out of this chamber, though. Only the blue screens. Ignos is calling it right—I don't have much leverage.

"Then what's the point?"

"The point? Kaishi. The point is you. Imagine what might happen if we sent a seed back to Earth with you inside of it? How simple it would be to take humanity at a single stroke? You and I had nearly completed the birthing pools in Damantum. We could finish what we started."

Insults die in my mouth along with defiant proclamations. Those won't do any good here.

"You still want to take humanity?" I stay in the middle of the room, my short spears ready.

"All species, Kaishi. All of them ought to have the chance to join the Sevora," Ignos replies. "Look at Malo. He lives because I allow him to. Without the Sevora, he would have died in that spaceport, where you left him."

"You caused all of that."

"Because you would not open your eyes. Now choose Kaishi. We want to come in. Nasiya and Jel, they do not trust you. I do. I know you'll see. Let the Sevora into your world, and your people will never lack for miracles. They will survive whatever evils the Chorus designs for them. Humanity will prosper."

I point my spears to the floor. Let them hang loose in my hands and give the door a slight nod. My shoulders slump, and I take a deep, hanging breath as my eyes close.

The door shunts open, and standing there is Malo, is Ignos, and my warrior-champion is flanked by a pair of Flaum holding miners. They're straight, quiet. Resolute in the way of total Sevora control.

Ignos walks into the chamber, Malo's arms reaching for the spears, and the two Flaum come behind. Malo's eyes are a defiant blue, even as the rest of him is still gaunt, starved and weak. Somewhere behind those irises is my friend. I left him behind once. I will not do so again.

"Humanity will be free," I whisper.

Ignos cocks Malo's head, and I move. My right short spear carries with my lunge, sweeping up even as I duck under the snap-quick turn of the Flaum's miner. When it fires, the Flaum's shot scores over my head. My short-spear does not go beneath its stomach.

Ignos, with Malo's body between me and its second guard, grabs at my left arm. Rather than trying to fight the pull, I let go of my short spear, let Ignos stumble back with its own strength. The Sevora clears the line for its ally, just as I brace and swing, with my right short spear, pulling the Flaum stuck on it to the left. It's body blocks the second miner flash, which fills the air with the stinging scent of burning fur.

The seed ship's lower gravity helps me push my Flaum shield forward, and the Sevora host takes another pair of miner hits to the back before I crash into the shooter. Before I drive my spear through one victim and into a second.

Before my own gets driven into me.

It's a numbing lance, a sudden wrongness in my back. There's pain, yes, but it's white-cold with shock. Ignos drives me forward with the attack, helping me impale the two Flaum and pushing us against the wall. Warmth doubles up with the chill, and it feels as though my stomach is leaking, spreading itself around me.

The mask isn't made to stop short spears.

Ignos withdraws the weapon and the three of us, the two silent Flaum and I, collapse on each other. The burned fur of my first one brushes my face—a desert yellow color, though now spotted with red. It is, though, the first soft, comfortable thing I've felt in a very, very long time. I could almost sleep.

"Stop it," Ignos says behind me. "Quit fighting."

No. I blink. No.

I hear Ignos backpedal. "We know your species. I am your mind."

Ignos is . . . my mind?

The question cuts through the pain's haze. The Sevora and its host are leaning back against one of the flames, still holding my short spear, its dark metal glistening with red wet. Malo's cerulean eyes see mine, and even from across the room, I know them.

I left Malo behind once. I will not do so again.

My fingers find the miner, pry it free. It hurts, it tears to turn myself, but I need the shot.

"Hey," I say, and my voice doesn't sound like me. It's soupy, strange and thick and it runs down my lips.

Malo looks at me. Ignos grips the spear, opens its mouth.

"Do it," Malo says.

I pull the trigger.

The journey to and from the nest the next day goes smooth, though Sax enjoys the jaw-dropping awe that comes over Plake and Agra-Red when they reach the lightning ball swirling in the back of the cavern. The nest has grown overnight too —there's a dozen or more glimmer worms here now.

Sax and Bas take one, reaching in and pulling it out from the swarm, then hand the limp worm to the Whelk and Vyphen. They take a second for themselves.

"Look at this, the Oratus find the treasure," says a voice from behind them, a squeaky, old one that belongs to the elder Teven from the yard. The creature's not alone, though; there's a pack of Flaum, Whelk, and others crammed behind him. "Told all of you it'd be smart to follow these two. The Amigga didn't fool around when they made Oratus. Not at all."

A moment hangs while both parties, the four and the two dozen, decide what happens next. With no weapons between them, it'd be a trivial exercise for Sax and Bas to rend their way through all the prisoners. What benefit, though, would such a massacre serve?

"We have an offer for you," Bas strikes first, and when she lays out the terms and conditions, there's not a single dissent from the bedraggled crowd.

The offer, though, requires the two Oratus to lead the flash-blue train of worm holders up to the cavern's front. At first, the half-dozen Flaum guarding the cargo skiff are shocked when the worms begin to appear, then, when every pair of emerging prisoners comes out carrying another, they get suspicious.

So Sax makes his move.

The Flaum guards are watching the next batch unload their worms into a suddenly-packed cargo skiff when Sax steps up behind them, takes his claws, and taps two of the guards on their shoulders. They turn, and start to stumble back at the sight of him, when Sax tightens his grip on their shoulder pads. With his foreclaws, Sax slams each of the Flaum against each other, mashing their miners and helmeted heads together and dropping them, limp and unconscious, to the ground.

This gets the attention of the other guards, who, launching into chittering alarm, start to bring their miners to bear on Sax. The Oratus is already moving to the next pair, while Bas, who's positioned herself behind the two closest to the cargo skiff—and farthest from Sax—neutralizes her targets.

The prisoners break into their own part of the play, lunging forward and grabbing at their oppressor's miners. A Teven pair jump onto the cargo skiff and knock off the pilot, smothering the shrieking Flaum to the ground, where a stunning blue flash numbs it a moment later.

A bellowing horn rolls through the courtyard as the resistance expands, and the far gate leading to the landing pad shunts open a moment later, with another dozen armed Flaum pouring out and into the yard.

And everything goes wrong.

There's no warning from the Amigga, no call to surrender—the Flaum guards simply advance beyond the gate and begin firing. The bolts aren't blue either, but the burning, killing red. Flaum, Teven, Whelk drop as they're struck.

Sax reacts with instinct. Before, he'd been trying to keep Chorus Flaum alive in hopes they would change their sides. Now, the stakes are mortal. Preserving life means taking it.

While some of the prisoners who've grabbed miners from downed guards take scattered shots back, the Oratus goes for a direct route; he takes two long lunges towards Bas, who kneels, sets her midclaws, then catches Sax as he jumps. The boost gets the Oratus high enough to catch the top of a heat stick.

Oratus are huge creatures, tall and heavy with endless cords of muscle beneath their scales. When Sax slams into the top of the heat stick, it bends, breaks and sends Sax riding back towards the ground. What the heat stick also does is blow bright, a shockwave of compressed light and energy suddenly loosed on the yard.

It's a blinding flash, accompanied by a burst that launches Sax, claws clinging to the heat stick's top, across the wet, muddy yard towards the Flaum. The momentary stun from the flare has the Flaum bringing their hands down from their eyes in time to see Sax leaping from his ride into the middle of their formation.

Mud, fur, torn armor flies into the air and skips across the ground as Sax whips and snaps. His claws tear, his tail trips, and with every bite of his mouth, Sax disarms an enemy. Bas joins in seconds later, crashing into the Flaum ranks from the other side. The enemy is outclassed, outgunned, and it's only moments before the prison's guards are nothing more than shredded snacks set upon by the remaining prisoners.

Sax meets up with his pair in the middle, her scales, like his, coated in all the evidence of their victory. After a quick confirmation that neither one of them bears anything more than the lightest of burns, they head through the open gate into the prison's landing zone.

The sole tower and barracks that makes up the prison's living space sits on the far side of the clearing. The Amigga's going to be in there.

"Ready?" Sax hisses to Bas.

"Very."

They lope across the landing pad, and are almost all the way across when a growing microjet whine has them stop, wheel around, ready for some new threat.

Instead, it's Plake, sitting at the controls of the cargo skiff. Agra-Red, assault miner re-acquainted with a power source, sits in back on top of a pile of pacified glimmer worms.

"Time to go," Plake announces.

"There's still an Amigga here," Sax protests. "It deserves the same as those Flaum."

"Oratus, now's not the time for your bloodlust," Plake replies. "Think bigger for once in your scale-brained life. We have to get out of here before that Amigga's reinforcements arrive."

Plake's right, of course. They ought to be jumping into that skiff and letting the Vyphen carry Sax and Bas away into the sky.

But.

"This prison ends now," Sax hisses, and he breaks towards the barracks as Plake fills the air with curses behind him.

The barracks and its tower have a wide double-door blocking the entrance, but it's not reinforced like the gates. There's no guards on the outside either, which lets Sax hit the barrier with all the force of his charging, tearing self. The metal rends, the door caves inward, then falls off its supports entirely.

Inside, there's a wide room, a mess hall and rec area coupled into one. A lift wide enough for the Amigga and its exoskeleton sits at the far end, and Sax makes a line for it. There's other people inside, more Flaum, but these are either the prison's support staff or they've decided getting mauled isn't in their interest, because they press back against the room's walls.

Sax is content to let them live. For now.

Someone's watching upstairs because the lift jolts before Sax can reach it, the doors shutting as it starts a journey up towards the second level. Sax keeps moving, digs in his talons and leaps, turning his shoulder as he flies so the Oratus crashes through the wall and the lift's doors, sprawling into the rising lift. Sax sweeps his tail in before it gets caught by the lift's movement, then swings himself around so that he's ready when the lift hits the next floor.

He's covered in mortar, dust and broken metal bits. So far, though, the mask keeps his scales intact, and aside from the constant aches in his bones from the falls, Sax is ready to go.

The feeling lasts until the lift's doors open and the Amigga, fully suited up, sprays laser through the opening doors. The fire stitches a line in the lift's back, missing Sax, who's hugging the ceiling. After a few seconds, the steady fire stops, and the Amigga's tuned laughter spills down the hallway.

"Are you going to cling up there forever?" the Amigga says. "Reinforcements are coming, Oratus. They'll put down your little uprising without difficulty."

An overconfident Amigga? Impossible.

Sax hisses, then uses his foreclaws to tear apart the lift's roof tiles, sending them cascading to the lift's floor.

"You won't even slow us down!" the Amigga continues. "I'll order up new collections and we'll have plenty more broken Flaum here collecting glimmer worms before another day is out. You'll have accomplished nothing, except killing innocent soldiers!"

Sax barely catches the last bit as he scrambles out of the lift and into the tight shaft around it. There's not much room above him, save the magnets keeping the lift stable. Sax, though, doesn't need much. The walls in this place are thin, clearly meant for convenience and not for standing up to assaults. He presses himself against the back of the lift's shaft, then slams forward, crunching through the wall.

As Sax breaks through, he pushes forward with his talons, leaping as the wall collapses. The Amigga stands before him, wearing its exosuit, with this one sporting a pair of rudimentary miners attached to gimbals on the sides. Nothing like the fancier assortment sported by the Amigga Sax and Bas encountered outside the mag lev station.

Not that any equipment could make a difference here.

The Amigga tries to adjust its aim, tries to backpedal on those treads, but all it gets is one quick, missing shot off before Sax collides with its exoskeleton. Sax gets his talons into the tiled floor and pushes, shoving the Amigga—now shouting, pleading with Sax to stop—across the floor, through the line of terminals and the forest of sparks they create as the Amigga's armor suit obliterates their fragile screens, and out the windows.

The Amigga plummets down, cracking against the ground in a shower of mud. Prisoners, having broken free of their yard, descend on the creature, beating and breaking apart its protection with the mad intensity of species knowing their lives are forfeit and wanting to spend their last moments in revenge.

"Ready now?" Plake cries as she swoops the cargo skiff in front of the shattered window.

Sax meets his pair, sitting in the back with Agra-Red, and Bas gives him a nod. That's all he needs. With another leap, Sax lands in the back of the skiff and Plake shoots them away. The Vyphen keeps them low, keeps their running lights off in the darkness.

It's easy to see, though, the Chorus shuttles descending towards the prison, and the night's broken when their heavy lasers start to flash into the yard.

At least they're too far away to hear the screams.

Ignos set its trap close to the gateway. The one that had closed behind me, the one that Ignos came through, that's wide open as I drag Malo's body towards it. Ignos said it was locked, that I was trapped. I shouldn't be surprised at another Ignos lie, and it just piles onto the rest of me.

Every footfall, even in the soft landing of low gravity, comes with pangs. My body's slowly going numb, and I stumble, but manage to get a leg out and catch myself. Not sure I could pick myself up again, after the bloody pool the first—and last—attempt produced.

My left hand hangs behind, clamped tight around the stone-frozen wrist of Malo. The warrior's still breathing, which means the Sevora inside his head is still alive too. Lan showed me how to swap between a miner's modes, and the blue flash worked as the Oratus said it would. Malo's alive, even though I might not be for much longer.

The gateway's a broad doorway when it's open, at the top of a ramp that's getting stained as I limp up it. I have my spear in my right hand—the miner's useless for me unless I'm within a meter of the target—and as I hit the top of the ramp, my right leg decides it's done and I catch my fall on the butt of the weapon.

"Guess we're crawling from here," I say to my friend.

Not that I have a plan. Maybe get back to T'Oli. In truth, I know I'm not going to make it that far. I hope, though, I can get close enough for T'Oli to find Malo. Maybe the Ooblot has a way to remove the Sevora. Do what I couldn't and save my friend.

I crawl through the gateway. Across the threshold to the gold flickers of the dead entertainment district. The low lights blur and stretch, winking away and whisking back to a beat of their own. The ship itself seems to tilt. Have the Sevora turned the seed ship on its side? Is this what would happen?

No. I've fallen over, that's what. And I'm not alone.

Four Flaum crest the ramp, each one carrying a miner. Two raise their weapons and point them at me, as if I'm somehow going to summon the energy to fight back. Every breath takes a toll, requires weaving through a tangled web of broken nerves and rattling bones. All I can do is stare as they rip Malo away from me. With Ignos safely clear, the two executioners set their sights for a mortal volley.

I tried, Malo. Viera. I tried.

My ears are ringing, my hearing shutting down too, so the flashes play out like a dream. Heavy crimson, the shots wash out the darkness. The two Flaum aiming at me go first. They're hit from behind and their stringy fur catches fire as the beams cascade into them. The other two, by Malo, barely get themselves turned around before the assault falls on them.

Smoke surrounds me as this district gets its first real show.

"Still alive?" T'Oli says, though the sound comes from another body.

Viera cleaves through the scattered smoke, lurching forward as the Ooblot moves her limbs, bends her knees and arms, though I notice her eyes blink of their own accords. Her mouth falls into a tight frown too when I offer her a smile, though since my face has gone numb, I don't really know what I'm doing.

"Unfortunately, I cannot carry three humans," T'Oli says, and the Ooblot lets Viera down gently next to me. "It does look like you're very hurt, Kaishi. I'm not an expert in human anatomy, but that is a lot of blood."

I open my mouth—I can tell I'm doing this because my chest isn't yet numb, and the whiff of air leaking into my body gives my motion away—but only manage a cough.

"Yes, that's the situation." T'Oli forms back into its creamy puddle, both eyestalks dodging around me, getting in for closer looks. "How about we plug the hole right here?"

A sudden, paralyzing cold hits me from my lower back. My eyes pop open, I suck in air, try to scream and only half manage it. Before I've come down from the polar sting, though, T'Oli laces itself along my body. I feel the Ooblot knead through my fingers as it spreads itself thin.

"You're going to have to help me, all right?" T'Oli whispers—a light slapping sound given most of its body is coating me. "I'm not much good at moving humans."

I want to tell the Ooblot I can't help myself, but then my hands shift a little; a push from T'Oli's hardening, contracting body. I go with it, lending my tiny strength to the effort. It's enough, somehow, to get me to my knees. From there, T'Oli pools itself beneath and behind me, then slowly hardens and shoves itself up, shifting me to a stand.

All the while, Viera blinks at me from the floor. I think I see her legs and arms twitch, but then T'Oli has me lurching around back into the residential district.

"Nobody's going to have first aid in the party town," T'Oli slaps. "But where they live? That seems more likely."

I thought I'd be dead by now, but T'Oli's support gives me energy, gives me hope, and I cling to it. The dark fuzziness still lingers on the edges, my muscles spasm and ache, my lungs feel like I'm underwater, but we go. Past the orange place where Ignos sought to trap me, to the next building, an ordinary square structure with oval windows and a dark door.

"Going to lean you here for a moment," T'Oli says, and the

Ooblot does just that, pressing me against the side of the building near the door.

The Ooblot slimes over to the door itself, a smaller, squat one I could barely fit through standing up, and presses itself against the metal. After a moment, T'Oli shivers, and the door shakes. There's a sound of tearing metal, and then something bursts in the far side and the door falls back inside the house with a loud thump.

"Good thing there's so few Sevora on this ship," T'Oli says as it returns to me. "Else we'd be overrun by now. Between us, though, I think we've knocked out a third of them. Not bad for a squishy species like yourself."

Unlike the home Ignos led me to, this building looks more ordinary. Straight halls with doorways lining the sides. Unlike the entrance, these are wide open in the lightless hallways. Ignos may have sent power to its chosen structure, but this one isn't turned on yet. In a way, I'm thankful for the dark.

I've made it this far, and now, I try to tell T'Oli, I'm done. My legs can't seem to rise anymore, even with the Ooblot boosting every step. T'Oli gets the idea, and we swerve into an open room where I collapse, with T'Oli's gentle assistance, onto what appears to be a large reddish sponge.

"Be back soon!" T'Oli chirps and the Ooblot vanishes.

With it, so goes my consciousness.


I wake with a rush, in the same dark room. The only light comes through the window, flicks of the scattered blue lamps throughout the section. The first thing I do is breathe, and it's amazing. Incredible.

I'm alive.

Somehow, I'm alive.

"Empress," Viera's voice is soft, and she's leaning against the wall across from me. "Kaishi. I'm sorry."

"Why?" I try to say and it comes out a scratchy, hoarse mess.

"I failed you," Viera looks down at the miners she has in each hands, as if admonishing the weapons too for their own failures. "I should have stayed on the bridge."

"It would have ended the same," I say. "How long was I out?"

Viera shakes her head. "There's no way to tell time here, but I don't think for long. T'Oli found some powerful creams. They woke me up the rest of the way too. I told the Ooblot not to give any to Malo."

"He's still taken."

"I figured, seeing how panicked his eyes were when I looked at him."

"Where is he?"

"Locked across the hall."

"And T'Oli?"

"Keeping watch," Viera says. "That Ooblot's vicious. After getting you back here and reviving me, T'Oli skewered each and every one of the Sevora inside those Flaum bodies. Said the only way to be sure is to get the little suckers themselves."

After what the Ooblot's been through, a genetic experiment forced to flee into the sewers beneath the Sevora city on their home-world, T'Oli's probably got rage to spare.

"Good," I reply.

Trying out my arms and legs is a cascade of miracles. Each one works, and while there's plenty of itchy, poking pain, I manage to roll myself out of the bed. Viera catches me as I fall off of the sponge, and she helps me stand. I'm wearing, now, a set of loose-fitting clothes, the vests and pants meant for a Flaum, and one of the legs slips beneath my feet and nearly trips me.

"Have a knife?" I ask Viera, and she produces a strange-looking blade, a serrated edge against a silver-black haft.

"Careful with it," Viera replies. "I took it off one of the Flaum. When you press this button here, it gets interesting." She does so, and the edge buzzes, soft and sharp.

I am careful, and I use the blade to cut away the clothes so they're less like a stifling, messy collection and more a set of functional, if ugly, rags. Nobody is going to confuse me for an Empress, but at least I won't trip and fall on my face.

Now there's two priorities. A few meters away from me sits the warrior I've been trying to get back since the moment I lost him. Farther afield, somewhere in this ship, are a pair of deadly Oratus being taken, every second, closer to their own capture by the Sevora.

I want to ask Viera what to do, but I already know. There's only one choice I'll regret if we don't make it out of here alive.

"Let's go see him."

Ignos, and Malo, are still stiff and stunned. Their body, Malo's body, is laid flat across another of the sponges, which must be what passes for beds around the galaxy. Malo's eyes flick towards me as Viera and I go into the room, though I can only tell they move because Malo's pupils catch the sliver of blue light from the window. Otherwise the room's too dark to tell much.

"Go and get T'Oli," I say after we stare at Malo for a moment. "It's time we gave Malo his body back."

Viera puts a hand on my shoulder. Squeezes. Then disappears away into the building. I adopt her stance, leaning against the wall and looking at Malo.

"Ignos, I could hear people while I was stunned, so I assume you can hear me," I say. In a way, the darkness makes it easier—it feels like I'm talking to Ignos like we used to, in the caverns of my mind. "You told me I was destined for greater things. That I would be the source of miracles, that I would save my tribe. You were lying, but you were right. You told me that Viera would be a good friend, that Malo had possibilities. You were using me, but you were right."

I stand, move over to the sponge. Place my hands against its soft surface as I lean over and try not to wince at the lingering pain.

"You stayed with me through the sessions on *Cobalt*, you told me not to be afraid, and even though you were only saying those things so I wouldn't leave you behind, you were right." I stare into those eyes and I don't know whether it's Malo or Ignos who looks back at me. "Because of all that, on Vimelia, I chose to spare you. I did the thing you would have warned me not to—I gave my enemy another chance."

I hear a pattering, slithering noise from the hallway. Times' almost up.

"You taught that final lesson when you came back for me. Thank you, Ignos. And goodbye."

T'Oli doesn't need a command to know what to do, and the Ooblot catches the vibe of the moment and says nothing as its creamy self sluices up the sponge, surrounds Malo's head, and slivers a piece of itself inside.

I force myself to watch. To see every small bit of the Sevora as T'Oli pulls it, struggling, out of Malo's ear. As T'Oli sets the squirming nest of pointed tentacles on the floor. The miner's barrel is almost larger than the Sevora itself.

I can't miss.


The three of us meet in the building's entryway. Malo's still flat on the sponge, nerves fried by the heavy stun I delivered not long ago. As such, my war council consists of three: me, wearing robes meant for another species and still weak from a mortal wound barely healed. Viera, the healthiest of us, holds a pair of miners in her hands and stares out the doorway behind me, eternally searching for the next threat.

Then there's T'Oli, a pearly blob decorated with two eyestalks. Out of any of us, I suppose the Ooblot has the most reason to be here. Made by the Sevora and abandoned by them, T'Oli's been on a slow path to vengeance since its creation.

"You're going to take Malo to the shuttle," I say to T'Oli. I'm not so much standing as leaning on my short spear, the ache in my side sapping strength from my legs. "The two of you need to get away and leap back to Earth."

"If you think warning the rest of the humans will help them survive," T'Oli replies, "you are overestimating your species. Any

Sevora raid will overtake them."

"We fought them off last time," Viera says.

"We were lucky, and the Sevora were distracted by the Vincere's assault on Vimelia. With their survival at stake, they won't play games. They will infiltrate, destabilize, infect and destroy."

"I preferred it when you weren't so depressing."

"That's why you need to get Malo back." I steal the conversation. "He's had Ignos in his head, he knows the Sevora, like you. And our people will follow him."

Like they followed me, when they needed to.

"We could all go for the shuttle, you know," Viera says. "We'd have time to get another message off, let that big ugly Kolas and the rest of their lizard friends save Lan and Gar."

I've thought about that option. Followed it to the possible ends— what happens if Kolas doesn't catch this ship? If the Sevora get away and restart this war that's been going on for so long?

"There's a chance to end it here," I reply. "If we stop them and take this ship, then the Sevora are done. There won't be another war, another species won't be lost."

"Since when did you get so grand?" Viera asks me, but she says the words with a slight smile. "The girl I remember only wanted a part to play in her own tribe."

"My tribe's a lot bigger now."

T'Oli doesn't put up any more resistance, though the Ooblot does help me break apart some more metal so I have a full-length walking staff to go with my short spear. Viera has her miners, and after we say one last goodbye to Malo, who blinks up at us, Viera and I head off.

Only one place to go, and that's back towards the central ring. From there we have to get lucky and find where the Oratus are. Then we have to get really lucky and catch the Sevora before they turn Lan and Gar into the deadliest slaves imaginable.

We trade the blue lights of the residential section for the soft gold of the entertainment district, and I try not to pause as we pass by the bodies of the Sevora Flaum.

"Guess nobody's looking for them yet," Viera says as we move past. "T'Oli really helped. I could barely move, Kaishi. Without that Ooblot, I wouldn't have been able to even pull the trigger on this thing."

"We picked the right sewer to dive in, back then."

Crossing the entertainment section takes a bit of time, as Viera takes the lead and scouts ahead, while I limp behind her with my staff. Whatever T'Oli used to get me on my feet, it's definitely not a total miracle. Maybe I should have gone to the shuttle and sent the Ooblot with Viera on the rescue mission.

But I'm not one to send someone else to clean up my own mess.

"Gateway's shut," Viera says when I catch up to her on top of the small rise leading back towards the central ring. Like the others, there's a black nub next to this one that doesn't react at all when I wave a hand towards it. "Tried that too. Either there's nobody watching, or they're content leaving us here."

"Well, I'm not content staying."

It doesn't take a long brainstorm to find a path through the gateway; Viera swiped two miners, but across all the burnt Flaum, there's several more. We take the extra weapons, stack them against the gateway and get well back. Viera sets up the aim, takes a look at me.

"Ready? Because there's no more secret mission after this. They'll know we're coming."

"I don't care."

Viera laughs. "Liar."

She's right, and she shoots straight.

The fireball is loud and short, full of warping metal and the starved crackling of momentary flames with nothing but steel to bite into. The smoke is momentary, a mist whisked away by unseen, unfelt breezes that leaves behind a blasted hole in the center of the gateway.

"These doors don't stop much, do they?" Viera says.

"Are your heavy doors deep inside your own home?" I reply, then heft my staff and walk forward. "Let's go. Lan and Gar need us."

"Yeah, you've made that clear," Viera replies, keeping her miners up and ready. "Just promise me one thing."

"What's that?"

"When we save their scaly butts, you'll get them to admit they needed our help."

The ring is more ominous when it's empty. Bright and silver, but all the seeds hanging above look like teeth out of a nightmare. That the vast corridor extends in both directions without end also adds an eerie side, as if we've stepped into a mirrored universe where things just go off forever.

"I think we have two options," I say to Viera as we stare across the black-steel floor. "We either try to get into the seed ship's core and hope we draw their attention, or we try and find which quarter has the Oratus."

"Or a third," Viera says, stepping in front of me. "We just start shooting."

The sound of booted feet on metal clanks towards us from our right, and a trio of Whelk, come slithering around the corner. Two of them have miners, and one bears a pair of what look like short black sticks.

Their momentum carries them into view even as Viera opens fire, blitzing down the first two in a hot second, their gel-like bodies super-heating and bursting into gouts of gooey liquid. The last, with its miner, attempts a scattered retreat, spraying shots that manage to etch a nonsense pattern of burns into the walls around us.

"Don't shoot it." I put my hand on Viera's arm. "What do you bet that thing's going right where we want to be?"

"I like the way you think, Empress," Viera replies, and then we're off.

Or, at least, Viera is. I tell her to go ahead, keep on the Whelk's trail as I stumble along. I'm not much use in a chase—no idea how good I'd be in a fight either—but my utter uselessness in this momentary encounter prompts me to ditch my short spear for one of the blasted Whelks' miners. I may not be much of a shot, but I might be able to distract someone long enough for Viera to finish them off.

The Whelk goes halfway around the ring—bypassing one large, closed gateway—before scuttling through a wide open portal leading to someplace new and different. I'm surprised to see, from the ring as I catch up, breathing hard, to Viera that this section isn't shrouded in dark like the others. It's even brighter than the ring itself; an almost scalding white.

"Together?" I say to Viera as she gives me a look that speaks volumes about how battle-ready she thinks I am.

"Kaishi, you can stay back. By my count, there were only a couple dozen Sevora on that ship. We've taken out almost half. Maybe more. I can handle this."

"I'm not leaving you."

"Then don't get me killed, either."

This time I grab her arm tight, make Viera look at me. "The Oratus are the priority. Not me. You get them out and they'll make sure the Sevora are finished."

I search her eyes, catch that lock of increasingly dirty and frayed white hair hanging down over Viera's forehead. Back in the jungle, so long ago, the constant humidity kept Viera's hair frizzy, at least until she caved and used the same ointments we'd cultivated from plants for years. Now, in the dry, dull air of these ships, it's almost perfect.

Minus the dirt, the sweat, the scattered flecks of blood and ash.

Viera doesn't have to reply. A simple, slight nod shows she understands.

Cavignum, during Aspicis' long nights, looks like a frozen fireball expanding into the sky. An orange, roiling glow somehow kept constrained into a mostly perfect sphere. The bottom cuts away into a mammoth structure lit by a glittering army of lights. Skiffs blitz in and out, though Plake hesitates, hovering low and nestled in some vines before adding their own stolen ride to the bunch.

"We can't just go in," Plake says. "We don't have any credentials, and I may be a smooth talker, but the rest of you are going to get us straight up shot."

"There's another problem," Bas says. "We need to let Nobaa and Engee know when to get into the station."

"Hope you remember the channel they're listening on," Agra-Red grumbles. "Cause I don't. Not after they took everything away from us."

Sax hisses a laugh. "I've had to remember so many codes and coordinates. Don't worry, Whelk. When we have the diversion created, we'll be able to send the message."

"Grand." Plake, dimly visible in the ambient light, waves a feathered arm up at the skiffs going by. "Any ideas on how we get inside?

I'm not going to ask about a diversion because I know your answer's going to be 'destroy stuff'."

"Can we use these?" Bas holds up one of the glimmer worms. "You said they might be batteries?"

"Maybe," Plake replies, and the Vyphen takes a long look at wriggling creature. "If nothing else, you could hide beneath them and let me get us inside."

"Or I could," Sax offers. "That way, if it goes poorly, I can fight."

"If you have to fight right away, we're all dead," Plake says. "If nobody's got a better idea, grab some worms and get cozy."

The cargo skiff isn't large enough to hold two giant Oratus lying down in it, at least not with any degree of comfort. Sax and Bas have to wrap entirely around each other, fitting arms and legs into any possible cranny, and encircling themselves with their tails. Plake and Agra-Red set about covering the pair with glimmer worms, each one hitting Sax like a squishy package of nutrient goop.

Agra-Red, then, squeezes itself down in between some of the worms, resting like a coating between the two Oratus. Whelks don't quite have Ooblot levels of flexibility, but they're pretty close. One advantage, Sax notes, is that Agra-Red can't talk when it's this spread out.

"Hope you're all comfy," Plake says.

Squeezed in the back of the cargo skiff, Sax can only tell what Plake's doing by the feel of his weight as the skiff drops, thanks to the slight breeze that manages to make it through the layers. He's not thrilled at being packed away like some piece of, well, cargo, but there didn't seem to be any alternatives, and—

"Sax," Bas says to him, and her hiss reminds him that their heads are actually touching. "Are you all right?"

"Perfect," Sax replies, which is both far from the truth and close enough that it doesn't matter.

"Good. It wouldn't be fair otherwise."

"What wouldn't be fair?"

"When it starts? I don't want to feel like my score doesn't count, just because you're hurt."

It's been a while since they tracked points. Casual missions feel so long ago; when their set dropped into a war zone or a Sevora facility with simple search-and-destroy orders. It'd been easier then to find some extra fun in the carnage. Not so much now, not when the consequences seem so much higher.

Then again, maybe the stakes mean their games are even more important. What would it matter if they came out of this conflict alive, but having lost themselves?

"I'm already winning," Sax replies. "I took at least seven Flaum down back there. And the Amigga."

"You didn't kill the Amigga, the prisoners did."

"But I—"

"The rules, Sax. I took five Flaum back at the prison. So you have a slight lead, for now."

"For now."

The skiff moves slow for a long time, with Plake telling all of them to keep quiet as they pass by another vessel. It's a dull ride, but Sax isn't disappointed by the soft moments with Bas. Before, with the Vincere, Sax always felt invincible. That he and Bas would always make it through to the next one.

Now that feeling's gone, replaced with a grim fatalism. The odds of success are so low, the importance so high, that Sax feels better assuming he's not going to make it to the end, replacing fear with a macabre determination.

"Coming up on the first gate," Plake says. "Looks like the landing platforms are beyond. Keep still."

The skiff slows, then stops.

"Manifest?" announces a squeaky Flaum voice.

"Uh, glimmer worms," Plake replies.

There's a moment's silence, then Sax sees a crawling blue light pass over their cargo area. It's a slow crawl, detailed.

"You hear about the other prison?" Plake says suddenly, loud.

"What prison?" the Flaum guard replies.

"Back that way, guess the prisoners rebelled?"

"You're a Vyphen, aren't you?" the guard says after hesitating. "Pretty strange to see one of you here, and running cargo?"

Plake's going to ruin it. Sax tenses, ready to burst up from the glimmer worm cover and take out the guard. Not that they'd make it very far after, but dying in a fight would be better than getting gunned down lying in the back of a cart and covered in worms.

"You see what's going on in the galaxy?" Plake says. "Everywhere's a mess. At least here, you can get a stable job. Running glimmer worms is a lot better than dying up there."

That, somehow, gets a laugh from the Flaum. "True. I was with the Vincere for a while, and I thought every day I'd be fodder in another attack. When the chance came to transfer here, I jumped on it."

The light hovering on their cargo hold clicks off.

"Looks like a good haul," the guard says. "Head to platform B, drop the worms there."

"You got it." Plake gets the skiff moving again, shifting its angle lower and to the right.

"I did not think we'd get through there," Plake says a minute later. "You all owe me your lives."

"After we saved you at the prison?" Sax hisses back. "We're even."

"Saved me? The Whelk and I were just fine. We didn't need your claws."

Sax knows Plake's playing with him, and he doesn't bother to reply. The skiff's slowing down now for the landing, which means their disguises are about to be ruined.

Sax can't wait.

"There's guards and staff everywhere," Plake says. "I have a new plan. Hold on."

"What?" Sax manages to say as Bas offers a questioning hiss.

Plake sends the skiff suddenly into a tight right slant, and a second later Sax hears a startled squeak followed by the crunch of metal-on-metal collision. Pops sound from their own skiff, which wobbles in the air as microjets try to compensate for their now-non-functioning fellows. The shaky moment gets cut short, though, when Plake throws the skiff forward, bending it into a hard acceleration.

"Cut out, now!" Plake yells.

Sax doesn't understand, but Bas does. His pair uses her claws to slice at the back of the skiff, breaking apart the thin railing into a shower of sparks. Sax twists his head so he can, for the first time, actually see out the back, and he catches the wide bronzed expanse of the landing platform, the various skiffs alighting on it, and all the people running towards another skiff that's apparently crashed and is burning away on the ground.

"Kick!" Bas hisses, and Sax follows her lead, pushing with his talons and scurrying out the back of the skiff.

On the way, with his tail, Sax scoops Agra-Red, pulling the Whelk behind them as they fall the few meters down to the landing pad's surface. They've barely landed when the cargo skiff strikes something behind, bursting into crackling flame. Alarms sound out immediately, though the disastrous procession of events seems to have Cavignum's guards confused.

Plake, well back from the other three, is already running up to the nearest guards, throwing her feathered self around and exclaiming outrageous threats about the skiff that allegedly hit hers.

"She's buying us cover," Bas hisses, though Sax thinks the gouts of smoke and fire are doing a better job than the Vyphen.

A look towards the explosion shows Plake didn't aim at random either—around the bent, broken wreckage of their skiff is the similarly destroyed shape of a loading gate leading into Cavignum itself. It's an opening that Sax and Bas are only too happy to use.

"Carry me?" Agra-Red says as the Oratus turn to move. "I can't keep up with your giant legs."

After a derisive snort from Sax, Bas takes the honors, scooping up the Whelk as they sprint towards the door. Sax closes his vents, holds his breath as they dash through the smoking sparks, and then they're through to the other side.

Into the largest power plant in the galaxy.

They have two objectives—find a way into the base that Nobaa and Engee can access, and then make sure that way is open when the pair of Teven try to make their escape.

"Does Cavignum have a control center?" Sax asks as they dash through the wrecked door and into a wide cargo corridor.

It's a silver space, metal tweaked and polished to handle the heat extremes possible in what amounts to a giant hole sucking heat from the planet's core. The temperature inside is plenty warm already, especially compared to the chilly night outside, and the corridor's ceiling is peppered with holes leading to vents top-side.

Sax gets this information from the mask without feeling it, as the transparent suit does its best to keep Sax's body at prime operating temperature. The mask also blunts the smell of burning things, letting Sax focus on what lies ahead—namely a forest of branching paths, doors, and ramps leading to other levels.

Nearly all of these entrances and exits have shifting signs next to, hanging over, or imprinted on the floor. Only a couple appear to be on, and that's because cargo sleds are heading their way, with the signs displaying shipment names and directions.

Except everything's stopped now, and dozens of eyes stare down the corridor at them.

"Are you always this obvious?" Agra-Red says. "Of course it has a control center. We just have to find where that is."

"I liked you better when you couldn't talk."

"I've never liked you at all."

Bas has no time for them, apparently, as she takes off running. Sax follows, because what else can he do except chase the one he loves? Behind them, Agra-Red yells for them to slow down, but every second means more guards, and the Whelk's not worth mission failure.

"Where are you going?" Sax hisses ahead to his pair as she pads past the first split in the corridor, with ramps on either side moving up and down.

"The Amigga are obsessed with being at the center of their creations," Bas says. "If this place has a control, it's going to be as close to that middle as we can get."

"What about the Meridia? The Chorus sits at the top."

Bas skids to a stop, glares at Sax. "They live in the middle. Trust me."

He's never had a problem doing that, and doesn't have a problem now, so when Bas resumes her run, Sax follows.

They pass by those cargo sleds, and the Flaum piloting them don't bother to shout. Neither do the uniformed workers moving from one station to another, nor the delegation of what looks like inspectors, leading their furry Flaum selves around the station in all-white uniforms.

No, the first obstacles come as they near the end of the corridor. A trio of Flaum, but ones in heavy exo-suits. Sax almost laughs—these are Vincere relics, used before the Oratus came to power to give Flaum some combat advantage. They're black-metal and give the Flaum an extra two meters of height, made for exploration and hostile suppression.

Normally, Sax would expect to see a wide shoulder rack sporting miners on the exo-suits. These don't carry any laser weapons, though, and instead look to have had those racks melted and refined into large hammers, making a pair of them per suit. Sax supposes they might have industrial applications, but these three are clearly lined up to prevent the charging Oratus from getting through the smaller door behind them.

It's hard to know what's funnier—the idea that three Flaum could stand up to the Oratus alone, or that they thought these exo-suits would give them a chance.

"Left," Sax hisses as they get closer.

Bas takes the hint, and when they're a dozen steps away from the Flaum, who are raising their slow fists to do . . . something, the two

Oratus leap onto the walls, their talons and claws biting through the sides as they keep scrambling forward.

The Flaum in their iron workhorses don't, can't respond fast enough. Sax is on the left, and his target makes a clumsy, lumbering step-and-swing at him. The aim is low, and would be barely enough to clip Sax's lower claws if the Oratus didn't jump from the wall and land on the outstretched, punching arm. With a twist as his claws tear through the metal, Sax rips the construct's arm out of its socket.

Unfortunately, the Flaum's machine has a second arm, and it backs up its fallen partner, swiping down at Sax, whose ridden his victim limb to the floor. Lying flat on his back, Sax digs in with his talons and kicks, scooting himself out of the way of the hammer blow, towards the Flaum and its suit. When the Flaum's fist hits the floor, it splinters the chromed tiles like they're made of glass. What the fist doesn't do is stop Sax from planting his foreclaws on the ground behind his head and using the momentum and their leverage to flip himself up and over.

Sax flips onto the exo-suit's chest, with the Flaum getting a terrible view of Sax's talons. The Oratus commences tearing, aiming for any wires. Sparks fly and pop into Sax's mouth, each one stinging with victory. He feels the exo-suit slant to the side as the right leg loses power, and Sax is about to scale up and go for the pilot when something slams into the back of the exo-suit and tips it forward.

Sax can't get away—his claws are all caught mid-rend—and the whole suit falls on top of him, pinning the Oratus to the ground. The glass shield blocking the Flaum shatters, pressing the furry creature against Sax's torso as the Oratus tries to breath. The exo-suits, it turns out, are heavy, and Sax isn't in position to move it.

The pressure on Sax's vents is too intense; all his air's going away. Sax snaps at the exo-suit with his mouth, but it's a futile gesture—all that's there is metal, and there's no way he'll be able to get himself free before he suffocates, even if the mask keeps the weight from crushing his bones.

Of all the ways to die. Killed by a Flaum.

Heat burns through the exo-suit, and Sax feels the Flaum pilot eject itself, run through the metal cage that had been stabilizing that glass windshield. The heat, though, doesn't die away, and suddenly the exo-suit feels lighter, a clanging bang sounding through the hallway as its other arm drops away to the floor.

"C'mon you dumb Oratus," Agra-Red's voice carries. "I don't have enough power to cut the whole thing apart. Lift!"

A bit of inspiration can go a long way when it comes to strength. Sax takes the Whelk's prodding and pushes. The exo-suit moves slightly. All four claws, talons and tail, though, aren't enough to get himself clear. Still, that tiniest of spaces is enough for Sax to open his bruised vents and suck some much needed air.

"Can't!" Sax manages to hiss.

"Your pair's busy with the other two," Agra-Red counters. "You want her to die? No? Then get yourself going."

There's another blast of heat, and the foot of the exo-suit falls off near Sax's head. Those few kilograms, coupled with the adrenaline-fear for Bas and the breath of fresh air, give Sax enough motivation to try another heave. This time, rather than lifting the suit straight up, he goes for a squeeze, sliding himself along the floor as he tilts the suit ever-so-slightly. Just enough for him to slip out.

Enough for Sax to stand, look and see Bas leaning against the far wall, laughing, while the Whelk is shaking its head, its heavy assault miner glowing from its own heat.

"She told me you have to learn to be patient," Agra-Red burbles. "You're diving right in without playing the battlefield. You could have waited for me to burn down each of those things from a safe distance—or did you not notice they only had big clubs?"

Bas . . . watched him? Sax nearly died there. He looks at his pair, knowing frustration, betrayal's showing on his sharp, gray-scaled face.

"Stop it," Bas hisses when she notices. "You almost got yourself killed. Next time you go leaping in without thought, you might risk all of us."

"What was I supposed to do?"

"See the strategy!" Bas roars back. "Communicate with me, with our allies. Work as a team, for once."

Sax shakes his head. Teamwork? Bas is his pair. They *are* a team, always. He takes a breath, is about to tell her exactly what she can do with her suggestion, when Agra-Red wheels around and takes a pot-shot with its miner into the heavy door blocking their way forward.

"Anyone have an idea for this one?" the Whelk asks. "If you're all done with your relationship problems, I mean. Otherwise I'm happy to wait until the hordes descend upon us."

Sax has a usual method for getting through doors; namely, his claws and hacking and slashing with them until an opening presents itself. This door, as Sax discovers with a few trial swipes, is both chrome-plated and full of thick, reinforced metal. There's no way they're getting through.

A quick glance back down the wide corridor shows a bunch of Flaum heading their way—Cavignum's guards finally catching on and coming to defend their station. Which means there's only one way for them to go: up the ramps.

"Follow me!" Sax hisses, and starts off.

Once again, Bas gets to play carrier for the Whelk, hustling the gel creature as the two Oratus run and leap up the cargo ramps. The first jump brings Sax up to the slanted surface, then a couple of steps gets him to another corridor, similar to the first but instead of a soft orange glow from pulsing energy, this bears a blue tint from the translucent cables lining the hall—the power starting to pump into battery packs and outbound connections.

Coupled with the chrome, it's a beautiful array of colors shifting between the cold spectrum. One that Sax could watch for more than a second if doing so wouldn't result in him being turned to molten mush by a pack of angry guards.

There's one more ramp set, though, so Sax makes another leap, hearing the shriek of Bas's talons as they grip the metal behind him. Then they're at the top level, and here the light's a standard, dull yellow-white; the energy by this point refined to its usable level. And, like the lower levels, there's a door.

The difference? This one's open.

Standing next to the control panel, with a small miner pressed to a Flaum guard's head, is Plake.

"Took you long enough," Plake says. "Let's go."

"How?" Sax manages to ask.

"Everyone went chasing after you, so I made a friend here who told me which doors would be the last to lock in an emergency. So we came to this one, and once I heard your manic hissing, I figured you'd be coming my way."

There's plenty of noise coming as the guards make their way around and up the ramps, so Sax, Bas, and Agra-Red—whom Bas dumps on the ground as soon as they stop—dash through the door. Plake slips through after them, dragging her hostage with her, and tells the Flaum to shut and lock the door.

Then they take a look at what's around, and Sax's hearts fall.

Batteries stack in front of them, the sapphire ends of the piled cylinders indicating they're charged and ready for shipping. This section is a vast ring, one that starts its curl as Sax looks to the left and right, a curl that slowly shifts in color, the stacked batteries showing less charge as the ring goes 'round.

The walls behind the batteries are massed cables, shunting energy refined on prior levels from pure heat to the batteries meant to store them. Above, through what Sax assumes must be meter-thick glass, glows Cavignum's great orange ball. This close, Sax can make out the thin lines holding together the nano-netting meant to capture and contain the heat coming from Aspicis' core.

What this technological wonder doesn't have for them, though, is terminals. Wherever the control center might be, it's not here.

"We need the control center," Sax hisses at Plake's hostage.

The Flaum cowers at first, but finds its spine somewhere in its dark blue uniform. "You're three levels too high. It's underneath, where it's safer."

"Any good ideas on how to get there?" Agra-Red says to the hostage. "Think hard, cause your life depends on it."

And, given the sudden banging on the door behind them, their own might too.

"Think while we move," Bas says, a suggestion they act on.

Unlike the earlier corridors, though, the central battery ring isn't lined with doors. As they move, Sax catches the battery colors fading from blue to green, and eventually to yellow and still no exit. Finally, with only an endless chromed wall on their left and infinite batteries on their right, Sax hisses for them all to stop.

"Is there a way out of here?" Sax asks the hostage, who lets loose a chittering cackle.

"One way in and out," the Flaum says. "The batteries funnel up here, and then they're taken out the door we came in."

"Funnel up from where?"

The Flaum, though, shakes its head. Plake shoves the miner against its side, enunciates the threat with a deadly whisper, but the Flaum only replies with another brisk shake.

"Not telling you anymore," the Flaum says. "I'm going to die anyway for getting you this far."

"We're trying to help you all," Plake tries, shifting to diplomacy from her more aggressive means. "Taking down the Chorus is going to help the galaxy."

"That's what you think? That taking away the only security we've ever known is going to help us?" The Flaum chitters another weak laugh.

Sax tears the creature from Plake's grasp, tosses it down the ring, back the way they came. "We don't have time for this."

Plake takes a look towards the hostage, as if she's thinking about getting the Flaum back, but then the furry creature gets to its feet and starts to run. Plake raises the miner, then shakes her head, holsters it.

"Let's go," the Vyphen says. "Some people will never understand."

"They will, when we win," Agra-Red adds as they get back to their run around the ring.

It's not hard to find the funnel the hostage mentioned; it's a wide gap in the line of batteries, filled partly by chromed scaffolding and a lifting mechanism. A look down shows dead batteries being loaded far below by precise conveyors.

"It's a tight fit," Bas says, peering in.

"You see another way?" Agra-Red says. "Cause I don't, and I'm not wearing a mask, so I'd rather not get shot."

As if hearing the Whelk, the rapid pounding of feet on metal echoes around the ring. Agra-Red slimes its way closer to the gap, starts to look at how it can fit in there. Plake draws her miner, covers behind them, while Sax and Bas look the other way.

"Can you make it?" Plake asks the Whelk.

"Not a problem for a gooey thing like me," Agra-Red says. "You're tiny too, captain."

"Don't call me tiny."

"Facts are facts," Agra-Red replies. "As for the big monsters, don't know about you."

"Go," Sax hisses. "We'll figure it out."

Adding to the mystery, the rapid footsteps have stopped, seemingly just around the ring's bends. There's a heartbeat or three of nothing, then a very clear scratching of a heavy nail on metal. A sound Sax knows, because it's one he's been making this entire time.

"Leave," Sax says. "Now."

"Don't have to tell me twice," Agra-Red says, and the Whelk disappears down the gap, slipping and sliding its slimy self along the bars.

"Get through this alive," Plake says as she follows the Whelk. "Never thought I'd say this about a pair of claw-mongers, but we need you."

The Vyphen, winged arms fluttering, disappears, leaving Sax and Bas alone in the hallway. The scratches are coming, deliberately loud now. Sax uses the threat to take his own look down the battery gap.

There's no question—the Oratus, standing more than three meters tall, with thick tails, are never going to fit through there. Not unless Sax gets to carving a wider hole, and there's no time for that. There's no time for anything, anymore.

On either side of them, standing alone in the center of the corridor, are two mirrored Oratus'. Their scales reflect the batteries and white lighting, giving them a shimmering appearance, with their outlines showing slight distortions in what Sax can see. With their every move, the light bends and twists around them, so Sax can barely tell where the creature is, much less where it's going to be.

"Only two of you?" Sax hisses, looking at the one facing him, knowing Bas is doing the same to the one looking at her.

Their tails touch, ever so slightly.

"More than enough to deal with a couple of Vincere traitors," says his Oratus, and Sax recognizes the voice, the same one from the train station. "Where's the rest of your band?"

"I told them we didn't need their help to take care of you."

Kah hisses a laugh—unlike Sax's own, it's a strange thing, distorted and mechanical. These creatures might be alive, but they are designed just like the machines moving the batteries around them even now.

"At least you still have your confidence," Kah says. "But do you still have your intelligence? The Chorus has an offer for you: in exchange for what you know about your leader, Evva, and her plans, the Chorus is willing to send you back to your former post."

"Not going to happen."

"No? We have a lead on the Sevora homeworld, Sax. Come back to us now and you can still make it to the end of the war you've been fighting your entire life."

The Sevora homeworld? Sax wasn't sure that even existed—he'd resigned himself to finding the last of the little slugs on some drifting seed ship somewhere. How the Sevora had managed to keep an entire planet hidden this long . . .

No. That's not the point. He's not fighting that war any longer.

"I'm not fighting for the Chorus anymore," Sax says. "I'm fighting for our species. For the lives we deserve to lead."

Sax expects another laugh, or another offer. What he gets instead is a slight bow.

"I respect a warrior with a cause, even if they are a traitor to their own," Kah replies.

"Can you kill him already?" Bas whispers. "Every second we're talking here, Plake and Agra-Red are in danger down there."

A single mirrored Oratus nearly cost Sax his life. Now there's two, and Bas doesn't know what she's up against. And unlike the train station, there's no space for a miner standoff. It's going to be up close and brutal. Before Sax can give her any warnings, though, their enemies burst forward, striking with a long swipe of their sharp claws as they dart in.

With slight pressure on his tail, Sax knows which way Bas is going to go, and he leaps right, dodging the swipe and ending up against the ring's outer wall. Bas clings to the inside, hanging above the empty hole for the batteries, while the two mirrored Oratus sit in the middle, each one turning to face their respective target.

Sax catches Bas' eye from across the ring, and goes low. He launches himself from the outer ring, aims for the ground and catches the floor with his left foreclaw, then his left midclaw, pulling hard to whip his body and, more importantly, his tail around towards the two Oratus. Kah, watching Sax, sees the strike coming, but the one watching Bas is busy ducking from her own leap, her high strike. Sax's tail sweeps the other mirrored Oratus to the floor, while Bas slams Kah, who jumps to dodge Sax's tail. Bas tackles Kah from behind and drives him forward into the outer ring, her claws and mouth putting in work.

It's a mad scramble then, as Sax takes advantage of the downed mirrored Oratus, grabbing its shoulders as the creature tries to get up and, using his talons to grip the ground, wheels and launches the Oratus into the outer ring, next to where Kah has just shoved himself away from the wall. Kah's trying to pin Bas back to the ground, but

Bas disengages, sidesteps the push-back so that Kah stumbles with no resistance, allowing Bas' follow-up tail strike to slap Kah left across the face.

The blow pushes Kah towards Sax, who delivers a talon-kick to the mirrored Oratus' right knee, knocking Kah to a kneel, then Sax bites in with his left claws and funnels the mirrored Oratus into its companion, just peeling itself off the wall. The two of them collapse into a pile against the outer ring.

"I forgot how nice it is to fight with you," Sax hisses towards his pair.

"Because you're always going off on your own."

"I'm here now." Sax says the words as they both turn, claws ready, while the two mirrored Oratus extract themselves from each other. "Ready?"

Bas nods. Sax tenses to leap.

And the floor explodes beneath them.

Through the gateway is a deep red and violet section. At first, I think the light's a cause of some alarm we've set off, some Sevora security mechanism alerting anyone here that a pair of rogue specimens are loose.

Then I see the vines.

They're cased in huge tanks; glass enclosures that rise from the floor and halt well short of the ceiling, where each separate tank joins with its fellows to create one large space where the vines snarl and twist among each other, an occasional large, purple flower blooming out. The red and purple lights crisscross between the thick stalks, casting shadowed versions of the plant patterns on every surface.

"Look," Viera says, pointing her miner at the base of one of the tanks. Each one is lined with a silver basin, and each one is full—some have overrun their sides, spreading the deep purple liquid across the black-metal floor. "Nutrient goop. Seems like nothing in this galaxy eats real food."

For now, I'm happy not seeing Flaum. Even though this space is big enough to match the entertainment and residential sections combined, there's not a single Sevora running through towards us. No miner shots coming our way.

"If you're worried about food now . . ." I start, and Viera waves my words away.

"Just joking, Empress."

"Then let's keep moving. The Oratus have to be on the other side of this section."

I don't know for sure, of course, but it's a feeling. It's a hope. Which is all I have right now.

Walking beneath the giant plants, I find myself re-evaluating a little about the Sevora. They clearly don't hate all life, and they're cultivating food here for their hosts. They have an entertainment district, and places for their species to live that seem viable, if not luxurious.

If it wasn't for the whole 'take over your mind' aspect, I'd find the species similar to our own.

We're getting close to the end of the section when I feel a sudden burst of pain from my abdomen, right where Ignos stuck its spear. I press my miner-wielding left hand to the spot for a moment, and the feeling subsides.

Viera, though, notices. Her nervous eyes give something else away.

"What are you hiding?" I say.

Her eyes flick to my wound. "T'Oli asked me not to tell you. The Ooblot said half the treatment relies on the person believing they're going to be all right. I, for one, think it's better to know."

"Know what, Viera?"

"It's a patch, Empress. T'Oli's boosted you with something it called stim, it found a packet on one of the Sevora Flaum and said it would keep you together for a little while."

Her words clear things up. Viera didn't argue when I suggested Malo go with T'Oli. Even the Ooblot didn't put up much of a fight. They know Malo's going to need to rally humanity if we fail, not because I *might* die, but because I'm going to.

"How long do I have?"

"T'Oli didn't know. It's never done this to a human before." The dim light makes it hard to tell, but I think there might be tears in Viera's eyes. "It doesn't matter, Kaishi. Let's focus on the mission."

"Easy for you to say."

"No, it's not easy for me to say."

I believe her, and respect her, so I turn away from the conversation. Shove away thoughts of a fragile mortality and reach forward with my staff. Go one step and then another. If my life's ticking away, then I plan on making the last moments of it useful.

The next gateway, like the one we went through to get here, is open. And again it stands clear, without sentries. Either the Sevora that escaped Vimelia with us are not soldiers, or Ignos took the only ones who were.

"Or it's a trap," Viera says as we head up the crescent steps towards the entry.

"The last section had plenty of good spots for an ambush. If they'd wanted to kill us, they could have attacked then."

"Maybe they're waiting for the perfect moment."

"Maybe you're giving the Sevora too much credit. Haven't they been losing this war since it started?"

Viera concedes my point as we reach the top of the steps. Here would be the ideal spot for a stream of miner fire to cut us both down, but instead all we get is a great view of something I've seen before, though because this section is so empty, it takes me a moment to fit the memory to the place.

When we escaped Vimelia the first time—that I have to add that qualifier makes me shudder—we did it through poisoning a Sevora hosting center; a place for hosts to be given up and new ones gained. This new section spreads forth in white and blue, a hard change from the darker shades we're leaving behind, and the colors pair, illuminating various pools. Each one, whether lit in sky blue or white, has metal poles leading to and from it, the angles making it obvious which direction is preferred.

Almost all of the pools, though, are empty. Except one, right in the center.

"They're not hiding very well," Viera whispers.

A dozen Flaum and Whelk, including our escapee, surround the pool, the only one full of the inky liquid I've felt too many times on my own skin. Nearer to us, splayed out inside the Sevora ring and still, apparently, stunned is Lan. Gar is nowhere.

Which means the Oratus is probably beneath those purple waters.

All eyes are on the pool. Given how many fighters they've sent away towards us, I'm not all that surprised. Who could imagine a couple humans and an Ooblot would stand a chance against the almighty Sevora?

From here, though, neither side will be doing much destroying. Viera might be able to land a couple of shots this far away, but I'd probably hit Lan. Or shoot the ink and zap Gar. Instead, I gesture with the staff towards the only other things in the room; racks and racks of clothes, armor, and weapons.

What's the first thing a Sevora would want to do with their new host? Outfit them in the right gear.

There's hundreds of miners lining tall stacks, and dozens of hanging robes, vests, and shells clinging to hooks on spindly structures whose base struts sport control panels that, I'm sure, could rotate a preferred item to Flaum height. A central gap leads through to the pools, and it's what Viera and I stared down when we first entered the section. Now we form up on the left side of it, on the backside of a miner rack. Viera takes point, peeking around the corner.

"Gar's still not out," Viera whispers to me. "We have a chance."

"Then let's take it."

Strategy sits back and lets instinct run with our attack. Viera slides around the rack, lifts her miners and opens fire, red bolts blitzing off towards the Sevora pack. I follow, my left hand aiming, squeezing the trigger, and adding to the chaos without hitting a single soul.

But that's fine, because what our onslaught buys us is panic. The

Sevora try to scatter, but Viera's picking them off, or at least she is until one clips her with a return shot. My breath catches as the right side of Viera's chest burns, but my friend never stops shooting.

If she can fight through her pain, I can fight through mine.

One of the Flaum breaks to my left, heading towards one of the empty pools and fires wildly along the way. I set my staff on the metal floor, brace my arm against it, and rest the miner on my right forearm. The Flaum reaches the next set of railings as I settle my sights, and the Sevora's choice to scramble over rather than dive under gives me the target I'm looking for.

This time, I'm blasting red. This time, I strike true.

Viera pushes me to the side and we both tumble behind a line of hanging battle suits not unlike the one Viera's wearing—all different sizes, all looking artificial and stiff.

"Are you all right?" I push myself back from Viera, keeping my eyes hunting for movement. I don't know how many Sevora are left, or whether they'll try to attack us, but I'd rather not die for lack of attention.

"I might be joining you in death's corner," Viera says, and there's plenty of tight pain in her voice. "But I'm not there yet."

"Then why did you push us?" I settle onto my chest, ignore the cutting sting my abdomen gives me, and aim beneath the vests. There's feet moving out there, looking like they're circling around us. Between the clothes we're next to and the rigid miner rack to our right, it'd be easy to trap us. "I'm counting at least four of them left."

"Because we were about to get torched." Viera gets up to her knees, still holding miners in both hands. "Setting your staff and standing still isn't the way to survive a firefight, Kaishi."

"Shooting the air isn't going to help either."

"Then go for the Oratus and leave the Sevora to me."

I'm a little surprised at the heat in her voice. The stress. She thinks I need taking care of, watching over. Heat hits my face as I realize here, well, she's right. I'm not going to be much help, but I can, at least, take care of myself.

"They're all yours." I crawl beneath the vests, get to the other side, and with the clothes hanging above me I set the miner against the ground and pop off a couple shots at the only Flaum I can see.

I miss, striking the white-washed far wall and leaving burned circles as evidence of my spectacularly bad shooting.

The Flaum raises its own miner, and I reach up with my staff, snag a pair of the vests and pull as the Sevora gets ready to shoot. The clothes fall over me as the bolts slam in, the heat sifting through to my right shoulder but not quite getting to my skin.

Chitters and screeches echo from elsewhere in the section, so at least Viera's doing work while I hide beneath the vests. Hoping, waiting . . . and there it comes, the telltale clacking of claws on metal as the Flaum comes closer. The vests laying over me shift as the Flaum pulls at them, and as soon as the last one goes, as soon as I see the furry face peering at me, I fire.

Turns out even I can hit at this range.

Lan looks untouched, still and perfect on the floor, her green scales glittering against the white tiles. Her eyes are open, and they track me as I walk up. Before I left the clothing cover, I waited until the shots died down, until the squeaking shouts stopped, and until Viera wandered back into view, her eyes casting about with her miners following.

"She's still alive?" Viera asks me—she's keeping away from the Oratus, staying where she can cover both the gateway into this section and the spaces between the other racks.

"Still alive."

"You can't tell if she's infected, can you?"

"Because I had one in me once?" I crouch down next to Lan, look hard into those eyes. "No, I have no idea."

"It would be easier now, you know," Viera trails off.

Execute Lan before she gets her potentially possessed self back. It makes sense, if you're heartless. Or hurt, tired, and fighting for survival.

"No." I straighten, turn to the pool. "We're not giving up that easily."

I expect Viera to protest, but she just wheezes out a laugh. "You never really change, Kaishi."

Any reply I'm thinking of goes away when the pool shows signs of life. The deep purple-black ink shifts, ripples going towards the edges. I back away, and briefly consider dragging Lan with me, but my wounded self issues a pang, so I leave the stunned Oratus where she is. Viera levels her miners towards the water.

"Don't wait," I say. "As soon as it's obvious Gar's taken, you have to kill him."

"No sympathy for this one?"

"Not this time."

Lan's still a question. A hope for the future. I know Oratus can be controlled by Sevora, and if Gar's been down there for that long, he's probably well in the hand of whatever parasite won the lucky lottery to take his mind.

A pair of thin claws appear over the edge, their points biting into the floor and leaving silvery scratches. Then a head. Gar's. Eyes open and blazing as the ink drips off of his scales.

"Stop," I shout to him. "Come up any further and we'll shoot."

"Then what am I supposed to do?" Gar hisses. It sounds like him, but Sevora don't change a host's voice. "Hang here forever?"

It's a sudden riddle—how am I supposed to determine whether a Sevora's inside of Gar? Is there a giveaway? Ignos could dig into my mind, my memories, and build up a knowledge of humanity. There's not a question I could ask that would give it away. I had hoped some plan would come to mind, that there'd be an obvious way, but I can't think of one.

So I go with the only sure thing I have.

"Viera, stun him."

The Lunare doesn't give any tics or tells, doesn't announce her shot with some battle cry or flourish, but Gar explodes out of the pool, leaping high enough that Viera's shots skate by beneath the Oratus.

But the gravity that gave Gar the boost betrays him now—the fall back is slow, and the Oratus is helpless in the air. Viera slides her weapons up, aims, pulls the triggers.

They click. Harmlessly.

"Viera?" I say.

"I knew I was getting low—you're up!" Viera says to me, then turns and starts back towards the other rack of miners.

I think mine still has power, and level the miner as Gar hits the ground. My shot goes, but Gar twists on those talons and I miss to his right, over the pool and into the section's back wall. I think Gar's going to come for me, but instead the Oratus darts towards Viera.

"Watch out!" I yell, stitching a line of blue bolts behind Gar and cursing myself the entire time.

Then Gar's gone from my view, down that center line. I get there with my staff, in time to see Gar catch Viera as she pulls miners from the rack. In time to see those claws dig into Viera's armor and launch her, flailing, across the section until she slams into the wall above the gateway we came through.

Gar turns to me, then. Stares my way, his mouth spreading in a razor grin.

"You're not Gar," I say, aiming the miner straight at the Oratus.

"But you know me, Empress of the humans," Gar replies, his hissing voice a rasp.

"I do?"

"I invited you into my home, once," Gar replies. "A home that you tried to destroy when we offered you peace. Now, we will go to yours and take what you would not give."

Jel. The Sevora leading the faction opposite to Nasiya, someone Ignos said was also on the ship. Of course, Jel's rank would give it first choice of new hosts.

"We should've killed you back on Vimelia." I fire the miner again.

This time I hit. Strike and burn into Gar's chest. The Oratus stumbles, but Jel keeps Gar on his feet. I try again, but, like Viera's, my miner clicks. Nothing, and I can't get past Jel to the miner rack.

The Oratus is stumbling towards me, Gar's right side twitching and dragging as Jel keeps the body moving.

I'm hurt, I don't have a miner, but I do have a staff.

"Your species is a mistake," Jel rasps through Gar's mouth as the Oratus comes towards me. "You were meant as a cure to our 'problem', but the Amigga failed. You saw Ignos. We learned how to take your kind, and we will take all of you."

"You tried that already." I shift the staff to both hands, holding it across my body. "You failed."

If Jel is crushed by my words, the Sevora and its Oratus host don't show it. Instead, Jel leaps at me, four clawed arms set wide, as if the goal is to crush me in a sharp, deadly hug. I can't match the Oratus for strength, I'm not faster, so I set my legs and jab the staff forward, trying to keep those nasty claws away from me.

Jel simply barrels through the charge, grabbing my staff and pushing me back until I trip and fall to the floor. Me, the staff, and a looming Oratus mouth, all teeth and leering anger. Jel hisses low and slow, giving me the full glimpse of my soon-to-be-doom.

All I can think of doing is buying time. Hoping that Lan or Viera will get up and fight. Even if I die, that one of them will finish Jel off.

So I push the staff between us. Fix my arms against its gray-metal line and interrupt Jel's snapping mouth. Until Jel bites the staff and snaps it in two. The bite comes through hard, and for a second the Oratus is right up against my face, Gar's smooth scales rubbing my skin.

In my hands, though, I now have two pieces. Two jagged pieces, and a target in the right place. I might not be all that strong in the galaxy's scale, but now, with all the desperation and anger and fear pulling me tight as a spring, I push and send each pointed fragment into Gar's head. Where those small dents, those tiny ear cavities, and a Sevora sit.

Jel jerks back, hisses loud and long, stumbles for a moment, and then collapses to the floor, snapping off one of the fragments while the other sticks up in the air like a terrible grave marker.

An instant of free-fall through a cloud of fire and rubble, a moment where Sax's stomach tries to leap out of his body, where he's thankful the mask keeps the shards of fracturing metal from stabbing into his vents and eyes, and then Sax hits the ground.

The mask can't blunt all the discomfort of landing on rubble, and Sax turns himself mid fall so his right fore- and midclaws suffer the brunt of the impact, but the explosion gives Sax the adrenaline he needs to push past the pain and force himself up with a swish of his tail and a dig from his talons.

Sax's first glance confirms Bas is alive and picking herself out of her own pile of cables and chromed floor tiles. His second looks for the source of the explosion and finds Plake and Agra-Red near a wide door leading out of the room. They're staring, though Sax finds Agra-Red's heavy miner aimed up towards the ceiling, suspicious.

The mirrored Oratus, though, didn't fall. The hole in the floor collapsed the center of the battery ring above, but left the edges for their enemies to peer over.

"We going to run, or you want to wait for those things? I didn't detonate those batteries for nothing." Agra-Red says.

"They were going to lose." Sax barely holds himself back, keeps his claws at his sides. "We had them."

"Probably a trap," Agra-Red shakes off Sax's glare. "You don't fight a mirrored Oratus. You run."

"Next time, leave us."

"This time, we're going. Now." Plake issues the order, and with the mirrored Oratus above apparently checking their wounds, Sax decides to follow it.

"Remember the mission," Bas hisses as she comes up behind him.

Why does that phrase keep getting in the way of his fun?

Beyond the battery room, it's clear they've entered a different part of Cavignum. No longer over the flowing energy source, the floors bear a design less suited for heat and more for pleasure; curling green and purple lines mimicking Aspicis' landscapes cover the floor, and the walls, between doors, are broken up with pictographs that Sax recognizes as sights from around the galaxy; various planets, highlights from the realms the Chorus controls.

"I'd almost call it beautiful if I didn't know what it represented," Plake says as they move.

Theoretically, they'll find some indication of the control room, but Sax isn't seeing anything other than locked doors with blaring red lights. A low-tone alarm starts up too, declaring Cavignum under lockdown. That it's taken whomever runs this place this long to call their insertion an emergency tells Sax just how confident they are in their forces.

Not that Sax hasn't proved a lot of people wrong on that bet.

"It's still beautiful," Bas replies. "We're not trying to destroy this place—if we take down the Chorus, this planet, this galaxy is still going to need Aspicis."

"They can have it," Agra-Red, sliming its way along the ground, says. "This planet is garbage."

As if hearing the Whelk's insult, the lights in the corridor flicker and die, plunging them into an absolute darkness. Sax flicks the mask over to night vision and scans back and forth. Finds the reason why.

The doors they've passed are opening, with Flauma and other species breaking into the corridor and running back the way they came.

Evacuating the hostages. The alarm blots out the sounds of footfalls, and there's no talking.

"Stop for a second," Sax says. He's not interested in the fleeing workers, but rather in the rooms they left behind. "Form up."

"You going to guide us?" Plake asks. "Because Vyphen can't see in the dark."

"Hold on to Bas' tail," Sax says.

He'll die before he lets the Vyphen hold onto his body. Bas gets it, releases a quick laugh, but doesn't argue. She knows Sax too well.

It's a quick sprint down the hallway and into the first open room on the right. The lights are still out, but the doors opening means Cavignum's not entirely without power. Terminals in the room still glow, and they're showing the kinds of graphs that make Sax think this is one of the places that controls the flow from beneath the surface.

Not what he cares about, but terminals are flexible.

Plake catches the idea too—which is good, as Sax has about as much trust in his own ability to use a foreign terminal as he does in Plake's chances one-on-one with a mirrored Oratus. While the Vyphen sets to work, Sax sets up watch at the door, taking the occasional chance to spook passing species with a low hiss.

Other doors along the hallway are open now too, with more and more staff streaming away. Sax could reach out and tear them apart. They shrink away from him as they pass by, running quick. A calculated gamble—Sax and the others haven't made a point of attacking random civilians, but they've caused plenty of destruction. Get out, save some lives.

Sax almost respects the Amigga running this place—he's sure there's one of the orb-like monsters here somewhere: saving lives always seems to be their last concern.

"Found it!" Plake announces with a thrilled bubble. "Close to here actually. Just down the hall, on the left." There's a pause, long enough for Sax to turn his head, about to ask why they aren't moving. "And Bas was right. It's in the center—only the center's not where the hole comes up."

"Great," Bas says. "Can we go?"

Plake gives the affirmative and they're back in the hallway. The remaining staffers turn and run back the other way at the sounds of Sax loping towards them, vanishing into side rooms where nobody cares to follow them. Eventually they make it to the door, the only one still locked shut.

"You have another battery bomb?" Sax asks the Whelk, knowing full well the creature has nothing.

"If any of you'd thought to grab another miner, I could make one," Agra-Red shoots back. "This thing packs a punch, but there's no way it's getting through a thick, heat-shielded door like this."

Sax places a claw against the door. It's hard, well-forged and constructed to stand against even normal Oratus claws. Then again, he doesn't have normal Oratus claws, not anymore.

"Cover me," Sax says, and gets to work.

The first scratches don't seem to make a dent—it's hard to tell in the dark if he's making any progress. One swipe, two, three and all Sax is wondering is whether his claws are going to break off, when there's a sudden change in tenor, a strike knocks off a long strip of the door's protective shell.

And his next swing bites. Tears off a good chunk of the metal.

"Finally found something you're good at," Plake says.

Sax doesn't get to reply. The hallway's lights come on bright and blinding, causing Sax to stumble back from the door, which works out well as the space he's been standing suddenly fills with red laser.

Apparently breaching the control room is a step too far for Cavignum's security, as they've sent a squad of Flaum—and Sax catches the telltale shimmer of the mirrored Oratus behind them—to the hallway, which they're now filling with deadly laser.

Agra-Red takes a couple of return shots as Bas hammers her weight and claws at a less-protected door on the opposite side of the hallway. A few swipes at the thin barrier and it breaks in, allowing the four of them to tumble inside the side room. Sax earns himself some burns, largely deflected by his increasingly-damaged mask, as the prize for last one inside.

"Nice choice," Plake says as they get a better look inside.

It's a break room. There are a couple of tables, a scattering of chairs, a large wall-screen showing some sort of local Aspicis news which currently features a meticulously groomed Flaum talking over an aerial shot of . . . Cavignum.

"We're famous," Agra-Red gives a hopeless, warbling laugh. "Never thought I'd die with a billion eyes watching."

"Not dead yet," Sax hisses, looking back out the door, across the hallway towards where they need to be. "If I can get another two or three swings in, I can open that door."

"You'll be charred slag before you get one." Plake doesn't offer a better solution, instead staring at the broadcast. "Are you all seeing this? They're saying repair crews are waiting outside as soon as this place is secured."

"Isn't that normal?" Sax offers.

"It's the solution for the Teven," Plake says. "We just need to make sure they're in that crew, then get out of here."

Before the glimmer-worm prison, they'd had communicators. They could've called Nobaa and Engee and told them the plan. Now, though, all Sax has is the mask, and its narrow-band wave isn't going to carry his words more than a few dozen meters.

The break room doesn't have any of those devices around either, but it does have a single terminal connected to Aspicis' global network and, beyond that, the galaxy at large. It's a small screen, and Bas looms large over it, her claws tapping away at the icons as they appear.

"I can reach them through this," Bas says. "Buy me a minute."

Sax knows how he can buy her several. He heads back to the doorway, peeks his head out of the hallway to see the security squad advancing towards them. A quick burst of miner fire has Sax ducking himself back inside as bolts strike the frame and ceiling around his head.

"Trying to get yourself killed?" Agra-Red, set up with its miner behind Sax. "How's that going to help?"

"Shut up." Sax hisses, then sticks a single foreclaw out, waves it up and down. "I have an offer!" Sax roars this loud enough to carry into the hallway.

When nothing tries to incinerate his waving hand, Sax tries sticking his head out again—at a different height than before, just in case—and he sees that the two mirrored Oratus have taken spots at the head of the Flaum column, with the furry creatures holding their miners ready behind them.

"What is your offer?" Kah asks. "Know that you have no other escape, and we could easily kill you should we choose."

"That didn't go so well for you last time." Sax steps into the middle of the hallway.

He's an easy target here, but he's hoping giving himself up is going to buy Bas the time she needs to send the message to the Teven. It also gets him closer to the control room door; even if this tactic fails, Sax figures he can get in one or two good swats before the mirrored Oratus or the Flaum burn him down.

That'll have to be good enough.

"Regardless," Kah says, and Sax likes the annoyance in its hissing tone. "Give yourselves up. Aspicis and its energy shouldn't suffer for your cause."

"I want the lives of my friends guaranteed," Sax says. "They should be allowed to leave Cavignum. This was my idea, and I made them do it."

Kah laughs and it echoes up and down the hallway. "Your idea? Sax, we have your records. You're not a mission planner, a commander. You're a set leader, a weapon made to carry out the tasks of those above you. Don't act like we're stupid."

Sax stiffens his spine. They're right, of course. Sax is a weapon. He's never been much of a bluffer anyway.

"Sent it," Bas hisses softly from the room to his left.

"So is that a no?" Sax asks Kah.

"We'd much rather have you dead," Kah says, stepping to the side of the hallway.

As the words come out of the Oratus' mouth, Sax lunges towards the control room door. Gets a strong swipe in that tears the uncoated metal to shreds. Flashes fill the hallway, and Sax expects, even as he continues flinging his claws, to get torched, but the fire doesn't come. There's plenty of flashes in his peripheral, and a couple glancing hits send burning pain up his side, but Sax lives.

"Keep cutting you big lizard," Agra-Red cackles from behind him. "I've got them ducking for now, but they'll find their spines someday!"

Sax gets in another slash, then another, until the door is a series of metal ribbons. He raises his claws again when something very heavy crashes into him from behind, breaking Sax through the remaining strips of metal and rolling them both into the control room.

"Couldn't stay away from you any longer," Bas hisses as she scrambles off of him, towards the big bank of terminals.

There are dozens of the screens in the big, empty space, along with chairs and netting to keep various species assigned to monitor them comfortable. Even the ceiling sports a projected, swirling display showing the current core temp of Cavignum. It is, as expected, very, very hot.

"Don't touch anything!" It's the monotoned voice of an Amigga, translated through its intercoms.

This one, an amber color and looking like a dried out piece of old fruit, sits in a chair at the room's far end. It's not so much a suit as a cradle, and Sax can't see a single weapon on it.

"If you destroy the wrong thing, then this whole plant could explode," the Amigga pleads. "Not only would you kill yourselves, but many, many more on Aspicis could die."

"Maybe that's what we want?" Bas says, her claws hovering over the screens.

"If so, then there's nothing I can do to stop you," the Amigga says. "But I refuse to believe Oratus would commit themselves to a mission of pure destruction with no other end. We did not fail so badly with your species."

Sax wants to strike the creature down for those words, but a yelp of Whelk-pain from the hallway reminds him they don't have much time here. Agra-Red's miner will run out of power eventually, and then they'll be swarmed.

Yet, they need to damage this place somehow, if Nobaa and Engee are going to have an excuse to come here as part of the repair crew. So Sax turns and slashes at the screens of the terminals. Cuts the glass, shreds the housing, but leaves the inside alone. Bas gets it, does the same to the screens next to hers.

"What are you doing?" the Amigga asks. "Please, don't cut too deep!"

"Find us a way out of here," Sax says. "Or we will destroy everything."

The Amigga has no eyes. No visible senses whatsoever, but Sax gets the sense that the creature is staring at him, trying to decide if the Oratus is serious.

"We've made our message," Bas adds. "Shown that we can strike anywhere, if the Chorus doesn't give in to our demands. Let us leave, and you'll keep your station."

Lying. Bas is so much better at it than Sax is, and her reasoning shoves the Amigga towards action. The creature's suit buzzes, and suddenly its voice blares out of speakers from everywhere.

"Hold your fire!" the Amigga shouts. "Allow the intruders to leave, or they'll obliterate Cavignum entirely."

The command does its job, and Agra-Red's shooting halts a second later.

"They'll escort you to an exit," the Amigga says. "Please, don't damage anything else. You've made our lives difficult enough."

"We don't care," Sax replies, though he doesn't move. "Bas, go with them."

His pair hesitates, looks at Sax. "What?"

"The only reason we're getting out of here at all is because these threaten the entire station," Sax says. "I stay, they won't hurt you. If we all leave, they'll take us the moment they've secured this room."

Her look only lasts a moment but it's a moment Sax holds constant in his mind as Bas sweeps out of the room, as she takes Agra-Red and Plake with her through some combination of passageways and out into the jungles of Aspicis.

Those pink-gold scales around her golden eyes. Sax saw in them the acceptance, the understanding of the mission. That it comes first.

Except, here, it didn't. Sax made the offer, Sax gave himself up not for the mission, but for her, because nothing else matters.

I wait, at first. Simply lie there with my head propped up and watch the body. Jel must be getting back up. It can't be dead. I've never seen an Oratus fall, aside from Sax's surprise blasting on *Cobalt* courtesy of Coorvin, the station's captive Flaum. Mostly, I can't believe I'm the cause.

Around me, the section buzzes. The ship hums. These throngs, the vibrations, are new. As if the Sevora ship is coming to life around me. Ignos said it would take time to get the seed ship up and running again. That it would happen gradually as the chosen one, the Sevora elected to helm the ship, began to merge with the craft itself.

The noises, though, remind me that we're not done yet. So I pick myself up, slow and gradual, first to my knees, and then to my hands —palms flat against the tile—before with a last push I get to a sturdy stand. Gar is still down. No motion. I look back towards Lan, and she's twitching. Her claws beginning to flex, her tail swishing ever so slightly.

Gar is her pair. What happens when an Oratus' pair dies?

I can't answer that question so I move past Gar's body and beyond. Past the racks of vests and clothes, past the weapons all neat and glistening. Ready for a war that I hope is over. Along the way I see the bodies of Viera's earlier victims. I would want anything than to be on the other end of her rage.

They're all down, all of them. Smoking, motionless.

But then, so is she. Viera lies flat on the ground, sprawled out, but breathing. There's a gash on the side of her head, turning some of her white hair pink, matting it. Her left arm hangs at an odd angle away from her body. And her eyes are shut as I get close and kneel down.

"Can you hear me?" I said to her. "Viera?"

I get nothing from her, so I set about tearing strips from her the robes she's wearing beneath the armor and making bandages. I don't want to move her arm, because I don't know what's wrong with it, so I do the best I can get her turned over. Staunch the bleeding, and lay her back down. I look back across the section, making sure nothing else is moving, and see I'm still the only one up.

Which means I'm the last one of us. Which means it's up to me to stop the seed ship.

First, I go back to the weapons rack. Take a pair of miners, take up the short half of the staff that popped out of Gar's head when he fell. And then I go. One miner slung across my back, the other in my left hand with my right wielding my half staff and using it as a crutch when I have to.

I go back to the ring, which feels emptier than ever before. For a hot second, I think about going back, finding the docking bay, Malo and T'Oli. We might be able to escape, the three of us. But no, that would only delay what needs doing.

I have to stop the Sevora. For Viera, Gar, Lan and all the others.

So I orbit the ring and walk beneath those glistening seeds pointed down like daggers over my head. I breathe steadily cleaner air as recyclers, newly activated, cleanse the ship of the musk of what must have been years and years of floating here abandoned in the black, waiting to be called upon. The last hope of an evil race.

I find my goal on the far side of the ring, near where the Sevora had nearly fought each other earlier. When Nasiya claimed its right to the center of the ship.

The silver walkway across the ring leads to a wide, square door in the deep gray central core. A door that Ignos said would be sealed. A one-way crossing for the Sevora that would give its life for the rest of its species.

"I guess you're too slow," I mutter, taking my first step on the walkway. Around me, beneath me, the ring extends down into the black void of space. I can see it all, infinite. It makes me dizzy for a moment and some part of me feels like I should just take a jump. Glide down and out and forget all of this.

And maybe I would have, except the walkway shakes. Something starts a process which cannot be undone. Behind me, at the edge of the ring, the walkway begins to recede. Pull back towards the center. I move. Hustle across the metal towards the door with no control panel. One that may not open, that may leave me stranded on a vanishing edge.

So as I stumble forward, the pain in my sides keeping me from moving too fast, I aim with my left hand, flip the miner to the third mode, one Viera showed me once but that I've never used. The trigger on the miner is light, built for smaller Flaum hands. When I press it, instead of scattered shots the miner bursts forth its energy in a solid beam as I run, racing my own plummeting doom towards the door.

The pattern I sketch, the opening I roast is not pretty. It's not large. But the elongated oval is enough, its edges burning orange with heat, for me to fall through and land on the inside. I've arrived right where I never thought I'd be. In the heart of my enemy.

It's a strange look, when I stand up. Pick myself from the floor and stare as, behind me, the thin door I cut through is replaced by slamming outer plates. A seal too thick for any miner to ever pierce. In front of me is a tall, black, walled cylinder. It's perfectly rounded, smooth. Without any way in that I can see.

I walk around the outside. Looking for an entrance and finding only what must be bins for nutrient goop, for food and drink. There are links to pipes coming from above, narrow and slight. Too small for anyone to sneak through. Except maybe another Sevora.

What I also find, though, is a total lack of an entrance. There's no door, no control panel. No waving flag saying here, here is what you're seeking. In the absence of all that, with only the thrum of the ship for company, and feeling so alone, I collapse against the outer wall and sit. One miner in my left hand, my short staff in my right, and my second miner looped over my shoulder harness. Armed, dangerous, hurt and pointless.

"What would you do?" I ask the air. I ask Viera, Malo.

Viera would probably just start shooting. Claim that there's no reason to fret as long as you have energy. As long as you can burn your way through. Who knows if that wall can be penetrated by a simple handheld miner? Who knows what's on the other side? If I burn through all my energy here, what happens? Would Nasiya simply tear me limb from limb? Could I beat a Flaum controlled by one of the most vicious Sevora with only my staff?

Malo might be more strategic. Hunt around for another way, but I didn't find anything obvious and I'm running out of time. I can feel it, as Viera promised I would; T'Oli's temporary cure is starting to fade. The pain's only increasing, and the edges of my toes and my fingers are growing weaker, more numb. I have to end this, and I have to do it quickly.

And T'Oli? What would the Ooblot do? Rattle off some facts about . . . No, wait. I look at my left wrist. It's right there, the answers I need. So I take what's left of my weakened spirit and send it into the Cache. Dig its depths to find the seed ship, and how I can destroy its core.

The answer is simpler than I'd realized: The central Sevora is protected by the main core walls. The only thing that's going to bring them down is a great force or, if necessary, provisions. The need for food and water, especially early, when the Sevora is still maturing. That's it. All I need to do is make sure the food arrives, and those walls will come down for me.

I leave the Cache and its emerald flash, and hope that Ignos' gift to me will be the end of its species. I stand and go back to the basin with the little pipes leading to it. Next to them is a small panel with only a very simple request. A green button covering the entire screen. I press it and there's a rumbling, a whooshing noise as deep purple sludge begins to drop from the pipe and into the bottom of the basin, collecting into a puddle. A trap being set by the Sevora's own ship.

I hear it then. The clicking, winding and whirring of gears out of sight. The black walls slide down one after another as I turn to see what a Sevora finally given a chance to grow looks like.

A younger me, more naive, would have screamed. Would have run at the sight of this thing in front of me. That it was a Flaum is evident, but it, very much, is no longer one. The furry body stands at a set of terminals and, springing from that fur, as if pores had opened into new life, stringy red and yellow and green tentacles arc up and down, clinging to the computers, lodging into spaces beneath the Flaum and the grated floor it stands on. Yet, the Flaum still lives. I see it tapping away, I see it breathing and I see those blood red eyes turn towards me as the walls finish descending.

"The human," Nasiya says. It's a voice far from the squeaky skitters of a normal Flaum and trending more towards a scratchy broken noise. Like a person in the morning after a too late night with too little water to drink. Muscles frayed and at the end of their purpose.

"Yeah, I am human," I say. "And I'm here to stop you. To stop your species. To stop this war."

"I don't care why you're here. I just care that you die." Nasiya punctuates the reply by stepping back from the terminals.

As the Flaum moves, the tentacles coming out of its arms and back and shoulders quiver and withdraw, until they arrange around the Nasiya's Flaum like a halo of scraggly hair. It's strange, but I'm too angry, too tired and hurting to be scared anymore.

I aim the miner and fire.

A long bolt of energy launches forth—I realize I forgot to switch the weapon from its single-beam setting—and cascades into the set of terminals next to Nasiya. The screens and their metal housings burn, exploding in sparks and raining fire across the central cylinder. My shot gets to Nasiya, who growls a hoarse, low noise as I leave a black burning scar across its chest, and heads towards me. But the Sevora has weakened its own host, and the Flaum lurches, stumbles even as those tentacles head my way. Even as my miner sputters out of power.

I use the basin and push myself to the side, continuing around the ring as Nasiya lurches out of its grated home after me. For every step the Flaum takes, its tentacles move even faster. They seem to be growing too, chasing after me like weeds reaching along the ground in my direction. With my left hand, I drop the dead miner and swing my shoulder, pulling my backup weapon around my chest where I catch it even as my right hand and the short staff keep me up and stumbling away from the creature.

"Stop and fight," Nasiya says behind me.

"It's not my fault you're slow," I reply. I give the miner a quick glance to make sure it's going to fire the quick bursts of bolts, and twist. I plant my feet and turn, ignoring the sting of pain that I'm so used to already, and pull the trigger. Hold it tight as red bolts stitch across the inside of the chamber.

Most miss as Nasiya crouches, but a pair strike its body, burn holes into its shoulders and Nasiya falls forward. But the tentacles don't stop. They wrap on my legs, crawl up my calves and over my knees and I swipe at them with my staff. A pair of green tendrils latch on to the gray metal stick as I strike, and while they don't pull it away, they stop its momentum. I have to let go to get my hand back, to push away another set of yellow vines getting close to my throat. I kick and push, but can't get away from the things as they multiply, seeming to come from everywhere and cover me like a net.

They're at my neck now. In a second they'll get to my eyes, my mouth, or choke the life out of me. I do the only think I can think of: aim the miner lower and pepper more bolts, more hot red, into Nasiya's body. Into the Flaum until it catches fire.

The tentacles climb over the bottom of my chin, I feel them in my hair, around my neck.

Now, finally, I scream. But it's not fear. It's anger, determination, desperation all coming out because I'm holding that trigger and I'm shooting my enemy. Not for me, but for my friends, for my species, for this galaxy that has apparently suffered so much at the hands of these evil creatures.

I just want it to end.

And even as the tendrils use the scream to climb into my open mouth, it does.

Nasiya has no final battle cry. There's no grand proclamation, no evidence of my triumph other than the harsh crackle of flames and the smell of liquefying flesh as the tendrils begin to shrivel black. They die away and I spit them out of my mouth, brush them from my legs and back and stare at what had once been the leader of the Sevora. At the last remnant of a species so hated by so many.

"Viera, Malo, I did it," I say to myself. There's no one else here. There's only me, trapped inside the central core. Any terminal I might use is burned and broken.

So instead I make my way to the basin of nutrient goop. Try a bit of the substance just to get the taste of Nasiya's tentacles out of my mouth. As my body gets looser, as the pain grows and my eyes start to water, as every breath gets harder than the last I press myself against the wall and watch as the Sevora's last fire burns out.

They stun him, of course. Barge into the control room with miners firing and they don't stop until Sax is a burned, disabled husk on the floor. Kah tears away Sax's mask, pausing only to sneer and offer up some insults at Nobaa's metal patches. Then they pick Sax up and haul him away.

Sax gets the whole experience fed to him like a dream; it's a series of blurry images as what's left of his senses struggle to piece together the scrambled feed. There's a mag-lev train in the basement of Cavignum that he's brought to, both mirrored Oratus taking point on his escort. They clear a whole car for Sax, giving the Oratus the most prized ride he's ever had on a transport.

The train shoots fast through the endless nighttime vine forest, and the inside is lit only in the low blues of a deep ocean, as their attack on Cavignum apparently carried into sleep cycle time. Not that anyone in Sax's car—except, maybe, Sax himself—gets any.

So everyone sees the Meridia as it comes into view. To say that the Meridia is a shaft of light would be too simplistic; it's a living space, a fortress, and a center of public governance all in one. There's all manner of blinking lights, yes, but each one sends a different message: the constellations of steady red mark countermeasure turrets, the wider, broader whites and yellows give hints to residents, while greens and blues illuminate docking spaces for messenger drones, small ships, and more.

The other defining feature of the Meridia is that, from the ground, there doesn't appear to be a top. The atmosphere and darkness of space beyond muddle away the definition of the construct well before it actually ends, like a mountain vanishing into clouds. As such, to Sax, it's as if the horizon's been split by an ax, rising thick and strong from the surface.

Like parasites clinging to the host, there's a vast city surrounding the Meridia, with plenty of other buildings shooting high and always, always looking miniature next to the galaxy's premiere structure. These, too, glitter in the night, and their lights peek in through the train windows or shine up from beneath as the track passes overhead.

The train isn't the only thing moving in the skies either—despite the apparent hour, skiffs, shuttles, and ships maxing out the limits for atmospheric entry clog the skies above the buildings, though again the Meridia acts like a filter, with only a few allowed to slip within the mandated perimeter.

The train isn't one of them, and it slides into a massive, slab-like station near, but not too close, to the Meridia's base. Sax, numbed again with a couple more courtesy stuns, is loaded onto a waiting cargo sled and, with the two mirrored Oratus continuing their escort, walked along a broad avenue towards the Spire.

Sax doesn't think his eventual end-point is all that high in the Meridia, but without windows, it's hard to tell. He's shuffled into a room, lowered through a ceiling to a cell, which is where his escort finally leaves him.

The Oratus doesn't bother moving—he knows what's coming, he's seen it plenty of times before; when the Chorus decides, Sax will have a simple death, sent out across the galaxy, to mark the end of yet another futile attempt to change the set course of the universe.

. . .

*Read on for an excerpt from* The Last Cycle, *the conclusion to the* Skyward Saga, *and find more adventures with Black Key Books:*

The first priority in a new, hostile space is target identification, followed by target elimination. Sax figures his death is imminent, and making that death expensive is the best move he's got.

The ring around his waist keeps Sax moving until he's closer to the level's ceiling, which leaves his talons a meter off of the floor. Without leverage, all Sax can do is wave his tail around, and when he sees his target, he stops. A single tail whip isn't going to do much to the mirrored Oratus waiting with a miner drawn and ready to deliver an instant execution.

"I beat you already, didn't I?" Sax hisses at the Oratus, whose scales would blend in more fully with the light, but whose recent scars leave long lines of puckered red and pink through his reflective coating.

Sax gave Kah those scars, and it's always fun to remind your enemies that you won. Sax would go even further, remind Kah about every thrashing blow delivered outside of the mag-lev train station in the vine jungles of Aspicis, but it seems like a waste of energy. Kah's not worth it.

"Is that why you're floating in our prison?" Kah hisses a reply.

"I gave myself up."

"Nobody cares," Kah says, but there's a sigh that whistles out of his vents. "But as you surrendered once, perhaps you'll consider doing it again."

A deal. This wouldn't be Kah's idea, then. No three-letter Oratus would strike a bargain with a captive. Better to eliminate the threat and move on to other things, especially when that threat is Sax, who, given an inch of freedom, will take every possible measure of revenge.

"Speak," Sax hisses.

"I was going to," Kah replies. "You don't have any right to command me here."

"They've kept you locked up in here too long. You don't know how to threaten someone properly."

"I don't need to threaten you." Kah gestures with the miner, as if the weapon's going to do his job for him.

"If you're just going to shake that miner, then at least give me a Flaum to scratch. I've gone too long without a real meal."

Kah gives Sax a hissing laugh for his trouble. "Your pair and that mass of prey are preparing to launch an attack on the Meridia. They will lose."

The words clear up Sax's fog. He didn't know whether the attack had started yet, whether Bas and the others had made it free from the Cavignum after Sax's gambit. Kah just confirmed both. Sax hopes a razor grin he can't repress doesn't give it away.

Kah, though, isn't watching him. Instead, the Oratus is glancing further back through the level. Kah's looking through the one side of the square cell that didn't rise, and while Sax doesn't have a view to what Kah's looking for, he can guess.

Mirrored Oratus always have masters.

"If you come out against the assault, if you help us turn their forces to our side." Kah turns back to Sax, his voice a low rasp. "The Chorus is willing to guarantee your life, along with your pair's. Your crimes will be forgiven, and you will have a choice of returning to Solis or choosing a planet of your desiring on which to retire."

Retire. Few Oratus get that chance, and the ones that do only receive it because of crippling injury. Any Oratus that can fight would, will, wants to fight. That is their purpose. That is their calling. Despite his life being tied to the idea, Sax snorts at the word before he considers what Kah even said.

"Perhaps," Kah allows at Sax's sound—he would understand, too, the insult in the idea of retirement. "We could arrange for a strategic post. Someplace where you could find plenty of entertainment."

Meaning things to slaughter. This would be better, except Kah's offer comes with a deal-killer: Sax isn't going to turn against his pair, against his former commander Evva and the cause he's joined. Not to go back to the Chorus and their pack of traitorous manipulators.

"You already know my answer," Sax says.

Kah glares in response. Matches Sax's eyes for a long moment before the mirrored Oratus dips his head in a nod that, Sax thinks, carries a tiny bit of respect with it.

"There is no other offer," Kah replies, though the words come rote; a question whose answer is known, which must nonetheless be asked. "Accept, or you will never see Bas again."

Her name this time. A sweetener, and if Sax were a weaker species, he might fall into the trap of possibilities; imagined futures laid out before him with a single, simple *yes* dividing their brilliant promise from his miserable present.

"There is no other answer," Sax says. "I will not betray her."

Again the nod. This time, though, Kah's motion is joined by a whirring noise from beyond the cell. The sound of micro-jets pulsing up, sending their cargo this way. Sax has sent the signal, and now he's going to see what the Chorus cares to do in response. Maybe they slaughter him here. More likely the Chorus will use the opportunity; a staged execution for all the galaxy to see. It's how traitors ought to be dealt with.

Sax has seen plenty of them himself. And cheered along with the rest of the Vincere when those dissidents were brought to fatal justice.

Kah steps across the room, behind Sax, as a pair of Flaum guards enter through the opening Kah's been glancing toward this entire time. These aren't average Flaum, small furry creatures with a penchant for squeaky conversation. No, these are armored in Chorus blue, carrying assault miners in their hands with secondary weapons attached around their waists. They stare at Sax with fierce focus that impresses the Oratus. If the average Vincere Flaum possessed this level of grit, it's possible the Oratus wouldn't be needed at all.

"So you *are* bringing me dinner," Sax hisses anyway, because it's more fun to keep the prey unbalanced.

"Quiet," Kah hisses slow from behind Sax. "This isn't time for games."

And when what's following the Flaum, when the source of those micro-jets, slides into the room, Sax can only agree.

*Continue the adventure with The Last Cycle, Book Six of the Skyward Saga, available now.*

## ACKNOWLEDGMENTS

This novel is the product of my family and friends refusing to let a dream die. My wife Nicole, for letting me write in the early mornings and making sure I didn't starve. My brothers and parents for their continual comments, support, and enthusiasm.

And, of course, you, the reader, for giving me a reason to write.

A.R. Knight spins stories in a frosty house in Madison, WI, primarily owned by a pair of cats. After getting sucked into the working grind in the economic crash of the 2008, he found himself spending boring meetings soaring through space and going on grand adventures.

Eventually, spending time with podcasting, screenplays, short stories and other novels, he found a story he could fall into and a cast of characters both entertaining and full of heart.

A.R. Knight plans on jumping through to other worlds and finding new stories to tell in the limitless borders of our imagination.

Thanks, as always, for reading!

*For more information:*
www.adamrknight.com

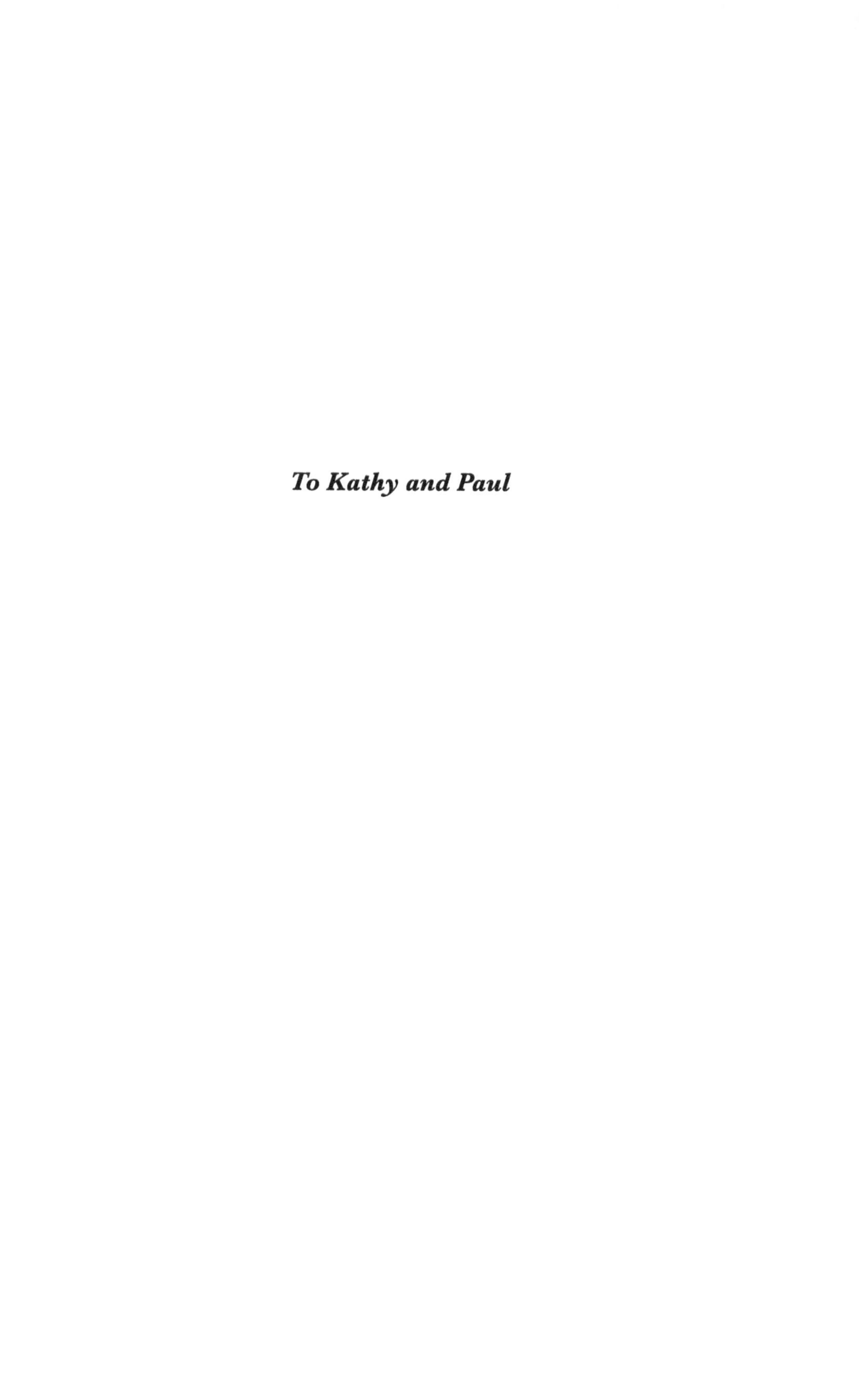

*To Kathy and Paul*